The Ripper

A Rudransh Ray Mystery Thriller

Anasua Ghosh

Ukiyoto Publishing

All global publishing rights are held by

Ukiyoto Publishing

Published in 2023

Content Copyright © Anasua Ghosh

ISBN 9789360495831

All rights reserved.
No part of this publication may be reproduced, transmitted, or stored in a retrieval system, in any form by any means, electronic, mechanical, photocopying, recording or otherwise, without the prior permission of the publisher.

The moral rights of the author have been asserted.

This is a work of fiction. Names, characters, businesses, places, events, locales, and incidents are either the products of the author's imagination or used in a fictitious manner. Any resemblance to actual persons, living or dead, or actual events is purely coincidental.

This book is sold subject to the condition that it shall not by way of trade or otherwise, be lent, resold, hired out or otherwise circulated, without the publisher's prior consent, in any form of binding or cover other than that in which it is published.

www.ukiyoto.com

Contents

The Body	1
Chapter – 1	9
Chapter – 2	26
Chapter – 3	41
Chapter - 4	51
Chapter - 5	59
Chapter – 6	81
Chapter – 7	92
Chapter - 8	107
Chapter – 9	116
Chapter – 10	131
Chapter – 11	139
Chapter – 12	145
Chapter – 13	157
Chapter – 14	167
Chapter - 15	182
Chapter - 16	188
Chapter - 17	202
Chapter – 18	210
Chapter - 19	220
Chapter - 20	233
Chapter - 21	245
Chapter – 22	255

Chapter - 23	261
Chapter - 24	272
Chapter - 25	285
Chapter - 26	294
Chapter - 27	300
Chapter – 28	309
Chapter - 29	323
Chapter - 30	326
Chapter - 31	337
Chapter - 32	345
Chapter – 34	355
About the Author	*365*

The Body

Just half an hour before he died from a massive blow on his head, he stopped to admire the dusking sky for the last time. The dying ray of the sun faded slowly, allowing heavy shadows to come alive and claim the throne of darkness. He stepped on the uneven rocky ground carefully with the help of his crutch, thinking, assessing, and calculating. Why had he been called here? The question nagged him, made him uncomfortable, and forced him to keep an eye out for any trouble. Even though his instinct screamed in alarm, he could not turn away. Not after coming this far. Not after putting in so much effort. He would have to see the end of this case. Or, this case would see the end of him. For a fraction of a second, his attention drifted and he paid the price immediately. A small pebble materialized under his crutch from somewhere, making him lose his balance.

'Fuck,' he cursed as he stumbled. His left arm shot forward in a futile attempt to regain his balance. As he fell, his eyes perceived the building where he would be meeting the group of people he had come to expose. The house was under construction for a long time. Its' naked walls stared at the world with the kind of blankness which spoke of depressed romanticism. The fall was not gentle. His body slammed on a heavily pebbled earth, drawing out a cry of agony from his dry throat. Pain shot up as sharp rocks pricked his flesh. It immobilized him for a moment. He looked around and considered getting away from this dismal setting. But his resolution to unmask the group of criminals stopped him. He had to try. Even if it killed him, he needed to make an effort to end the evil that threatened to engulf his country.

With effort, he pushed himself up on his feet, trembling from the intensity of the fall, cursing his useless leg. Particles of dry dust clung to his blue denim pants and dark blue shirt. Quickly he brushed himself clean and began to walk towards the lone building which stood on the highway like an abandoned warrior.

His unease grew with each step. For a moment, for one frightened moment, he considered calling for help. But he did not reach for his phone. Instead, with firm determination, he approached the sorry-looking building which would witness his violent death in less than ten minutes. An unseen clock ticked in the background. Even though he could not hear the sound, his heart knew that his end awaited him at the other side of the threshold. A few more minutes, he told himself, then he would walk inside to shake hands with death.

'Hello,' he called as he reached the front door of the building. 'Anyone there?' In his mind, he went over, not for the first time, through all the possibilities. Even if he died here today, his evidence would be safe. He had sent the files to the right person and in due time the package would reach its destination. Getting no response from anyone, he decided to cross the threshold. Inky darkness greeted him the moment he stepped inside.

'Hello,' he called again. From the corner of his eyes, he detected a movement, a stealthy, sure, and deadly movement. He turned quickly towards the approaching entity. But it was already too late. They had written his death warrant a long time ago. Fortunately, darkness veiled his vision and did not allow him to see the cricket bat that came down on his head with enough force to crack his skull.

A homing bird cried somewhere in the distance, painting the scene a shade darker. It made him remember the days of his childhood which he had spent in utter isolation and longing. He tilted his head and looked down at his feet where the body lay lifeless. Blood oozed out of the crack where the cricket bat had landed. Even in the falling darkness, he could make out the darkish-red liquid oozing out of the wound he had caused. Blood, he inhaled deeply. The smell, the coppery, heavy smell of blood, brought something out from within. Not something, someone, he corrected himself. It had been a long time since this individual came out to claim his place in his heart. It had been a long time since he had this much pleasure killing a human being. Before he could stop himself, his hand reached inside his jacket where he carried his most prized possession - his knife. With a slow, yet deliberate motion, he brought the blade out. His heart thumped against his ribs, forcing him to breathe fast. It had been a long time since he had done this. With ceremonious slowness, he bent forward, and with a swift movement of his wrist, he slit the throat of the dead body. More blood gushed out of the wound, flowing free on the ground. It should have satisfied his lust for gore. But it did not. If anything, it elevated the urge to do more, to get more, and to rip more. He drew a deep breath to collect his strength, and then he attacked the body like a hungry animal looking for meat to devour.

His companions gasped as he used the stainless steel blade to rip the dead body apart. It took him twenty minutes to work the knife down to reveal a blood-soaked interior. Others watched in muted horror as he made his art. They would be speechless for a long time, he knew that. They had seen him kill before. But they had never seen him rip people up. He had not displayed his full talent to any of them before. With effort, he had controlled the beast which lived inside him. But it came out this evening. Despite the strongest leash, the beast finally tore itself free. He could not stop the beast any longer. Before his eyes, the guts, raw and vibrating, stared openly at the world, begging him to take them home.

Unable to ignore the call, he reached down and thrust his right hand inside the open rib cage of the dead body, and with a strong tug, he yanked the heart out of its designated place. The organ was still warm. It pulsated in his palm, making him feel alive and hungry. Twice he squeezed the pulpy organ. Then he tossed it aside like some useless object.

Three pairs of eyes stared at him. He could feel their penetrating gazes on his back. Horror dripped from their eyes. They took a step back when he turned. Fear, he could smell it in them like perfume. It was there, in the depth of their hearts. Now, they knew what he could do. They knew the length of his madness. In time they would get a test of it too. One by one, he smiled silently.

With his right foot, he kicked the body hard as a last goodbye. Quite a sight the dead man had made, he thought, tilting his head. Humans looked funny when they died, all motionless and incapable. But when they lay mangled in their own flesh and blood, with bones crushed, eyes bulging out, they made real sights.

Sights to behold.

Somewhere in some distant house, a clock chimed. In this isolation, the chime sounded ghastly, elevating the sense of horror. He looked down again, not yet ready to leave. He liked what he saw. His art. His masterpiece. He created it with his own hands.

'We gotta hide the body,' said one of his companions. He could hear a slight tremor in the tone.

Fear. He loved it. He loved the feeling of being feared. Yes, he could kill them all like the way he had killed the man lying at his feet. Then he could rip them all apart.

Time.

Time came. It did not go.

'I think, we should burn the body,' said the second accomplice. 'Once we reduce it to ashes, no one will find it.' The poor soul tried to sound smart.

'Burn it?' asked the first one. 'You gotta be nuts. Fire will attract attention in this darkness.'

'So what do we do?'

'Bury him,' said the fourth one of the group, the wiser one too. 'In this abandoned highway area, no one will find him. It will be another one of those missing-person cases. No one will ever know about the murder.'

'Wise idea,' said the ripper. 'Bury the bastard.' In the secrecy of his heart, he wanted to leave the body in the open and take some photos for social media. People should know about it. People should fear. They needed to know that death could come in gruesome masks when they least expected it.

Later, he promised himself. The time would come soon.

The Cops

'Whoa, what had happened here?' asked a young man dressed in the white Kolkata Police uniform. 'It looks like the act of some lunatic.'

'Must be some lunatic,' agreed his partner. Tonight he gave his uniform a miss and stood wrapped in a dark brown thick woolen jacket and a pair of jeans.

They waited for the force to come and join them. Their hands froze. The wind rose and the temperature dropped with each passing moment. In a futile effort to stay warm, they huddled deeper inside their winter coats.

'Never before have I experienced such winter in Kolkata,' said the first officer. 'It will freeze my heart.'

'Frozen heart,' joked the second officer. 'The ice queen.'

'Who?' asked his partner.

'No one.'

'Who?' insisted the young man.

'An animation heroin.'

'You watch animation movies?' came the question laden with disbelief.

'Yeah, when good porn is not available.'

The white headlight of a rushing car halted their conversation. The first officer checked his watch, past two in the morning, almost two thirty. It must be the force. In half a second a white Hyundai i20 pulled in front of them. From the driver's seat descended a tall, thin man in his late fifties. He looked at them through his black wire-rimmed glasses.

'What happened?' he asked.

'A murder,' said the plain-clothed police officer.

'A violent murder,' corrected the other one.

'Why am I called?' asked CID chief Chetan Bajaj. The frosty wind ruffled his white hair. He rubbed his hands to keep them warm.

'Sir, please have a look inside.'

Inside, a coppery smell greeted everyone. A strong smell of blood. Chetan looked down at the body lying on the floor. He rubbed his chin. 'Have you identified the body?'

'No, we have just been called. The night patrolling officer found him…this way.'

Chetan Bajaj rubbed his chin again. His face had a troubled expression now. 'This is a case befitting Rudransh Ray,' he muttered to himself with a worried frown.

Chapter – 1

Winter wind exploded as Rudransh Ray stepped out in the open. He stood still to relish the frosty air. People would call it madness to be out in this weather at this time. But Ray loved cold air and crispy nights. His love for cold and darkness would never make sense to him. Whenever the sun went down, he felt a tug inside his heart. It dragged him out. It made him run. Run to what? Run from what? He hardly knew. Frankly, he hardly cared.

He pulled the hood of his dark gray woolen jacket over his head. Not to protect himself from the biting cold, but to shut the world out for a while. To check the time, he turned his right wrist. His silver-plated Rolex watch said that it was half past midnight. People of Kolkata retired early as the winter chill set in. Unsurprisingly, not a single spark of light was visible from the tightly shut windows of the skyscrapers.

Sometimes there is no light at the end of the tunnel.

Before the sour mood took over, Ray hit the road. No sane man would go for a run at this time of night in mid-December. Then again, no sane man would spend his life chasing killers and enjoy the thrill. Ray did enjoy the thrill of chasing criminals. He enjoyed the thrill of cornering vicious murderers and leaving them no chance to escape. But what he enjoyed most was the task of putting together pieces of puzzles to uncover the faces of the perpetrators.

In the darkness, Kolkata looked different. The warmth, the classic mysticism, and the brush of nostalgia, which defined Kolkata disappeared when night deepened. In its place, emerged a slumbering city, with countless shadows and tightly shut windows. Ray inhaled deep, but the smell of his city remained. Even in frosty winter, Kolkata smelt like home.

Familiar road signs disappeared as he sped past them. Ray took no notice of the scattered pieces of beer bottles and cigarette butts. With darkness, came out the rebels. It was the story of every city. Kolkata was not an exception either. He increased his speed.

Half an hour later, a burning sensation down his calves warned Ray that he was going too fast, that he should slow down. But, if you knew Rudransh Ray, you would know that he never did what he should have done. Thus, he kept running, ignoring his thudding heart, ignoring the burn down his legs, and of course, ignoring the cold. Fuck. Fuck them all.

His iPhone screamed for attention by the time Ray entered his eleventh-floor apartment. Like a machine programmed to move, his eyes turned to look at the wall clock in his living room.

Three in the morning. The Devil's Hour. A long breath escaped his heart. Someone, somewhere lay dead. No one was calling him with a wedding invitation at this time of night. With a reluctant hand, he picked up the phone. Siddhant Thakur, CID Senior Investigator, and his best friend.

'Sid,' Ray greeted after pressing the call receive button.

'Having sex, fucker?' was the first question Sid asked Ray.

'No playing with myself,' Ray replied. 'What's up?'

'Someone's down,' Sid shouted. Ray could hear the sound of hissing wind from the other side of the phone. Driving. 'Or so I heard. You gotta cover it. I am stuck near Kolaghat. Will take a couple of hours to reach there. Besides, the Chief wants your ass down at the crime scene.'

'Who died?' Ray asked, already heading for his bedroom.

'Some business man or so I heard.' Sid continued to shout.

'What else have you heard?' Ray pulled open his wardrobe and scanned the row of hanging clothes. What to wear?

'That the murder is befitting Rudransh Ray.' And the line went dead.

That hit the wrong place inside Ray's stomach. A murder befitting Rudransh Ray was bad news. With the thought in mind, he reached for a dark gray sports coat. Gray had always held a special place in his heart. He did not know why he was so drawn to this color.

Probably, he had more gray in his mind than black and white.

To go with the coat, he picked a light blue Channel dress shirt and a pair of faded blue jeans. Yeah, he liked clothes. His grandfather taught him to dress well. The old man made Ray a brand freak too. He started to check the time but then shook his head. Whoever had died would not go anywhere.

Should he shave? He ran his hand over his face to feel the depth of the stubble which had patiently grown around his lower face. It had been five consecutive days he had not shaved. Maybe he could wait a couple of more days before taking a decision. It took him fifteen minutes to get ready. Before getting out of the room, he checked his reflection in the mirror. He had a date with a dead body after all.

The smell of blood and death blasted over Ray's face as he hung by the threshold of a wide, square-shaped room. He inhaled through his mouth. A lungful of odor-laden air could make anyone throw up. The Cry of a stray dog ricocheted, shattering the doom-like silence for a moment. Ray craned his neck to catch a glimpse of the animal. But in the thickening winter fog, the world appeared smoky. Mysterious even. It bloated out the sky and muted the moonlight. After he was done searching for the dog that barked, Ray turned his attention toward the room which awaited his entrance.

The barking sound of the dog died, and a death-like silence rushed over to fill the void. Nothing moved. Rows of houses stood in anticipation. Not even a flicker of light came to view from the spot where Ray stood. Doomed. Of course, to be up at this hour of the night and in this weather, one either had to be a thief or a cop like him. He was not a cop anymore, he reminded himself that. Not in the traditional sense. But he could be called a cop, in the technical sense. He assisted the cops and helped them solve crimes no one else wanted. Right now, he was about to enter a crime scene that no one would want to face. His forlorn heart cried in protest at the thought of disturbing the artistic mayhem inside. Once again he would have to place himself inside the head of a killer and think like them. It hurt the human self which he had kept alive with effort.

Tragic, Ray inhaled. Not through his mouth this time. Immediately, he regretted his carelessness. Five years in CID Crime Branch had prepared him for anything. Or so he thought. The crime scene in front of him had come out of the blue. CID and criminology had not warned him of this and had not taught him to deal with something like this either.

Every case was new. Every victim had a different story to tell. What story the man lying dead would tell him? What went wrong? Ray wanted to ask. But the time to ask questions would come. Time came. It did not go. He blew foggy air to give his racing heart a little respite.

And the day had just begun.

'Morning shows the day huh?' asked Akash Bajaj from behind.

Ray turned to look at his research assistant and business partner. 'Thought you don't believe in it.'

'Nope, I don't.' Akash shook his head. He shifted his weight before giving a nervous laugh. 'What the fuck do you think happened here?' He pointed at the two-story house they stood facing. Its front door was open, giving them a generous view of the dead body, they had come to meet or rather to take a look at.

'Someone died,' Ray said. His hand itched for some reason. One of the coldest mornings in Kolkata, yet, he felt nothing. The lack of ability to feel anything bothered him sometimes. It made him feel less like a human being.

Though his voice remained calm, he experienced something down his heart. It seemed a lot like fear. What his eyes saw each time they looked inside could frighten anyone. But a leader could not show fear. No matter how hopeless. No matter how close to death they stood. They must always wear the mask of courage. So, he did it too. He chuckled for no reason at all. Just a hairpin curve and he appeared to be the bravest hero of the force. Then he wiped the smile from his face and wore the mask he usually wore to hide his weaknesses and sorrows.

Stony or frosty, it served its purpose. Ray felt his heart thudding against his chest, fear and something close to excitement made him flex his hands. It was fascinating too. What sort of man could do that? The basic, he thought, always came down to the basic.

Everyone lingered by the threshold. No one had dared to enter the building yet. So, Ray took the onus of entering the territory of dread. He took the first step. Being the first one to step ahead had been a childhood habit. Numerous times, he had stepped forward for the wronged and helpless ones. So he, Rudransh Ray, had been branded as the hero who fought for the weak. Someone was yet to fight a fight for him. But then again, being a hero served his purpose. It helped him catch offenders and kill them too.

Ray slowly crossed the threshold and entered the crime scene. Others followed. They always did when someone is crazy or foolish enough to lead them ahead. Doom or destiny, did not matter. They just wanted to follow someone. Ray always made sure that it was he who did the leading.

'This is like…' Akash said. His voice held a fusion of fear and awe. 'This is pure barbarism.' Ray heard the touch of panic in the tone. He did not blame Akash for reacting like that. Anyone would panic in this situation. Ray himself would have panicked, had he not been a cop.

'You write true crime stories,' Ray said to lighten up the mood. 'Don't you?'

'I do.' Akash buried his hands deep inside his pockets. 'But I don't write such fucks' He pointed at the body lying on the floor. 'This is inhuman.'

'Try writing travel,' Ray said before turning his focus on the crime scene. A massive wooden table was set by the door. Near this table sat three leather executive chairs. The reception area of the office showed clear signs of success and wealth. By the opposite wall across the table lay the dead body.

'Who is he?' Ray asked. 'You IDed him yet?'

'Samir Shrivastav,' Vivan read from his notes. 'He is…was a businessman.'

'What sort of business?' Akash asked. To this question, Vivan gave a shrug.

After checking everything with a shift of his head, Ray approached the body. Samir or what was left of Samir lay in a pool of blood. For a better view, Ray squatted down, careful not to touch anything even though he had been wearing rubber gloves. The body, rather the carcass, had gone through a serious post-mortem operation after the murder took place.

The face had turned into a mash of flesh and bone. 'Blunt object.' Ray heard Vivan mutter.

Sure enough, blunt object, thought Rudransh Ray. Possibly the killer had used a cricket bat to kill Samir and then beat down his skull till it turned soft. The force of the bat had not only broken Samir's facial bones but also smashed his skull. Ray turned his eyes away from the body for a fraction of a second. They said morning showed the day. But they never said anything about what the darkness before dawn showed.

'Sir.' Rudransh Ray looked over his shoulder at the call. A uniformed cop in his late thirties or early forties stood by the threshold. The way he kept blinking his eyes, anyone would tell that he had not seen many dead bodies.

'Yeah, what?' Ray asked. Even to his own ears, the response sounded a little harsh.

'I found a cricket bat lying in the backyard.' The officer paused. 'It has blood stain.'

That explained the blunt object. 'Send it for fingerprint analysis.' Ray shifted his attention back toward the dead body.

'What are the chances of finding a fingerprint on it?' Akash asked. From experience, he knew that fingerprints rarely helped in catching a killer.

A lot depended on finding the fingerprints of the perpetrators. Not that it would help them find the killer. It would surely tell them about the man who had killed Samir. 'Let's wait till the report comes.' Ray muttered, looking at the body like the way an artist looked at his artwork. What kind of a man could do that? He thought and he had no doubt that the offender was a male, possibility in his late twenties or early thirties.

His watchful eyes ran down the cut which had revealed Samir's guts. It was deep and long, unhesitant, sure, confident, Ray noted with unease. The slash had opened Samir up, giving the world a view of his internal system. The offender had not stopped ripping his victim apart. He had torn Samir's heart out and tossed it aside like an unimportant piece of junk.

'This is what? A ripper copycat?' Akash asked.

Ripper copycat, Ray considered for a moment. The MO and the signature would bring this question he knew that. Yet, something about the murder, the entire scene, and something else he could not explain right now, made him wonder. Jack the Ripper or something deeper, someone with unusual wits.

Unease down the pit of his stomach made him get up on his feet. By now the smell of blood, stale flesh, and death all had become an integral part of the air that he inhaled. 'Ripper was not known to his victims. At least there was no indication that he was.' Ray looked around to capture the image of the scene in its full vividity.

'You think this guy knew Samir?' Vivan asked.

'You see any sign of forced entry?' Ray asked. Their wits sometimes bothered him. These were the people Kolkata betted her security on.

'Nope.' Vivan shook his head.

'Common sense my dear is very uncommon. Try to gather some.' Ray felt his eyebrows rise with the comment. 'I want to know everything about Samir. I want to know who he dated. I want to know who he ditched.' For a moment his words trailed. 'I want to know his bank account details as well.'

Vivan took it all down in his notebook. The kid had all the qualities of a good secretary. Should have joined a corporate to take down notes. With a long breath, Ray made his way toward one of the file cabinets placed against the corner of the room. The offender left the murder weapon behind, he thought as he stood in front of the metal shelf which housed files and dust. But he had taken the sharp object, possibility a knife with him. What type of man would do that? He knew the answer would come eventually. But what he did not know was, how many more would die to provide enough clues to develop a strong criminal profile.

The cabinet was staked with dusty files. A splatter of blood had created an unusual decoration on the dusty surface. 'He played with the blood or what?' Vivan's question intruded into his thought and brought him back to the present.

'These blood stains came from the knife.' The slashes bothered Ray. There was something about the way they ran down Samir's body that made him wonder. First crime? Definitely not the last one.

'He danced with the knife or what?' Vivan looked around for a moment then said with a scowl.

'Or what,' Ray said. 'Seal the room. And go through the cabinet. I want a thorough report of these files.' Ray stopped to look at Vivan. 'ASAP.' He added.

'You gonna get it EOD.' Vivan gave him a thumbs up. This gesture everyone got a lot from him. Frankly, Ray hated to look at the raised thumb of anyone.

It was 4.30 in the morning already. Not even a flicker of light pierced the darkness of the sky. Even the stars remained aloof like the solution to the murder at hand. Maybe he should give up hunting criminals and start writing poetry, thought Ray with disgust.

For the last time, he checked the room. Nothing else to see, nothing else to discover either. Vivan stood in the middle, contaminating the scene and taking notes. One could not help crime scene contamination. Footsteps, movement, and even breathing contaminated crime scenes. The challenge was to prevent it as much as possible for the CSIs. Ray scanned the room for no reason at all. Once again, he had the disturbing sense of overlooking something. Probably, he should go home now and get some sleep.

'Who's gonna inform his family?' Ray asked. He hated this job. So many years later, he still remembered the first time he had performed this task. It had burned his soul that day while delivering the news. The scar still throbbed against his ribs. He could still feel the agony deep in his heart. It was a tough job. One which he wanted someone else to perform.

'He does not have one,' Vivan said. 'According to the data base, his father died five years ago. His mother is an Alzheimer patient. And there is a house keeper.'

Ray reached for the packet of cigarette which he carried inside his jeans' pocket. He had to fan the gray matter of his brain. 'Get me the address I wanna talk to them.'

Vivan looked at Ray with a blank expression on his face. 'His mother is nuts. What's she gonna tell you?'

With effort Ray controlled the bubble of irritation that threatened to come out. When would this kid learn? 'Sometimes insane people make more sense than the so-called sane ones.' Ray's eyes fell on the dead body once again. His hands itched inside the rubber gloves. But he did not like to take them off on crime scenes.

'Understood.' Though Vivan did not argue with Ray, his eyes remain confused. Rudransh Ray did not wait to explain anything.

One last scan and Ray had had enough of the bloody scene. Without another glance over his shoulder or another word, he walked out.

Wind, free of any odor, enveloped Ray in a tight embrace. He dragged a lungful of frosty air. Over his head the dark night sky seemed to loom down in malice. He could smell wet soil. Gonna rain or what? Ray hoped for a storm which lasted for a whole day.

The long suppressed yearn for a smoke came rushing to him. This time even with his strongest push it did not vanish. What the heck, he thought, fishing a cherry red packet out of his pocket.

After a generous drag of his cigarette, his heart felt lighter. Vivan came to stand by Ray. 'Where is Akash?' Ray asked.

'Inside, still taking notes.' Vivan kicked a tiny stone. It rolled to stop near a puddle. 'What do you think of the killer?' he asked after a long pause.

Criminal profiling could be tricky and, most of the time misleading. One could never be certain about the nature of a human being from modus operandi alone. Of course, one could get a probable character sketch of the person. The fun was in building an entire picture from just a few scratches. The behavior showed a man with outrageous passion. The post-mortem operation did not seem planned. This meant, the offender killed Samir, and only after a while thought of ripping him apart. Something had triggered the behavior, Ray thought looking at the sky.

'It is way too early to say anything,' Ray said through clouds of gray smoke.

'Still there must be something,' Vivan said, his eyes shone like marble. The kid was fascinated by criminal profiling and claimed to watch everything remotely related to serial killing.

Before Ray had a chance to say anything, a black i20 pulled in front of Samir's office building. A tall young man unfolded his lean masculine frame from the driver's seat. His bony face showed signs of sleepless nights. He looked at the house with measuring eyes for a fraction of second, then his attention turned towards Ray.

'Here comes your boss,' Ray said to Vivan.

CID Senior Officer Siddhant Thakur joined Ray and Vivan. 'What's inside?' he asked.

'A dead body,' Ray answered.

'Befitting Ray?' Sid asked. He reached for the cigarette Ray was smoking. They had shared numerous fags together.

'The body had gone under the knife,' Ray said.

'Sexual murder?' Sid asked.

Ninety percent time, post-mortem operations occurred due to suppressed sexual frustration. But this time Ray felt something else. The crime depicted excruciating rage, which might be sexual, might be something else. Samir and his blood-bathed office room flashed in his mind. The offender had been trying to prove something by ripping Samir apart. It flashed in Ray's mind like a lightning bolt.

'Not entirely.' Ray shook my head. 'Sexual aggression is there in the behavior. But there is also something else.'

'A disorganized offender?' asked Sid, keeping his eyes on the darkness ahead.

To this Ray did not reply immediately. His hesitation did not go unnoticed. Sid narrowed his eyes. 'You think it's an organized offender trying to layer his act?' he asked.

Sadly Ray had no answer to this question. 'It's too early to say anything.' What Ray was about to say next would startle Sid. But it was his job to reveal the unpleasant truth. 'This is not a first time offender we are dealing with.'

Sid was about to toss the cigarette butt on the ground. Ray's comment stilled him. His hand hung in the midair. His eyes widened. 'You know what you are saying right?'

'Yeah. Those slashes are not the handy work of any amateur.' Ray fished out his cherry red packet of cigarette again. 'Our guy has done it before.'

'Cool,' Sid said. He ran his hand through his thick dark brown hair. 'How come we haven't heard anything about the similar MO?'

'Must have hidden the body well,' Ray said.

'Why not hide this one too?' Sid asked in a calm voice as if they discussed the weather.

Hiding a body required resources. Making it disappear required time. 'Someone must have interrupted the act.' Even to Ray's own ears his voice sounded to be loaded with worry. 'Hold the mutilation part from the media,' Ray said.

'Yeah, I know,' Sid nodded. 'People will get panicked.'

Panicked? Ray had to chuckle. 'Panic has nothing to do with this fuck.' Sid glanced at Ray at the comment. He stood straight and waited for the next bomb to explode. Ray admired his patience. 'The media attention can send the unsub on a killing fiesta. You know there are prices to fame.' That stopped them all.

Sid stood still, frozen against the backdrop of the inky black night.

Ray's heart thudded against his ribs. The surge of blood made his veins throb. Down the pit of his stomach, he sensed a twist. Adrenaline hit. The hunter within was coming to life. Ray curled and uncurled his hands. His jaw tightened automatically. With his right hand, he touched the waistband of his denim. Hidden inside his gray woolen sports coat was his favorite toy, his Sig Seur P250, loaded to go on at any given chance. The race had just begun.

Chapter – 2

The drive to Samir's house took Rudransh Ray less than fifteen minutes. Empty road and adrenaline worked together to make him fly his Honda City. No one would call Ray a reckless driver. But no one would certify him as a safe driver either. When he got his car flying, people usually hung by the edge of their seats. Like right now.

'You wanna die or something bro?' Akash asked. His face revealed no trace of fear. By now, he had become accustomed to fly around in Ray's car. Akash was guilty of rash driving himself. So, they made a perfect match to run their business together.

'Nah, not today.' Ray slowed the car near a narrow lane, following his mobile's GPS. Through this rift only a single human minus obesity would pass without obstacle. So, Ray would not even dream of going inside with his sedan.

Samir lived in a middle class housing area of VIP Bazar. The locality remained crowded throughout the day and a deeper part of the night. But in this freezing winter morning, not even a single soul appeared outside.

'Where are they?' Akash asked eyeing the rearview mirror. Sid had promised to follow them. But somewhere down the road, Ray had lost them.

The street stood empty. Ray's watch said five thirty in the morning. The sky remained stubbornly gray with thickening cloud. With each passing minute the gray turned a shade darker. Wind slammed against the trees in occasional intervals. Akash shuddered as a gale of frosty air hit him hard.

Soon, snowflakes would start falling, Ray thought. The thought popped suddenly, making Ray chuckle a little. As a kid he hoped someday Kolkata would see a blizzard. He even spent hours in bed lying awake fantasizing a snow covered City Of Joy.

Sid's car pulled right behind Ray's Honda City. Ray opened the driver's door and stepped out on the street. Akash followed. For a while, they stood in silence, letting their eyes do the job. None mentioned cold, frosty wind or feeling strangely numb from inside. Samir's death had hit them all real hard. But they would have to proceed without speaking about the horror because it was their job to swallow trauma and move forward. No wonder so many cops went for counselling. Ray clearly remembered his own sessions. The shrink did not know what to do with him. He was completely unresponsive to the treatment. But thankfully, he came back in right order. Well almost in right order, Ray corrected himself. To keep the momentum going, he pushed the memories away. No, he would not think about the fall. No ways. Instead he set his eyes on the work at hand.

Samir lived in a lower middle class neighborhood. Houses both old and new assembled to create a colony. Old ones had long lost their usual paints. Now, they only bore heavy marks of assault of time and weather. The new ones would soon follow the path of their old companions. Some of the houses had parking spaces which housed motorcycles and cycles. They could not see any four wheeler from where they stood.

'Not a safe place to leave the cars,' Vivan said. His face wrinkled in worry.

They slapped police stickers on the windscreens before heading for the narrow lane. Because none of them had an ounce of extra flab their journey through the rift was non-descriptive. At the rear of the track was a deep drainage which served the purpose of garbage dump. Smell of month old food and who-knows-what loaded the surrounding air.

'What a fucking mess,' Vivan said. He shook his head to the unthinkable sin of dumping garbage on the street. 'Can we coach these people somehow?'

'And teach them what?' Sid asked. He looked at Ray with a wide grin. Vivan came from a rich family which hardly tolerated this type of behavior.

'Being human.' Vivan made a face.

'Mission impossible 10,' Akash said. His grin made them all loosen up a little. If anyone could make a grim situation light, it was Akash.

Ray halted on his way and checked his phone once again. According to the given direction they stood just a couple of houses away from Samir's place. Ray's eyes moved up to see a two story building with falling paint, clearly a member of the old construction team. Once it must have been painted pink. Now, blackish stains had engulfed most of the exterior. The house saturated against the dark horizon. What a place to live in, Ray thought.

'Bleak house,' muttered Akash and Ray could not agree more. Bleak and guilty of hiding secrets, Samir's house stood at the farthest corner of the street.

'Sure you wanna enter that?' Vivan asked. He scanned the road with doubtful eyes. 'I mean it's only five thirty in the morning. The mother must be sleeping given her condition.'

'Sure you don't wanna patrol by the car?' Sid asked. Though he kept a nonchalant demeanor, Ray could feel his tension. They had worked side by side for a long time. Before joining CID, they had played soccer in the same team. They could read each other better than an open book.

'We should have brought a female officer along with us,' Akash said. He wrote true crime stories and screamed about women being thrashed at the hands of law enforcers all the time. His books had never received academic praise because of graphic violence and touch of storytelling. But general people liked his writing.

'We are here to deliver the Samir's news and take a look at his belongings,' Ray said.

They approached the front door with caution. Front door meant a piece of frail wood which would not withstand the next monsoon. This Ray would have to knock with the hope that it would not fly off at the pressure of his hand. A colorful curse formed at the thought of what he would find at the other side of the door.

'Careful,' Vivan said as Ray raised his hand to knock.

Instead of using his open palm, Ray curled his fingers to tap with his knuckles on the door. A faint tapping sounded at the contact of his finger joints and the wood. As expected the door trembled like someone had sent an electric shock wave. Ray pulled his hand back afraid of causing serious damage to the door. They waited for someone to move at the other side of the door. They even strained their ears to catch the faintest sound. Nothing. No one moved. Only death like silence loomed inside.

The horizon in the background turned a shade darker. It looked black and vengeful now. To keep up with the gloomy mood of the sky, wind hissed in rage. Sun would not rise today. The promise of a bright morning vanished into oblivion. Now, the city looked up to an angry expansion of the horizon and waited for a downpour which Ray doubted would stop any time soon. He inhaled deep, allowing his lungs to get full. Crisp winter air worked like energy drink. Ray felt refreshed immediately.

He raised his hand again and tapped. Harder this time. The wood trembled again. Akash chuckled. Surprised at the sound Ray glanced over his shoulder.

'The door is a female,' Akash said. 'It trembles for more of your touch.'

To this everyone laughed. Everyone but Ray. 'You have the sense of humor of a pornographer,' he said. To this no one laughed.

'Tap again,' Sid said. 'If mama has hearing problem we will be standing here forever.' He threw a worried glance at the sky.

Bracing himself for the impact, Ray curled his hand into a tight fist. 'Police open up,' he shouted as his hand slammed against the surface of the door. It almost flew off at the blow.

For a moment everything thawed. Even the air stalled. Then they heard a rustle from the other side. Skin against attire, Ray tilted his head to listen clearly. Someone moved carefully, probably through furniture. Slow drag of heavy feet, screech of a chair and then the door screeched. Moment later, it cracked open to reveal a woman's face. They could not guess her age. She could be fifty, she could be eighty too. Wrinkles and tiredness had given her a faded look. She blinked at the sight of four men. Fear, disgust, and withdrawal came and went in sequences.

'Samir is not at home.' Ray had to strain his ears to hear what she said.

'Yeah, I know.' Ray began with confidence. The he looked at Sid for identification. Like always Ray was not carrying anything to solidify his right to be there. To be frank, he had no right to be there. He did not work for CID anymore. Years ago, Ray participated in every gruesome murder case actively. But now he came to picture only on request. Only when something befitting Rudransh Ray happened, he stepped forward to solve the unsolvable. Samir Shrivastav's death had sent a tremor of shock which made Chetan to call Ray down for investigation. That was the only reason he had butted in to interview Samir's mother and house keeper. The truth was, criminal profilers did not do it. They did not interrogate people or speak to victims' relatives. But he was Rudransh Ray. He had the license to break rules and make some of his own.

At Ray's signal, Sid stepped forward armed with his ID card which proved that he was from CID and had a right to knock on any door any time. He thrust the card at the woman's face making her flinch. 'Police?' She said finally. Her eyes travel up to set on Ray. Questions stormed in the dull depth. Ray braced himself for her reaction when she learned about Samir's death. But there was no way of cushioning the news. A death was a death. An end. How would anyone cushion this news?

'Samir Shrivastav...' Ray paused, groping for words. Numerous times in his life he wished to take the job of an accountant at times like this.

'He is not at home.' She held the door tightly in her vein protruding hand as if she had the strength to withstand their combined force.

'You are Mrs. Shrivastav?' Ray asked. He had his doubt. And she confirmed it.

'No I am the housekeeper.'

'Mrs. Shrivastav home?' Ray asked.

Those doubtful eyes became defensive now. 'She is. But she cannot talk.' A pause materialized in which the old woman's face relaxed. Then she became aware of Ray watching her. 'She is unwell.'

'We are aware of her condition,' Ray said. He was a criminologist not a psychiatrist. Hence he was ill equipped to handle sensitive situations like these. 'We just want to take a look at Samir's things. That's it.'

She blinked at the request. Because Ray stood just a couple of inches away from her, he witnessed the passing apprehension. Scared of what? Even though the question attempted to push out of his mouth, he held his tongue. Not now.

'Why do you want to go through his things?' she asked.

'I am sorry to inform you that...' Vivan started with a calm demeanor, then mid-sentence he lost his control, and paused. He looked at Ray for assistance. This he did not get. Ray looked away and showed no intention of getting into this conversation.

The house keeper's hands tightened on the door frame. They were losing her. If Vivan did not hurry, she would shut the door on their face. Ray's probing eyes found Vivan's hesitating face. He looked at his companions and then down at the leather boots he wore.

Fortunately Akash lacked everything that people called human emotion. When no one showed any willingness of getting the news out, he stepped forward. 'We have found Samir's muti...Samir's dead body this morning. He was...' For a moment, just for a moment, he appeared to be out of words. However, the state of indecision did not last for long. And like always Akash gained his voice back. 'He was murdered. We are investigating the case.' That being said the true crime writer moved back and allowed his friends to take over.

The old woman's eyes narrowed as she tried to digest everything Akash had said. She turned her gaze towards Ray for confirmation. He could see series of questions storming in her eyes. But her mouth did not utter the words.

'We will not bother you for long,' this Ray said in his mildest and gentlest voice. Sometimes he surprised himself. If she did not let them in, they could always come back with a warrant. But he did not want to take the matter to that level.

In her eyes, Ray saw for the first time something other than worry. He saw acceptance. She looked at Ray for another minute before letting go of the door. As the wooden barrier opened, they had the liberty of looking at a long, narrow corridor; half lit by a white zero power bulb. Under the muted white light, the corridor looked like a setting from a cheap horror movie where the ghosts puffed white powder over their faces to look menacing.

This passage they would have to cross to enter the depth of Samir's lair. Ray could already feel a profile taking shape in his mind. Places where people lived reveal a lot about them. Samir, despite his wealthy business setup, lived in a gloomy and depressing house, which was dominated by shadows. The interior of Samir's home matched its exterior. Year old furniture and dirt-covered showpieces crowded a wooden shelf in the hall. Even the interior air had a dusty, mold stricken smell. It took Ray half a minute to scan the room.

Four of them stood for a while, trying to decide their next move. Asking question to this woman might get them information, but Ray wanted to have a look at Samir's things. He needed to know who Samir Shrivastav was in his life. Criminal profiling heavily leaned on knowing two individuals, the offender and the victim. To know the offender, a criminal profiler needed to know the victim and the victim behavior. Frequently victim profile took a back seat in crime shows and movies. No one focused on the one who had been on the receiving end of the crime.

'Where is Samir's room?' Ray asked.

'Upstairs,' she said and disappeared inside an adjourning door to the hall.

For another heartbeat they stood contemplating their next move. Should they take the stairs and go searching Samir's room? Or, should they go back for a female officer? In the end, they decided to go snooping. It would take a couple of minutes only. What could they find inside a business man's room?

'I believe we should hurry,' muttered Akash under his breath. His face had lost the confident control. His team followed his suggestion and hastened up the stairs.

An attic served the purpose of a bedroom for Samir. The decoration of Samir's room surprised Ray. By this time a vision of the entire apartment had formed in his mind. Automatically, he had imagined this room to be a similar companion of the downstairs' living space. But Samir lived in a luxurious room, large enough to accommodate at least twenty people. Freshly painted gray walls looked like blank movie screen. Samir had chosen to paint his ceiling white and hung an enormous chandelier from it beneath which stood Samir's bed, covered with black satin sheet. Even for the pillows Samir had chosen black satin covers, noted Ray. Samir seemed like a man inclined towards darkness which did not tally with the personality of the business man lay dead in his New Alipore office space.

A dresser also painted in black snuggled at a corner of the room. Vivan pulled the lid to reveal rows of shirts and neatly folded trousers. Vivan quickly took inventory of the possessions and bent forward to check the lower level of the dresser.

'Pretty masculine,' Akash said looking around. 'Gives a negative vibe too.'

Yes, that was the word to describe the room. Dark and negative, it felt like the walls wanted to tell tales of many misgivings. A framed photograph caught Ray's attention. It hung over the bed.

He got closer for a better look. A young man with a fair bony face and brown eyes beamed from the photo. Samir in his life. The vision of Samir in death formed in Ray's mind which he had to push away for the moment. It was not the right time to think about the carcass which he had seen just a few hours ago.

'What has he done to deserve to die like that?' Akash asked. He came to stand beside Ray. Together they had mourned a lot of lives. Together they had also rejoiced a lot of deaths. Whether to mourn Samir or rejoice his death, Ray had not decided yet. But he had his suspicion that before the sun came out, they would see Samir Shrivastav in a different light.

'Collected movies,' Vivan said from behind.

The bottom drawer of Samir's dresser was loaded with DVD's. 'Good God,' Akash said. 'Must have been a movie buff.'

'Don't touch them,' Ray said as Akash reached down to retrieve a DVD. 'None of them comes with any title written over them.'

'I will get them checked,' Sid said. 'Gotta be porn.'

Ray squatted to take a look under the bed. 'You think the killer will be hiding there?' Akash asked still staring at the stakes of DVD's with a doubtful expression. Others gave a nervous laugh.

No, he did not find the killer hiding under the bed. He came upon two large suitcases instead. With his right hand Ray gave one of the suitcases a casual yank. It did not budge. Cursing, Ray pulled again harder this time.

Ten minutes later, they stood surrounding two large leather suitcases, loaded with five hundred rupees notes. For a long time none of them spoke. They had the same thought in their minds – was it money that slashed Samir throat to navel.

'How much?' Finally Vivan asked.

'More than crore.' Ray took a wild guess.

'Wow.'

Sid looked at Ray. They exchanged a quick glance then Sid fished his phone out of his pocket. 'Check Samir's bank account details. I want to know about every transaction he has made till he died.' He paused to listen and then said. 'Yes, everything, debit and credit card transactions included.'

Ray's gaze fell on the DVD piles. Already, a nudge deep down his stomach had started to rise. 'This murder is gonna fry our asses.' He muttered under his breath. 'And then twist our nuts like fresh berries.'

Downstairs, they stood facing the housekeeper again. This time the conversation took place inside the room where she had disappeared earlier.

'Where is Mrs. Shrivastav?' Ray asked breaking the thickening silence. His lungs screamed for a fag. But the time was not right. Hence, he had to shove the urge away. Tough task, but, you gotta do what you gotta do, he thought with irritation.

In answer to his question, the old woman looked at a connected door. 'She is in there.' After a pause, she added. 'Bathing.'

Bathing? In this cold? At this time of the morning? Ray felt the questions tumbling out from inside. But before they came out, he put a tight lid on his mouth. It was not his place to question whether Samir's mother would bathe in icy cold weather or sizzling heat.

'Someone has killed him last night.' Sid took over, sensing Ray's unease. To this the old woman did not react. 'Do you know anyone who may want him dead?'

While the woman thought, Ray took the room at a glance. There was not much to see. A single bed at one corner, a metal wardrobe, a wooden chair and a plastic table perched against a fading wall were everything the room had, a far cry from the dark bedroom upstairs.

'A lot.' The two words were spoken in such a low voice that Ray almost missed them.

'Can you name some?' Ray asked, startled.

'No,' she said. 'But they used to come here to talk to him. Some threatened to kill him. Ishant can tell you.'

'Ishant?' Ray asked, looking at Vivan.

'Ishant Mallick, Samir's business partner. He is in Mumbai right now.'

'When is he coming back?' Ray wanted to know.

'Day after tomorrow.'

'He brought home girls as well…' Before this went any further, the bathroom door opened. A woman in her late fifties walked out wearing a pair of pink slippers. Only a pair of pink slippers.

All four of them froze. But only for a moment. Then they regained their wits and flew from the room like kids caught stealing fruits from neighbors' garden.

Chapter – 3

Hard wind turned harder by the time they drove out of Samir's neighborhood. The murder scene bothered Ray. Something did not make sense. In his mind Ray kept seeing Samir's mutilated body. The fact that the killer left the murder weapon behind yet took the object possibility a very sharp and very long knife which he used to rip Samir apart with him, did not fall into place. Why did he leave the cricket bat which may possess finger print, yet took the sharp object away?

What was he chasing? A disorganized killer? A man who had lost touch with reality? A man so driven by passion that could not relate to his human side now? Or, a man so shrewd that he thought no one could match his wits? Both were dangerous offenders. But for others sake, Ray hoped it was a psychotic killer they had been dealing with who could not plot or plan out his acts. A confident psychopath would be harder to profile and catch.

The murder scene pointed towards a disorganized killer. Yet, somehow Ray could not agree. His heart kept contradicting the disorganized killer theory. This could not be a murder of passion. Of course, the murderer had passion. But passion seemed like a secondary motive here. Deep down inside, the story had some other backstory. Something brewed under the layer of the vicious MO and the post mortem operation. Something he could not touch right now. But it glared at him, challenging him to unravel it.

'Samir's office will be full of fingerprints.' Akash said.

'It's an office. Of course, there will be fingerprints,' said Ray. He was not bothered with finger prints. Even if they got finger print of the offender inside the office, they would not be able to get a match unless the offender had a police record.

'How will we separate the ones not belonging to the employees?' Akash asked. Then he remembered. 'Oh, I forgot, Samir did not have any employee. Only Ishant.'

'We will fingerprint Samir and Ishant to find the visitors.' Ray rolled the window down. Cigarette, the need for a smoke increased by the second. Without any guilty feeling he fished a cigarette out.

'At that rate, you will die of cancer in next two years.' Akash narrated his warning not for the first time.

'If I am lucky,' Ray said. His silver plated Rolex said it was eight in the morning. By the look of the sky, no one would be able to say that. With gathering clouds, wind had picked up pace. Mother Nature wanted to tell them something, Ray thought. All hell would break loose or life would yield to death or your ass had been royally fucked. He did not know which one of the expressions would be good for his mental health.

'Where are we going?' Akash asked. 'To the station or office?'

'I gotta go to office.' Ray held the steering wheel with one hand and lit his cigarette with the other. 'Will email my report from there. You go down to the station.'

'To do what?' Akash asked.

'To talk to Chetan. He needs a direct update.'

'Chetan meaning Chetan Bajaj?' Akash asked. 'The CID chief?'

'Ditto.'

'That's my father who hates me.' Akash grinned.

'Great.' Ray pulled the car at the side of the road. 'Get out.'

'Not fair man,' Akash moaned.

'Life isn't buddy,' Ray said, not wishing to extend the conversation at all. You let Akash rant, he would take all your morning and your entire day too and then he would ask to spend the night at your place.

'Fine.' Akash pushed the passenger door open. 'I will give an update.'

Lightning began slashing the horizon to pieces when Rudransh Ray pulled in the front yard of his Raja Basanta Roy Road office. Smell of wet soil still hung in the air. He looked up and drew a long breath inside. It felt good.

Every conscious breath is meditation…

Her voice rose from the past. Then it went silent. Every conscious breath…Ray dragged another lungful of conscious breath. Funny, he never tried to do it when she was around. Don't even go there, Ray told himself. A couple of more steps and downhill, he knew it. Better to start working. Inside, he found his office already buzzing.

'Hey boss,' called Chirag Malhotra, a tall, lean, young man in his late twenties. A promising lawyer, he worked closely with prosecutors and helped them implicate criminals. Chirag had a team of young lawyers working under him on freelance basis.

'Hey, what's going on in the legal front?' Ray asked, taking off his coat.

'Nothing hot,' he said. 'Waiting for something to come up.'

'Or else, he will have to chase ambulance,' said a golden brown eyed young man. He stood six feet three, an inch taller than Ray. Through his beige woolen coat, his masculine arms and wide chest came to view. This was a guy who worked out every day. Karan Shergill was a topper in criminal psychology department. Now, he worked for Rayon Corp.

'Never,' Chirag said. 'I am not gonna chase ambulance.' He threw a pen at Karan which missed its mark.

'You were on call boss?' The question came from a willowy girl, sitting at the corner of the hall. Her pale gray eyes reminded Ray of a cat he used to play with when he was a child. Then one day, someone drove a truck over it. Upon coming back from school, Ray had found a thick patch of blood where the cat used to sit waiting for him to come back. Ray's grandfather had paid a garbage cleaner to take away the tiny body. But the blood did its job. Ray understood that his friend would never come to greet him ever. Fiona Gilbert reminded him of that cat, hungry, lonely, and waiting for someone to run her over. She worked as the field executive. Her job description included gathering information, following people around, and keeping a tab on suspects.

'How do you know?' Ray asked.

'You drove your Honda City.'

Oh, yeah, his field car. 'Yeah Sid called me at 3 and sent me on a case.' Ray looked around and gestured the entire team to gather in the conference room.

'Where is Akash?' Karan asked.

'He went to meet the chief,' Ray said. 'To update him.'

'Shouldn't you update him?' Karan asked.

'Later,' Ray said. 'This case is gonna twist a lot of nerves. I don't wanna worry the chief.'

'That bad?' Karan asked.

'Try gruesome.'

'Wow.'

The conference room of Rayon Corporation could accommodate at least fifty people. Ray stood at the head of a long wooden table with his back turned towards a large white board that they used for planning, strategizing and scheming. He gazed out the only window of the room. Clouds had turned black. Soon a downpour would begin.

Chirag entered the room with a white tray in his hand. He served coffee to the team. 'Where is Lavania?' Ray asked.

Lavania Banerjee was the research analyst. She knew her work. But she was yet to know about professionalism.

Chirag shrugged. 'She has not called.' In other words, none of them had called her.

'Might got late putting on make up,' Fiona said in a deliberate slurred tone.

Before, anyone could comment, the door of the conference room opened and Lavania breezed in. She wore a lime green rolled neck knitted sweater over a pair of skin tight faded blue jeans. Chirag whistled. 'Looking good babes,' he said.

Lavania flashed a smile that said she knew how she looked. Then her eyes turned towards Ray. She hovered near her chair for a moment then dropped on it.

'Learn to be on time,' Ray said.

Her face fell at the order. 'Yes boss.' She nodded.

'Have a seat.' Ray looked at a lanky, young man sitting quietly beside Karan. 'Nilesh, find me everything you can about a man named Samir Shrivastav.'

'He died?' Karan asked.

'Yeah and went under a knife,' Ray informed.

'As in?' Karan asked.

'Post mortem operation.'

'Sexual murder?' Chirag asked.

'Not necessarily,' Karan said. 'What exactly happened?' he asked, turning his gaze towards his boss.

'This.' Ray tossed his iPhone on the table.

Everyone clustered around the phone for a glimpse. Chirag whistled. 'My, my, Jack is back.'

Karan looked at Ray. His gaze reflected the fear his boss felt inside. 'This guy has done it before.'

'How come we have not heard about anything like this before?' Fiona asked. Her wide eyes showed no trace of fear. Ray could feel a growing restlessness inside her. A field job would calm her down.

'He has hidden the body well,' Ray said. That was the only possible answer he could give them right now.

'What happened this time?' Chirag asked. 'Got company?'

'Could be,' Ray said. 'Too early to say anything.'

'But from the look of the body…' Karan leaned forward for a better view. 'It seems like it is a young man.'

'Not very young,' Ray said. 'In his mid to late twenties.'

'Gotta be a strong one.' Karan inspected the wounds carefully.

'Labor of some kind?' Lavania asked. 'Some say Ripper worked in a butcher shop.'

Karan looked thoughtfully at Lavania. 'Someone who works for a butcher shop knows their strength. They would not hesitatingly slit the left side of their first victim's throat. Then left and then right side of the second victim's throat.' He shrugged. 'Ripper gained enough confidence to slit his victim's throat in one swift motion from his third victim only.'

Ray heard in silence. It was an ongoing debate which will continue till the eternity. Who was Ripper? Why did he kill the way he did? What made him choose his victims? Why did he stop? No one knew and no one would ever know. Probably, not knowing made Ripper so interesting to everyone.

'But he had learned his craft from somewhere, right?' Ray finally asked. 'Someone had taught Ripper to slit and rip people apart with knife. So, the butcher shop theory sticks close. But we will never know, right.' He looked down at his phone. 'As for this offender, this guy works out regularly. He is strong. Cannot be a labor or a blue collar worker. His slashes are methodic, sure, and confident. This is an educated guy we are dealing with.'

'What's your plan?' Chirag asked.

'Pull out everything you can on Jack the Ripper,' Ray said to Lavania. 'I want to have everything about the Whitechappel murder case.'

'You really think this is a copycat?' Fiona asked.

'No, I don't,' Ray said. 'This offender is fascinated by the signature of Ripper. Or, else he wouldn't have slashed the dead body open after killing Samir Shrivastav. It is asking for attention and trouble.' Probably, the guy sought attention.

'Okay, I will find you everything I can,' Lavania said. Her eyes lingered on Ray for a fraction longer than a second. Then she looked away.

'Fi, you need to check on Samir. Find every dirty detail you can,' Ray said to Fiona. Her eyes brightened. She had come to Rayon Corp five years ago, looking for a job. Though Ray had a feeling she would be useful, where to put her had been a big question. Her qualification did not help either. Being a standard eight pass out, she had nothing to show for herself. Everyone roared in protest when she still got hired. In five years as a field executive, she had not disappointed Rudransh Ray or his band of crime fighters. 'Karan, you will assist me in this case.'

'My pleasure, skip.' Karan bowed.

Rudransh Ray looked at his team. They all waited. 'This is going to get worse.' Ray delivered the worst. 'The guy is going to strike again. We need to be prepared for his next blow.'

'How do we find him?' asked Chirag.

'If we fail to find him, we will let him find us,' Ray said. 'Either way, the guy gets what he deserves.'

Karan raised his brows in a question. 'What he deserves?'

Ray looked at Karan with a humorless smile. 'He deserve to be behind the bars Karan.'

'Of course.'

Chapter - 4

A flash of lightening divided the heaven into two. Shraddha Basu closed her eyes in disgust, expecting a boom of thunder. But it did not occur. Rain drops beat steadily against the window pane. She placed her hand on the glass and stared out. It looked like a thin curtain enveloping the earth. The rainfall would bring down the temperature even more. She wrapped her arms around herself and shivered happily.

Vibration of her cell phone made her look back. Must be the customer care, she thought. Why they called on the first place? She moved from the window to check the number.

Oliva Sinha, her ex colleague and best friend. 'Hey buddy, how are you?' Shraddha greeted, genuinely happy to hear from Oliva.

'Shraddha,' said Oliva. 'I need your help.'

Olivia's tone stabbed inside Shraddha's heart. Her stomach twisted. She felt a vomiting sensation even though she had no idea what her friend would say next. 'What…what happened?' she asked.

'I am coming to Kolkata,' Oliva said instead of telling her what went wrong.

'Great,' Shraddha said. 'But what happened? Why are you sounding so low?'

'It's Raghav.'

'What happened to Raghav?' Shraddha remembered Raghav Sinha, a promising young journalist with talent to make it to the top. The only setback Raghav endured was his right leg. He could not walk without the help of a crutch.

'He disappeared.'

'He what?' Shraddha moved towards the window again hoping to catch Oliva's voice better.

'He had disappeared. It's been six months I have not heard from him,' Oliva said. Her voice trembled.

'Six months?' Shraddha could not believe her ears. 'And you are telling me now?'

'You know Raghav don't you?' Oliva asked.

'Yeah, I do.' Raghav had worked undercover several times. He had helped breaking a lot of cases others did not dare to put their hands on. 'But he had disappeared many times before what makes you think…?' Shraddha did not let herself finish the sentence.

'Before, he never forgot to send flowers on my birthday.' And Oliva burst into tears. 'I am coming down to Kolkata.'

'Sure,' Shraddha said, trying to digest everything Olivia was telling her. 'But what makes you think he is in Kolkata?'

'Faisal told me.' Faisal Iqbal was the chief editor and the CEO of Delhi Chronicle, a daring newspaper known to fear no one.

'Listen,' Shraddha said, trying to calm her friend down. 'Let me talk to Faisal first. Let me check what he has to say.'

'Okay,' Oliva said.

'Once I get all the information, I will do a rain check.' Even though her voice sounded soothing, she did not feel exactly confident that something meaningful would come out of her investigation.

'Shraddha, I am scared,' Oliva whispered.

Shraddha could understand what her friend felt right at the moment. 'I know what you are feeling. But baby you need to hold on. Can I ask you a few questions?'

'Yeah, sure.'

'Raghav told you anything about the current case?' she asked.

'No.' Oliva's word sounded distant as she blurted it out through sobs. 'He never discussed his cases with me. Oh Shraddha…' She dragged a long breath. 'I am pregnant.'

That halted what Shraddha wanted to say next. She stood with one hand resting on her leather executive chair and another clutching the cell phone to her ear. What would she say to her friend now? Congratulation? Or, words of courage that Raghav would come back?

'This is Samir Shrivastav,' said Akshaj Aparajit Mukherjee. Shraddha stared at the bony face smiling at the camera. The rugged handsomeness of the man in the image grabbed her attention. Although extremely good looking, Samir's eyes sent a sense of chill down her spine. 'He died last night.' Akshaj continued. She looked at her boss. The CEO of Kolkata Breaking made sure that he dominated the room.

'What's so unusual about his death?' asked Kevin Gray. The senior crime reporter had his notebook spread open before him. He hadn't shaved for a couple of days. The greenish stubble did him good. Girls stopped for a second glance and Kevin being a ladies' man, knew the effect.

'We have nothing yet,' Akshaj said. 'But Rayon Corporation is investigating the case. Rudransh Ray had been spotted at the murder scene. And then later at the victim's house.' He paused to look at Shraddha. 'He made sure that no one saw him. Yet, there are ways to find the truth out.'

Shraddha sat back swallowing. Rudransh Ray, she drew a deep breath. Memory of a hard man with expressionless eyes came back to her. five years had passed since the dreadful office trip. Lisa's dead face formed in her mind. She still had nightmares sometimes. Rudransh Ray had been there to investigate the case. Even today, after so many years, she still remembered everything, moment by moment. With effort she made herself to speak, 'There is more to it, right?' Shraddha asked, shrugging away her discomfort. For the last five years that man had maintained a no-contact moto and she respected his decision. He did not want her. She was fine with that. 'Or, else you would not have called us here.' She flashed a smile and Akshaj smiled back. In these past two years, she had come to know her boss pretty well. The man had a hard face and a soft heart. He could not tolerate injustice of any kind.

'Yeah,' Akshaj agreed. 'There is more to it.' He nodded. 'We know unofficially that Samir was killed. Also, he went under knife after his death.'

'You mean to say…' Kevin sat straight now. His eyes picked up the signal. 'He was…'

'Ripped apart.' Akshaj chuckled as Shraddha's eyes widened.

'Wow,' Shraddha could not help saying it out aloud. Her heart slammed against her ribs. 'Ripped apart? How you know?'

'I have sources my dear,' Akshaj said. 'There are friends up there and down there. Both.' He smiled again.

Despite Oliva's depressing call in the early morning Shraddha felt a nudge of excitement. She leaned forward and waited for her boss to continue. Had she been able to see her own face, she would have seen a woman glowing with exhilaration. Akshaj looked at her face a moment longer then tore his eyes away.

'I want you two to cover the case. I want proof that Samir Shrivastav has been ripped apart. I want to catch the killer before Rudransh Ray does or maybe alongside him. I want to print the story before any other newspaper.' That defined Akshaj. He wanted to do it before anyone else. 'Can I depend on you two?'

'Hundred percent,' Kevin said, already jotting notes.

Shraddha said nothing. She sat pondering the issue. Where would they begin from? The link? 'Do you have Rudransh Ray's number by any chance?' she asked. 'Rayon corporation is investigating, it is the link to the case. We should begin from there I guess.'

'Yeah, but Ray is not an easy man to deal with,' Akshaj said. 'He will block you out if he gets to know that you know about the MO.'

'I would not tell him that I know about the ripping,' Shraddha said. Her stomach twisted at the prospect of meeting Rudransh Ray again. Had it been within her control, she would have avoided going in front of Ray. But her job demanded that she met Ray and she would. 'But first I think we should visit the crime scene once.'

'Cops will not let you in,' Akshaj said. 'And the house does not have any special feature which people will be interested to know about.'

They sat in silence. Akshaj led from the front and he took all the decisions. So, they knew eventually Akshaj would tell them what to do. 'Begin from Samir's home.' He looked at Shraddha with hard eyes. 'Kevin, you drop by and take a look around.'

'Sure,' Kevin said, rising on his feet.

'Shraddha stay for a few minutes,' Akshaj said. 'I need to speak to you once.' Kevin threw her a sympathetic glance before disappearing from the room. Once alone, Akshaj looked hard at Shraddha. For the last two years, this man had trained her like a coach, protected her like a father, and pampered her like a big brother. Why Akshaj felt so strongly about Shraddha, no one knew. No one had the courage to ask the question either. 'Shraddha, you are not a journalist,' Akshaj said. 'Meaning, you don't have any degree to back yourself up.'

'True,' she said. Her qualification had been the talk of the newspaper office since she had joined two years earlier. Everyone including Akshaj's younger brother, a major shareholder of the paper, had raised strong protest. They wanted her out. All of them but Akshaj and Kevin.

'But it does not matter,' her boss said. 'I don't believe that degree can make someone write. This case is important. I want you to break it and bring me evidence that Samir was ripped apart within two days. If you fail, I will assign someone else. But I want you to work hard and prove that you deserve to be here.' He leaned his back against the chair and looked at her for a long time. Then he said in a mild tone. 'Don't let me down.'

Now, that hit her hard. Don't let me down, her father told her too. But she could not prove her worth to her father. He died too soon. She moved her eyes from the man sitting across her. She owed him a lot. She owed him the job. He had hired her when she had nothing. Five interviews she had flung before coming to Kolkata Breaking. And he hired her. She still did not know why. And now, he wanted her to prove that she deserved to be here in the paper.

Her silence made him smile. 'Don't worry. If you fail to break the news, I will not fire you.' His mild tone made her smile too. 'Maybe I will penalize you by making you write weather forecast. But you will not be fired that is a promise from my side.'

'I will break the news,' she promised, more to herself than to her boss. 'I will surely prove that I deserve the job.'

'You deserve the job. I have no doubt about that. It's about time you prove it to yourself rather than to others.' He waved his hand in a go-away gesture. She nodded and got up to her feet, feeling a rush of blood down her stomach. Prove it to the bitches and assholes of the papers, sure she would. With her head held high, she walked out of Akshaj's room. It was time, she paid Rudransh Ray a visit.

Chapter - 5

Samir with his mangled skull looked at Rudransh Ray. Blood gushed out from Samir's mouth. He pulled his lips upward in a grotesque smile. Then he raised his blood soaked right hand for a shake. Ray's eyes flew open. He sat up straight, gasping for breath. Crime fighters did not fight only crime. They fought their nightmares as well. Ray rubbed his face with his sweaty palms.

The wall clock of his living room said it was half past three in the morning. He arched back to give his spine some movement. A sharp sensation of pain made him grimace. Carefully, he tried to stretch. But the muscle of his back screamed in protest. The leather couch was not the right place for an over six feet man to sleep. This habit needed to go. If only his heart mustered enough willingness to sleep in his bed.

With a gasp of irritation, he lay back. The rain had subsided long ago. Now, only a smell of wet soil lingered in the air. He snuggled deeper under the blanket, thinking that tomorrow being Sunday, he did not have to go to office. He could work on his book. Maybe if he had enough Sundays, he would be able to finish it too. With the thought in his mind, he turned and closed his eyes.

A face from the distant past formed in his mind. It formed each time Ray was alone. It had been five long years, yet, he could not forget Shraddha. Her mousy face, and wide innocent eyes, still made him wonder what she was doing now. He did not stayed in contact after Lisa's killer was caught. He wanted to. But something inside his heart pulled him away from her. He did not want to contaminate her world of fiction with his dirt. One life had already been lost. He could not take another one. With force, he pushed Shraddha Basu and her thick paperbacks away from his mind. They would never meet. Not in this lifetime at least. He would never allow himself to go near her. Never. With that resolution, Ray drifted into a restless state of slumber.

Next time his eyes opened at a shrill sound. For a moment, Ray could not fathom the cause of the sound. Then he understood that the doorbell of his apartment was buzzing. Someone continued to ring it without interval. Automatically, Ray gazed at the wall clock – past eight in the morning. Strange he did not wake up again last night. A rare feat given the fact that he could sleep only four hours a day.

'Ray, open up,' Sid's voice came booming from the opposite side of the door. 'I need to talk.'

Before he woke up the entire Southern Avenue neighborhood, Ray bolted out of the couch, calling. 'Coming. Hold on.' His voice sounded thick with sleep. His head pounded. Every instinct told him to lie back, pull the cover over his head and drift to the land of nowhere. Ray stumbled, limped, and then walked towards the front door. His still trying to adjust to the gloomy interior of his living room.

Sid looked no better than what Ray felt. His face, pale from lack of food and sleep. His hair needed immediate brushing. He gazed at Ray with tired eyes. 'I watched those videos.' For a moment Ray failed to attach meaning to the statement. What video? Then the fog of sleep thinned and Samir's dresser popped up in his mind. Amidst the mayhem and a futile attempt to profile Samir's killer, Ray had completely forgotten about those videos. But from Sid's expression, Ray understood that the video content possesses enough brutality to drag the CID senior officer to his doorstep so early in the morning.

'And what have you found?' Ray asked, tilting his head a little, just to work on the cramp which threatened to give him a stiff neck soon.

'You gotta watch this.' Sid waved a DVD before Ray. His face broke into a humorless smile. Everything about Sid screamed low energy. Whatever he had seen in those videos had rattled him to the extent that he had ran to Ray's doorstep this early in the morning. Ray scanned his best friend's face once again. Then he turned away, not wanting to know the content of the DVD's. But he would have to know. His demanded that he got into gore and found solutions to save the mankind.

With reluctance, Ray, finally, stepped back and allowed Siddhant in. 'Make some coffee,' Ray said. 'I will be back.' He hurried inside his bedroom, painfully aware of the fact that his head was nicely working up to conjure a massive ache. If he did not gulp down at least five mug of strong coffee and smoked at least thrice, it would knock him down for a long time. Headache kept him company while he worked on a case. So, it was nothing new to him. The only problem was, it was the first time he had been facing a killer who used knife to rip his victims apart. The mental state of the man who had caused this mayhem disturbed Ray. He had seen a lot of violence in his life. But this particular murder had the potential to send him back to therapy.

Sid had two steaming coffee mugs waiting when Ray returned from bathroom after brushing his teeth and splashing ice cold water on his face. His stomach growled. 'I am hungry,' he said.

'Yeah me too.' Sid got Ray's laptop going on the coffee table. It was ready to run at any command. 'Watch this.' He put the DVD and let it run.

The screen came to life with a direct view of a master bed. Ray recognized Samir's room immediately. The same dark gray walls, same black bed sheets, and the same chandelier, deep inside his stomach something rolled, making him want to throw up. Before Ray could react, the camera focused on a man, standing naked by the bed.

Ray let out a deep breath at the sight. The man had a joker mask on his face which kept his identity hidden. However, that's not what made him set his coffee aside. Despite his hardest effort, Ray could not help looking at the masked man's cock which stood hard and strong.

'What's this?' Ray asked, tearing his eyes away from the screen. The day had just started and his head already promised the ache of the year. 'He made porn?'

'He made violent porn.' Sid grinned. 'Busy guy.'

A gasp of fear made Ray look back at the screen. The masked man half dragged and half carried a woman towards the bed. She wore nothing but a pair of red high heel pumps. He threw her on the bed and a moment later two more men wearing same joker masks joined him.

Ray tapped the mouse pad with his index finger, not really ready for the scene to unfold in full motion. 'So, Samir made porn movies.'

'Yeah, he did.' Sid agreed with a smirk. His face broke into another humorless smile. Lately all his smiles look humorless to Ray. 'Think one of his victims popped him?'

'Not likely. The killer cannot be a woman.' Ray closed his eyes and forced himself to return to the scene of murder. Samir's dead body made a comeback to his mind. Nope, he did not think it was a woman.

'What makes you think so?' Sid argued. 'Women don't get nuts?'

'We all get nuts. But the hit on the skull looked masculine.' Again Ray allowed himself a sneak peek of Samir's dead body in his mind. *Look at artwork to know the artist.* 'That and the cut down the navel. I will bet my money on a man. A tall, strong man skilled with knife.'

Samir Shrivastav was a tall man, over six feet. To hit him on the back of his skull and crack it with one shot, the offender needed to be tall and masculine. Someone in his late twenties, Ray thought. The accuracy with which the offender had blew the Samir's skull spoke of a calculative, and practiced hand.

'I see.' Sid lit a cigarette. Long suppressed temptation came flooding as the smoke the living room area. Ray's hand too reached for his signature cherry red packet. 'So, what's the plan?' Sid asked.

They had banished the possibility of a hired gun. The offender was known to Samir and it was apparent from the lack of struggle in the crime scene. Samir died without knowing what was coming. Only someone familiar could cause that type of damage.

'That's the saddest part,' Ray said. 'I don't have any. Samir knew his killer. And we need to find out how.' He paused for a long drag of cigarette. 'Also, it is difficult to create a geographical profile.' He held Sid's stare for a moment then let the smoke out. 'Not enough resources.'

To get a geographical profile of a killer, a profiler needed at least five bodies. Ray did not want the matter to go to that extent. But from the way Samir had been mutilated, he could bet that soon they would get a geographical profile of the offender.

'We need to know about Samir.' Sid looked up at the ceiling and dispersed three smoky rings in the air. Ray followed suit and released four to outmatch him. It had been their college time competition who could create more smoky rings. It was fun. Life was fun. Then everything went downhill.

'He made porn,' Ray said, watching the rings fade in the air. 'What else he did?'

'I will have to check.' Sid leaned his head against the sofa and closed his eyes.

'When was the last time you slept?' Ray asked, thinking about the murder.

To this question, Sid said nothing. He let out clouds of smoke. 'I will not be in town from tomorrow,' he said. 'You will have to take care of the investigation.'

'Yeah, what else is new?' Ray asked. 'Most of the time I take care of the investigations. Little good leaving CID did to me.'

Sid let out a long breath. His eyes found a spot on the wall. Ray followed his gaze. 'Yeah, I removed her photo.' Ray's voice sounded hollow in the silence of the morning.

'You don't think she deserves to be remembered?' Sid asked.

'I think it's about time I move on,' Ray said. His eyes still hung on the spot in question. 'I think she deserves to be set free.'

Sid's eyes moved away from the wall. He looked at Ray with a strange expression. Ray could not identify the emotion. For half a second it lingered. Then Sid got up to his feet. 'I gotta go now.' He grinned. 'Take care of that ass of yours buddy. I don't want to have a platter full of crispy ass fry upon my return.'

Sid walked out without speaking another word. His behavior have started to worry Ray. Siddhant Thakur had always been a happy go lucky who took life as a journey to enjoy. Ray turned his head to look at the empty space above the television set. Once, a framed photo of his wife Rusha hung there. Now, only a dusty reminder of what had been, glared at him.

To push the memory away from his already wrecked mind, he got up to his feet. The wall clock struck nine thirty in the morning. Ray stood in the middle of the room with his hand on his stomach, considering. Was it too late to go for a run? The chill outside and today being Sunday people would not amble out in the street. Still it was morning, and running would be an unappealing task, Ray thought. Rather than going for a run, he decided to hit the gym. His body ached for a sweat blast.

The trainer, a tall slender girl in her early twenties, smiled at him at the gym. 'Hello Mr. Ray.'

'Ray please.' Ray smiled back. She looked sweet in a pink tracksuit. Funny, he had not noticed her before, thought Ray. He had noticed only one woman after Rusha. A sharp knife stabbed inside his heart, making him drag a deep breath. No ways, he thought, not now, not ever. The firm inner voice, however, failed to instill its authority as his heart continued to crave for the only woman who had succeeded in reviving his soul from the land of death. What did she do to make him fall so hard? Wondered Ray, even today. Only, he had no answer to that question.

'It had been a long time since you came here,' she said. A lock of silky brown hair fell over her eyes. She tucked it behind her ears. A futile effort, as it fell back again.

'I had been here,' Ray said. 'But to the Taekwondo workshop.'

'Oh,' she said. Her eyes turned softer as she looked at him. 'What's the difference between Karate and Taekwondo?' she asked.

Ray raised his eyebrows at the question. Though athletic, she did not strike him the type to go around kicking and punching. But since she had asked, and he had knowledge, he decided to enlighten her. 'The kicks. In Karate kicks take a backseat. While Taekwondo is all about kicks. Punches take a backseat in this form of martial art.'

She nodded as if that made sense to her. Probably it did. Ray did not stay around to find out. Instead he walked over to the treadmill, jammed his ears with a pair of headphones and started to run.

Two hours later, Ray finished his work out. Sweat flooded out of his system like water coming out of a tap. It felt good. he thought better when he sweated a lot. The blood pump cleared his head. The possibility of a headache had subsided. Ray breathed easy now that he had his blood pumping in his veins.

'You don't quit do you Ray?' asked the gym teacher.

In reply, he pulled his mouth up in a smile. Poor kid, did not know the half of it. 'Not always,' he said. He would have asked her out had he remembered her name. it had been ages since he had been out with a woman. Time to move on and stay moved, Ray thought.

'How about a cup of coffee?' she asked without skipping a beat. When Ray raised his brows up she looked down at her feet, embarrassed.

To make her feel at ease, Ray said, 'I would have asked the same question.' It made her look up with a bright smile.

Her name, Ray found out later, was Ekta Patil. They drove to a CCD and sat outside so Ray could smoke. She sat silent. Occasionally her gaze found his and she smiled. Shy, Ray thought with the same beat *not my type*. A forty inch television set was broadcasting Samir's death news. They had not found out about the ripping part, yet. Ray did not know how long the news would stay hidden. Someone from the police department was bound to go bragging about it. All hell would break lose when the news came out.

Ekta's face tightened at the sight of Samir's photo on the screen. She sat straight with lips slightly parted. Ray felt his stomach turning up with anticipation.

'You know him?' Ray asked.

She did not answer. Her eyes wide with surprise and hatred did not move from the screen. He waited for her to come back to this world. She knew something. In situations like this the biggest challenge was to be patient. You pushed it, you lost it and Rudransh Ray was a patient player. His colleagues called him The Vulture for the reason.

Life had taught him to be patient. Impatience might be the new life of the new generation, yet, it led to nothing but destruction and failure. No matter what, the world must wait for the sun to rise, tide to turn, and clock to strike. Ray watched her in silence. She did not tear her attention from the television screen.

'You know him?' He asked again when she regained her composure and turned her gaze towards him.

Instead of answering she looked down at her hand. This she did a lot. 'No,' she said in a small voice that he had to strain his ears to catch. 'I thought he looked like someone I knew once.'

A lie, the wolf in him could smell it. Some people are yet to master the art of lying without getting caught. If your face did not give you away, your voice surely would. A perfect lie was a fusion of right expression and tonality. His instinct held him back from pushing it further. Let it be, he thought. Later he would grill her to tell him how she knew Samir or what he did to her.

Ray drove slowly back home after dropping Ekta at her doorstep. His mind whirled with possibilities. How she knew Samir? Why was she afraid of talking to him? He pulled the car at the side of the road and fished his iPhone out.

Fiona answered at the first ring. 'Fi, I want you to do a thorough BGB of a girl named Ekta Patil. She is a gym instructor.'

Fiona did not sound offended to be called on Sundays. Crime fighters did not allow the luxury of vacationing or relaxing at home. 'What exactly are you looking for?' she asked. 'Which angle should I focus on?'

'She knew Samir,' Ray said. 'But she is afraid of something. I want you to get the details and report back to me.'

Next he called Nilesh, his tech guy. That was the sophisticated way of saying Nilesh hacked computers – ethically, whatever that meant.

'Nil, I have work for you,' Ray said.

He too did not sound offended. 'What can I do for you skip?'

'I want some details about my gym instructor Ekta Patil. She knew Samir and I want to know how.' Ray tapped his index finger on the steering wheel.

'You will get it skip. I will report back on Monday.'

'See ya.'

A surprise awaited him at his door step. A petit woman in her early thirties stood in front of his apartment building. Ray froze at the sight of her. A rush of memories greeted him and took him five years, four months, and eight days back in time. He had counted each moment that he had spent away from her. There had been times when he almost picked up the phone and made a call. But each time that urge took him over, he forced myself to remember Rusha. He had ruined an innocent woman and he was not going to ruin another one. So, he stayed away from Shraddha all these years, even though it killed him from inside.

'Mr. Ray,' she said when he got out of my car. 'Do you have a moment?' Her voice was cool and nonchalant. It did not give any sign of recognition. But he saw it in her eyes. He saw questions crowding there. Questions he would not be able to answer.

He approached her in slow and hesitant steps. She wore a pair of skin tight ice blue jeans and a black rolled neck knitted sweater under a knee length red woolen coat. For her feet she had chosen a pair of nude colored boots. A vision to behold in serenity. Her long, dark hair rested loose on her back. Ray looked into her eyes, trying to connect this polished woman to the mousy girl who he had met five years ago. Nothing of the old Shraddha remained in her now, saving the eyes. Her wide, innocent, and vulnerable eyes. His heart twisted, turned, and then began to race.

His heart continued to thud against his ribs as he came to stand before her. She stood there, dazzling against the backdrop of his apartment building, looking at him as if he was a stranger who did not matter to her.

Probably, he did not. Of course, he should not. Yet, that did not reduce the ache down his soul.

'What can I do for you ma'am?' He heard himself saying to her.

'I am Shraddha Basu,' she said with a humorless smile. The last information was added after a pause. 'From Kolkata Breaking. I want to speak to you about Samir Shrivastav murder case.'

'I remember you Shraddha.' His voice sounded soft. He did not recognize this voice. Neither did he like it. He should walk away now, he knew it. But his feet did not obey his command. They remained planted on the ground. 'You are a reporter now?' he asked in surprise.

'Yeah, I am,' she said. Cool and composed, the Shraddha Basu he knew had changed completely, from inside out. Ray let out a breath. Would he fall harder for this version or was the old one better? He asked himself with discomfort.

His back ached from a previous injury. 'Why don't you come upstairs?' he said. 'We can continue over a cup of coffee.'

'Sure,' she said without hesitation. 'Coffee will be good.'

Like a programmed machine Ray turned and walked towards the entrance of his apartment building. His head felt heavy all of a sudden. All these years he had remained away from her hoping that it would save her from crime and violence and now here she was dealing gore from the center.

Inside he offered her a seat and went to fetch coffee. He kept checking all the details he gathered till now in his mind. Sadly, nothing led to the next step. He returned to his living room with two mugs of coffee.

'You want sandwich?' he asked. She looked to be starving.

A smile played on her face at the question. 'No. Thank you.' She shook her head.

'Here is your coffee.' He set a mug in front of her. 'Don't worry it's not spiked. You know me right?' he asked. 'I cannot do that to a woman.'

She brushed her hand through her hair which went past her shoulders and reached her narrow waist. 'Unless you are questioning them and trying to extract information to solve a case.' She laughed then. The warm and melodious sound filled his dead living room and he found himself joining her. It felt good to laugh with someone.

'I try.' Ray nodded. 'You are from Kolkata Breaking.' He dropped on the couch across her and looked at her face. She barely looked twenty even though he knew she was well past thirty. Her wide eyes and parted lips, forced him to look back in the mazes of past. His gaze brushed the empty space over the television set.

'Yeah, I am.' She rested her hands on her lap.

'A big shift huh?' meaningless questions, yet he could not stop himself from probing a bit into her life. Was she single? Dating someone? Married? In love with someone?

Her eyes lost focus for a fraction of second, trying to remember. 'Yeah.' She paused. 'A big one. I gave up content writing five years ago and worked for a small newspaper as a fashion reporter. Joined Kolkata Breaking two years back.'

'Yes. And in this short while you have been assigned to Samir Shrivastav's murder case?' Ray asked. She did not look equipped with enough bitchiness required to handle a high profile case like this.

An expression crossed her face. It vanished before he could read it. But it looked very close to confidence, combined with pride. 'Yes, I am.' He expected her to retort, to come back with some wisecracks. But she said nothing else. She just flashed him a smile and nodded. The girl he met had grown up, he noticed with regret.

'Ok.' He nodded, reaching for his coffee. 'Please, help yourself. This is not spiked.'

She lifted her shoulders in a nonchalant shrug. 'I know it's not.' She made a face.

Despite the polished lady like exterior, there lay a touch of innocence in her which he had found appealing before. 'How do you know that Rayon Corporation is involved in this case?'

'My boss informed me.' She took a small sip from the coffee mug, leaving a smudge of her pink lipstick on the rim.

'Your boss?' He raised his brows in question.

'Akshaj Mukherjee.' She set the coffee mug down and looked around the hall. Ray sat back allowing her to take inventories of his personal space.

Once she was done scanning, he asked. 'Who?' The name did not ring any bell. He made a mental note of checking on this person later on. 'I thought Dharam Agarwal is the owner.'

'Sir bought it from him.' She cracked her knuckles. Nervous. Ray almost smiled at her unease. Poor girl, should not have been brought in this mess.

'Do you know what your boss has dragged you into?' Ray asked, watching her face speaking to her. The old Shraddha had an open face, easy to read. But this woman, who sat across him had no expression at all. Only her eye reflected the inner turmoil which she went through.

Her eyes narrowed, losing her composure for a second. It passed quickly, but not before Ray caught it. She had a volcano striving to come out from within. He would have loved to pry it out. But now did not seem like the right time.

'He said it is a sensitive case since Rayon Corporation is involved.' Her voice calm and serene, had an electrifying appeal.

'Yes, it is a sensitive case,' Ray said. 'More gruesome than sensitive. You have no idea what had happened to Samir.' He smiled at her. 'Don't get involved in this. You might get into trouble.'

The wall clock of his living room ticked in the background as she sat in silence. Ray sipped his coffee watching her face. It did not crack. Her facial muscles did not reveal anything. The only expressive features were her eyes. They reflected every thought that passed through her head.

'You know what?' she said.

The moment she said this Ray knew what came next. 'Yeah.'

'My job depends on breaking this case.' She looked up to stare into his eyes. 'Either I get the information or I lose my position forever. My boss trusts me and my ability. I cannot let him down.'

Her boss, Ray would love to meet this man once. 'You have no idea what might happen.' Trying to talk sense into her would not be easy. Yet, Ray could not allow myself to let go. He just could not shrug and say - not my problem. 'He is using you.'

'He gave me a job when I had nothing. He hired me as a journalist even though I don't have a degree,' she said. Her face revealed the first touch of emotion, anger. 'Would you have hired me?'

His mouth pulled up in a smile. She looked radiant with the touch anger. 'Yes, I would have.' A lie, being near her all day long would ruin his peace of mind.

'Will you tell me about the murder?' she asked, without further ado. Her right hand went inside the black leather hand bag which she carried with herself. It came out with a thick, hard covered, black A5 notebook and a pen.

'Sure, I will.' Her eyes widened with surprised, not ready to believe him yet. Ray was not ashamed to admit that she was not wrong in not believing him. Someone believed in him and died for doing so. His eyes travelled up to look at the empty space again. She deserved to be remembered. Sid was right. But each time he looked at her framed face, smiling at him, he felt something dying inside. She died. He lived. Unfair, life was.

Shraddha waited for him to tell her something which would save her career. Something he had no respect or weakness for. He did not live for limelight. Yet, media could be helpful. They could assist them in shaking the offender out in the open. His gaze fell on her eager face. A plan formed in his mind just then. It could be risky to pull something like this. But he had no other option right now. With this single move, he could drag the offender out and save Shraddha's career in crime reporting together.

'Before, I say anything, I want your word that my name will not be involved in this.' He cracked his knuckles as he said this. She leaned slightly forward towards him.

He did the same, automatically imitating her body language, getting comfortable with her in his living room.

'You have my words.' Her voice barely above whisper rang in the silence of the room. They sat eleven stories above the ground. Here silence ruled as the sound of zooming cars, people passing by or any other sound failed to intrude. Those searching for silence would find solace here. They too found serenity in seclusion.

Making a quick decision, Ray got his iPhone out of his pocket. With his index finger he scrolled down. Twenty images, useless downloads from WhatsApp later, he stopped. His eyes stared down at Samir's body lying on the floor, ripped and exposed. His stomach rolled at the sight, once again.

'This is Samir.' He turned the phone over so she could take a look. What he expected he had no idea. But he certainly did not expect the reaction she showed.

Shraddha leaned further towards the screen. Her eyes, wide and surprised, took in everything, even the backdrop of the body. She licked her lower lip with her tongue. Then Ray witnessed the transformation. Surprise gave way to curiosity. Her eyes brightened and mouth turned up in a smirk. Before his eyes she changed, radiated with energy and passion. Even with his best effort, he could not look away from her face. Hell, she was stunning, ravishing even, he thought. Working along side with her would be difficult.

'The Ripper,' she said. 'Can I have that image?'

'What you gonna do with it?' he asked, struggling to keep his voice calm. Blood rushed everywhere in his body, making him feel alive again. He wanted to kiss her, deep and long. As the thought passed his head, he became aware of the fact with unease that it was not all physical. What he felt for her was beyond the flesh level. His soul, his long deceased soul demanded her. The yearning was so strong that he had to draw a deep breath to maintain control. 'You cannot print it,' he said and congratulated himself for not showing his emotion.

She leaned back, reaching for her coffee. 'Of course, I cannot. I will edit the image before printing.' She looked him in the eyes and said. 'Public has a right to know what they may face. He is already dead. He will not mind being printed.'

'Yeah, he is dead.' He agreed, still watching her.

Her eyes narrowed and the smirk vanished. She looked at him with a thoughtfulness that almost made him look away. 'So, why are you showing me this?' she asked. 'Why suddenly you want to talk to the media?'

Her questions had a valid point. Ray did not want to speak to the media. He had always avoided facing the mike, unless it helped him solve a case. But this one was different. The media personality was different this time. But he could not tell her that. So, he repeated what she had just said. 'Public has a right to know.'

'Aha, cool. If you believe that why not talk to the media right away?' she asked. 'Why this private conversation which no one can hear?'

'You want the image and the information?' he asked.

'I do.' She shrugged. 'But I also want to know where you are pushing me. You know before getting into the wheel trap…'

'What trap?' Ray asked, caught off guard.

'You don't know Mahabharat do you?' she asked.

Hell no. 'I don't have time for that.'

'Make time.' Her smile widened at his expression. In her eyes, he saw yearning. What did she yearn for, he wondered as he smiled back.

'Fine, I will make time,' he said. Then he leaned forward. 'Look, this case is a sensitive one. Don't be misguided by the façade of safety. No one is safe here.' He put his phone back. 'The killer may come after you once your writeup gets published.' He looked at her for a long time. She looked back. He did want to save her career. But he wanted her to be safe as well. 'Your boss will not be able to protect you if things go wrong. So, think about it more than once before getting too deep in this case. We are dealing with a madman who will strike again.'

Chapter – 6

The last ray of the sun died a long time ago. Wind whined like a dying old woman. The temperature, though already frosty, dropped even lower.

Shraddha sat hunched on her writing desk. It was half past seven. She had her laptop switched on. The blank screen screamed for her attention. She had things to write. She had her novel to finish. Only, there was nothing she could think of writing at that moment. In her mind, she kept seeing Samir and his body, ripped from the throat to navel. From childhood she had a thing for blood and gore.

Whodunit had been a childhood companion which taught her that anyone could be the bad guy. Or, rather the genre had taught her that the most innocent looking man or woman in the room had to be the killer. But that was different. Whodunit stories featured people with wits and ability to plot. Rarely the murders in her beloved mystery novels got her stomach twist in fear.

She closed her eyes. Immediately, Rudransh Ray's face formed in her mind. His dark, and deep eyes, his unshaved face, and his wide smile, came back in a rush. A smile played on her face as she thought of Ray. It was probable a bad idea to lust over a man she hardly knew and did not trust. But Ray had that thing about him which screamed easy confidence. There was something more to the man then just a rugged appeal, or maybe a hidden vulnerability. Whatever it was, Shraddha found him to be a storybook hero who had no place in this real world.

Vibration of her cell phone brought her out of the trance. For a moment she thought of letting it go. Then she thought otherwise. It was her younger sister Trisha.

'Hey Trish, hows you?' she said, happily. They had a routine of speaking to each other every evening.

'Hey babes, things are going fine,' said Trish said with a touch of smile in her voice. 'I have sold a painting.'

Shraddha felt her heart warmed at the news. Trish had worked hard for this exhibition. Her sister deserved success. 'I am so happy for you Trish.'

'Thank you.' Shraddha heard a catch in her sister's voice. Something was not right.

'What's wrong?' she asked. 'You don't sound too happy.'

'I am happy,' said Trish. 'It just that I have received a job offer.'

'Job offer?' asked Shraddha, confused. What type of job offers artists got?

A pause materialized on the other side. She could hear Trish's breathing and zooms of cars. 'Yeah from an art gallery in Paris.'

Everything vanished for a fraction of second. Shraddha blinked. Her vision cleared moments later. 'Wow Trish,' she yelled. Her voice rose, shattering the silence mounting inside. 'I am so happy. You are going to Paris.'

'No, I am not,' said Trish. 'I can't.'

'But why not?' Shraddha asked, puzzled at the answer. 'We have savings. Money is not going to be a problem. Besides you will get paid from the gallery.'

'It's not money I am thinking about,' Trish said. 'The salary is enough for two of us.'

'I earn a lot of money from my job.' Shraddha said. Since the day their parents died in a car crash, together they had ran their home. Each supporting the other with strength and affection.

'I cannot leave you alone there.' Shraddha heard a touch of desperation in Trisha's voice. Trisha had always been over protective, even though she was the younger child.

Trish, Shraddha thought, you have to go. 'I am leaving Kolkata in a few months as well.' She blurted out.

'What?' Trish asked. 'Where are you going?'

'Bangalore or Pune,' Shraddha said, thinking fast. 'My boss is transferring me soon. So, if you come back, you will be alone here. I am going anyways.' She paused for a breath. 'So, it's better that you accept the offer that comes your way. And go.' Her heart ached as she said this. Trisha was her only family. They loved each other more than life but they both were driven by their passions. Prisoners of their own desires, she thought. 'You will never get this opportunity sis.'

Trish went quiet. The silence stretched. 'You are lying right?' Trish asked finally. 'You can never leave Kolkata. That city is your life.'

Of course, they knew each other better than their own shadows. 'Yeah, I am lying. But if you come back because of me, I am gonna move out.' Shradha paused to drag a breath. 'Now, it's your choice.'

Trisha was quiet for a long time. 'Then promise me to come to Paris when I settle down there.'

An image of Paris from the videos and pictures she had seen formed in Shraddha's mind. She dragged a deep breath. Could be good to relocate. 'We will see about that.'

Long after the conversation with Trish, Shraddha sat staring at her laptop screen. She had sent her article on Samir Shrivastav murder case. She had even attached an image of Samir in his last slumber. What Akshaj did with the image was none of her business anymore. She would wait for the next order from her boss. Right now, all she could think of was Raghav. Where did he go?

She had tried to talk to Faisal in the morning while waiting for Rudransh Ray. But the editor in chief was not in his office. She tried to get his cell phone number, but the receptionist refused to offer any help. She called Oliva for the cell number. And found her friend's phone switched off. On the second attempt to find Faisal, she had been told, not very politely, to leave a message. She did. It was almost ten in the night and no one called.

Tomorrow, she promised herself and the unseen entity up there. Tomorrow, I would fight again. Right now, her eye lids felt heavy. She needed to get some sleep. As her hand reached for the laptop, her cell phone started vibrating. She kept it on the vibration mode all the times because cell phone's ringtones made her want to scream at someone. It had been the same since her childhood days. She had an aversion to noise and high pitch sounds.

Who could it be? She thought in irritation. It was already too late. She checked the caller ID, Delhi's number. With shaking hands she pressed the receive button. 'Shraddha Basu.'

'Hey,' greeted a male voice. 'Faisal Iqbal.'

'Hey,' she said. Her mouth turned up in an automatic smile. Faisal's ruggedly handsome feature formed in her mind. The guy looked good enough for fashion magazine. 'I need to talk to you,' she said.

'Raghav?' Faisal asked.

'Yeah, Oliva called. This morning.' She narrated the conversation.

'I am worried too.' Faisal's voice dropped. But Shraddha did not miss a single beat. 'This time…' He let out a breath. 'I have failed to contact him. He has just vanished from the face of the earth.'

'Do you have any idea what he was chasing?' she asked. 'There must be something important. Groundbreaking.'

'You know us, don't you?' Faisal asked. 'We chase things no one else dares to chase. Raghav was excited. He said that he would bring great scoop from Kolkata.'

'Hasn't he sent you anything during his mission in Kolkata?'

'Yes, he has sent me mails.' She heard him hitting some keys on a keyboard. 'But he did not explain anything to me.' He paused. 'I am forwarding everything to you. Even the last mail where he expressed fearing for his life.'

'He feared for his life?' Shraddha asked.

'You are working as a crime reporter right?' asked Faisal.

'Yeah.'

'Make friendship with fear. This is our constant companion.' Again she heard some keys being punched. 'I have sent everything. See, if you can find a clue. But…'

'But what?'

'Don't dig too deep. I don't think it will be safe.' With that warning the line went dead. Shraddha sat looking straight at the window which overlooked a dark and fast emptying street. Winter nights in Kolkata, she thought without any emotion.

In six months Raghav had sent only fifteen emails. Only the last two had something of value. In these two emails he had expressed his fear for life. He also said that someone had hacked into his computer. But she found nothing which could lead her to a name or a place.

Raghav must have stayed somewhere. He did not live on the street. If only she could find the place where he lived, her hand reached for her cell phone. Would Oliva be of any help? Then her eyes turned towards the wall clock. It was past twelve thirty in the morning. No decent person should call another at this time. Added to this Oliva was pregnant.

She curled her fingers in resignation. Her phone vibrated at the exact moment. Talk about decency. She checked the caller ID. Akshaj Mukharjee. At this hour?

'Sir,' she said, frightened at receiving a call so late. 'Is something wrong?'

'I read your article,' boomed Akshaj's voice. 'It's brilliant.'

Shraddha's face warmed despite the chill at the appreciation. 'Thank you sir.'

'But this article might attract unwanted attention.' Akshaj let out a breath. 'I saw the image. It is pretty disturbing.'

Samir's body, she closed her eyes and tried to push the image from her mind. But the horror stayed, stubborn as pimple mark. 'Yeah, what happened to him was pretty brutal.'

'True.' Akshaj said. 'We are printing it. But right now you stay anonymous. I cannot reveal your name. It might be risky.'

She could see Akshaj's eyes, narrow with worry. The omission of her name disappointed her a little. She had dreamed of rising to fame from this article. But then again, somethings in life should wait for the right time.

'You there?' Ajshaj asked.

'Yes sir very much,' she said, flushed.

'Why are you awake so late?' asked her boss.

She laughed at the question. 'You are up too.'

'Yeah, but I am printing the biggest story of the newspaper's history,' Akshaj's high energetic voice erased the last string of tiredness from Shraddha's mind. 'What are you doing? Waiting for your boyfriend's call?'

No I was trying to get famous, she wanted to say. 'I am trying to find someone.'

'Boyfriend?' came the instant question.

'No, a friend's husband.'

'What happened?'

'So he came to Kolkata and then he vanished?' asked Akshaj Mukherjee. He sat in her living room, a coffee mug in his hand. She insisted that he did not have to come. He insisted that he had to. Like always, she lost the battle. And here she sat across her boss and a sleepy eyed Kevin at 1.30 in the morning, in her living room, discussing Raghav's disappearance.

'According to Oliva and Faisal, yes,' Shraddha said. She could see it in her boss' eyes that he smelt a story behind the disappearance. 'I just don't know where to start looking for him from.'

'If we find out where he lived…we could have…' Akshaj's voice trailed as he pondered this over. 'Faisal knows anything about it?'

'No,' she shook her head. 'I haven't talked to Oliva, yet.'

'Talk to her.' Akshaj said. 'We could run a missing person ad with a photograph, if everything else fails.'

'What a cliché,' she said making a face.

The comment made Akshaj smile a crooked smile. 'Sometimes clichés work better than witty twists.'

'Will remember that.'

Next morning came with lot of excitement. Samir's death which made it to the third page in other newspapers became the show stopper for Kolkata Breaking. To make people gape in horror, Akshaj printed a photo of Samir's dead body. To avoid legal charges, he ordered to blur the image. But people got it. Samir was killed. Samir was ripped apart. The killer was roaming free. The police had failed to come up with anything useful. They also had pointed out clearly that celebrity criminal profiler Rudransh Ray was profiling the offender. As an afterthought, Akshaj decided to print Shraddha's name which made a lot of people angry in the newspaper room.

'How you got hold of that image?' asked Shivani Guha. Shivani had been working for Kolkata Breaking for the last eight years. In her opinion, she possessed the divine right to work on all the high profile cases. She did so before the change of ownership.

'I sort of found it lying on the pavement near College More bus stand,' Shraddha said. She munched on a grilled chicken sandwich and sipped cold coffee to wash it down her throat. People commented on her liking for cold coffee. It was too frosty for cold beverage. But Shraddha loved her cold coffee and she would have it despite any weather condition.

'You think I am a fool?' Shivani took a step closer.

Ugly too, this Shraddha did not blurt out. 'No, I think you are impossibly clever.' Saying this, she walked away before the conversation stretched further. As she reached Akshaj's cabin, she turned. Shivani stood her ground, glaring at her. 'That's your biggest tragedy.'

With that she opened Akshaj's cabin and walked inside, leaving the former star reporter of the newspaper frowning at her.

'Good morning,' she said in a soft voice.

Akshaj looked up from a thick leather diary he had been studying. His face broke into a smile at the sight of her. She felt herself smiling too. Looking at him no one would say that he spent the entire night planning to find Raghav.

'Congratulation,' Akshaj said. 'You did a good job of breaking the case.' He stared at her for a couple of minutes. 'How come Ray gave the image to you?'

'He must have a plan.' She could think of no other reason than that.

But it did not satisfy Akshaj. 'That or he liked you?'

Shraddha laughed at the question. 'You know something?' she asked. 'You are like a horribly possessive father.' She paused to look at her boss. 'You just don't want to admit it.'

Akshaj leaned forward, still staring at her. 'I am like a horribly possessive father. I am admitting it.'

'Very good.'

Chapter – 7

The front page of The Kolkata Breaking made Ray grin. He leaned back in his living room couch and relished Shraddha's writeup. Not for the first time Ray noticed that she was an outstanding writer with a tendency for melodrama. A perfect fit for the media, he thought with approval.

His cell phone vibrated. Chetan Bajaj, the CID Chief. He had been expecting this call. 'Hey chief,' Ray said, still grinning.

'Rudra, have you seen the paper?' Chetan barked in the phone.

Fuck yes, he did. 'Yeah, I am going through it. They have captured the news in stunning accuracy.' He put my feet up on the coffee table which sat in front of him.

'How they got the scoop?' asked Chetan. Ray could hear a touch of suspicion in the old man's voice, he knew Ray had a role to play in this entire scenario, but, he had nothing to accuse anyone. They never had anything to accuse Ray or hold him accountable for the calculated mayhems he had created all his life to solve crimes.

'I gave it to them,' Ray said. Chetan had trained him. Under his guidance Ray had worked for more than eight years. And when Ray drifted from the reality and almost died in depression, Chetan helped him get back on track. He had always been the father Ray never had the chance to know.

'Why Rudra?' he asked. 'People will be terrified.' Chetan trusted Ray. But there were times when Chetan found it difficult to agree with Ray's radical ways.

'I know. But it will shake loose the killer as well.' Ray did not know what would be the consequence. But if his gut feeling was to be taken seriously, then this feature would drag the offender out of his lair.

'You think it would drag the man out?' Chetan asked.

'This girl, Shraddha Basu came to me asking about the ripping part,' Ray said. 'They already knew about it. I just added some details.'

Chetan went silent. Ray could hear the sound of his raspy breath from the other side. 'I am having a bad feeling about all these,' Chetan said finally.

Ray did not have the heart to tell Chetan, so did he.

His phone was screaming for attention when Ray reached his office building. It was Sid and therefore something nasty must have happened.

'What?' Ray asked upon receiving the phone call.

'We traced the money through its number,' said Sid.

Ray stepped out of his car. Today the sun did not deprive the world of its golden light. The untimely rain had given the trees a much needed bath. Green leaves, brown tree limbs, and even the tattered streets of Kolkata dazzled with new life. He leaned his back against his car and waited for Sid to continue.

'That money has come from Gurgaon.' Sid like it was his habit shouted the information. Ray failed to understand why his best friend always shouted. Even after repeated reminders nothing changed, so now, everyone simply endured Siddhant's way of speaking over the phone.

'Ok,' Ray said waiting for the prologue to end. Being patient had its own disadvantages. People expected you to sit through everything they had to say. They always thought that their version of the story was that damn interesting, that was their tragedy. You would have to solidify their belief, that would be yours.

'Even CBI is trying to trace this money.' Sid paused for a breath. 'It's ransom money.'

'Ransom?' Now, why he was not surprised. 'Who paid it? And when?'

'Tejyas Ranwar, a Gurgaon based diamond merchant vanished last month. His family got a phone call a couple days later. Hold on for moment.' Ray heard Sid speaking to someone in not so low voice of his. 'So, the caller asked for ten crore.'

'This is a part of that ten crore?' Ray asked, calculating.

'Apparently.'

'Samir ran a kidnaping racket?' Ray asked to no one particular. 'What happened to Ranwar?'

'He was found unconscious in front of his door step the morning after the ransom money was paid.' Sid's answer should have shocked Ray. But somehow he was not baffled by the development of the case. Slowly, he was getting a clear victim profile. Samir Shrivastav lived a dark life which welcomed violence. So, it was not surprising that now he lay dead in the autopsy room. One day, someone would have pulled the trigger. But who had ripped him apart in such a vicious manner? What type of a man could do that? A violent, angry, abandoned man? Could someone that near the line of insanity plan this type of a murder?

'Fucking brilliant. What a dick that bastard was.' Ray immediately felt bad for cursing like a teenager. But the things just got better for him. First a mutilated body. Then a violent porn video. And now a kidnaping racket. What else remained? Ray thought. Sadly, he did not have to wait long for the answer.

'Anything on Samir?' Ray asked Fiona.

'Yeah,' she said. 'I found a lot about him.'

'That's our Fi,' Karan said with affection. His eyes got softer whenever he looked at her. Ray sensed a brotherly protectiveness in Karan. But Fiona's eyes made him uncomfortable. He did not want the kid to fall in love with Karan and get hurt.

'So, what do we have?' Ray asked.

'Samir's father was a businessman. He made money. He died…somebody stabbed him to death. Samir was in his early twenties back then.'

'His killer?' Chirag asked.

'Found nothing on the stabber.' Fi gave a little shrug. 'Did not get caught.' She looked at me. 'Anyway, Samir was busted for drug possession twice.'

'He served time in jail?' Ray asked.

'No, the possession quantity was not sufficient to send him to jail. It was grass.' She added after a small pause. 'Once he got arrested and almost went to jail for trying to molest a woman. But lucky for him the girl refused to press charges and he went free.'

'Talented guy,' Karan said.

'Natural born criminal,' Ray said. 'Can you pull up some records on his father's death?' Ray asked Fi. 'I am having a bad feeling about the entire scenario.'

'What good his father's death will do to us?' asked Chirag.'

This made Ray smile. 'It will satisfy my curiosity.' His eyes turned towards Karan. 'I believe you have seen all the photos. I haven't got the report yet.'

Karan pulled his phone out of his pocket. 'Sending boss.'

Chirag fidgeted in his seat. Ray sensed his unease from the moment he entered the room. 'You wanna tell me something?' Ray asked.

'I received a call this morning.' Chirag looked around the waiting faces. 'The caller said he knew Samir and wants to talk.' Everyone waited. 'He will be coming in about thirty minutes.'

'What's his name?' Ray asked.

'He did not tell me.' Chirag flashed an uncomfortable smile.

The door burst opened and Akash entered. 'People are pretty unnerved by the images.' He declared. 'They have gathered in front of the police station demanding an arrest.'

'So, what else is new?' Ray asked. 'Someone is coming to talk to me about Samir.'

Akash had found a seat by the corner of the room by then. 'How come you allowed Kolkata Breaking to flash our name?'

'We need promotion,' Ray said.

'We do?' Chirag asked.

'Even Audi does, what are we?' Ray asked.

Before he could dismiss them, Akash dropped the bomb. 'So when did Shraddha Basu make a comeback to your life?'

Ray had been expecting this. But he did not expect Akash to sit in the conference room amidst the entire team and ask him about Shraddha. He could feel questioning eyes on him.

'Who is Shraddha Basu?' asked Karan. His face broke into an amused smile.

'The girl who wrote the piece on Samir's death,' Fiona said. She looked curious like everyone else.

Ray thought about giving them something to keep them quiet. 'I met Shraddha five years ago on a case.'

Chirag leaned forward. 'Which case was that?'

'Lisa Brown murder case,' said Ray. Before the conversation stretched, he waved his hand. 'Enough. Go now.'

It worked, they all scrambled out of the room in hurry. Ray heard Chirag's voice from outside. 'Got a copy of Kolkata Breaking?'

'Was that necessary?' he asked Akash after everyone left.

'Why not?' asked Akash. 'It's not like you are in a relationship with this woman. Why are you getting worked up about the question?'

Ray had nothing to say to this. Quietly he chose to drop on a chair and stare outside. The sunray looked warm and affectionate. It had been days since the city had the honor of meeting the monarch of the sky. It felt good to look at the molten gold sunray.

'The inside news is not very appealing,' Akash said, making him tear his gaze away from the scene outside.

'They are bringing special force?' This had happened many times before. Ray had the chance to rub his shoulders with cops who admired him, cops who loved him, cops who loathed him and copes who simply hated him.

Akash got to his feet and paced the length of the conference room. He could not sit still. A habit that had irritated many, but, Akash being the man he was did not bother to change. 'Not yet. Dad has succeeded in pushing the matter off, but, it will happen. We can lose the case.'

As if that worried him. 'Does not matter.' Ray got up to his feet, checked his watch and looked at Akash. 'Now, we watch the situation. This man, being a fucking attention seeker will surely make a move.'

'You sure?' Akash asked. In his eyes Ray witnessed a resigned fright. 'I just hope all hell does not break loose due to the news report.'

News channels went crazy with the news of the ripping. One of the channels aired a lengthy show on Jack the Ripper. It also promised an elaborate report on some famous serial killings. Ray stretched, thinking about Shraddha. Kolkata Breaking had printed her name in small letters, pretty easy to miss. It pleased Ray. He did not want her to be in the middle of this case. If he could, he would have sent her miles away from Kolkata right now.

His phone vibrated then. The caller app traced the number, it belonged to someone named Shivani Guha.

Must be press, he thought as his index finger hit the receive button.

'Yeah,' Ray barked, making his tone rougher than it already was.

If the greeting bothered her, she did not show it. 'Mr. Ray, I am from Kolkata Breaking.'

Aha, his mouth almost turned up in a sarcastic chuckle. Press. 'Kolkata Breaking?' he asked. 'I already talked to your paper.'

'You haven't talked to me.' Ray heard a hint of smile in the caller's voice. 'You have talked to an amateur.'

He would not mind talking to that amateur again. But this he could not tell her. 'How can I help you?' he asked instead.

'I would like to meet you,' she said. 'How about discussing the case. You know the progress.' Her desperation glared at him. Professional rivalry.

'I will give you a call.' He promised which he would not keep and he believed she knew it. 'Right now, I am busy.' With that Ray disconnected the call.

A black Audi A4 pulled in the parking lot of his office. An elderly man climbed out of the driver's seat. He stood straight. For a moment he looked undecided whether he wanted to enter the building or drive away. But he did neither. Instead he stood still, scanning every corner of the front yard. Expecting a tiger to come out any time, Ray thought. Business owner, with a lot of money, he sighed.

Satisfied that he was not being monitored, he turned towards the entrance of the office. Ray moved away from the window and took a seat. Somehow snooping on a man did not feel right anymore, though this had been a hobby he enjoyed when he was in college and nothing else succeeded in amusing him.

The front entrance opened. Footsteps resonated at the corridor. Karan asked the old man for his name. Minutes later, he peeked inside the conference room. Akash sat in one of the chairs oblivious to the arrival of the guest. He typed the report of Samir's case.

'Hey skip, the guy Chirag talked to,' he said. 'Is waiting in the front office.'

'What's his name?' Ray asked.

'Prakash Tejas,' Karan said. 'A businessman.'

'Bring him in here.' Ray moved to a chair beside Akash.

'Who is this guy?' Akash asked.

'Will find out soon enough.'

Prakash Tejas was in his late fifties. His face had begun to display all signs of aging. From wrinkle to worry, everything could be witnessed on his face. He sat measuring Ray and Ray allowed him. Rich people liked to belittle other rich people. Initially it struck him funny. But now he got used to it.

'Coffee?' Ray asked.

'Later,' Tejas said. 'You are investigating Samir Shrivastav's murder case?' he asked, finally.

'We are assisting the cops in tracing his killer,' Akash corrected.

'Samir...' Tejas stopped. His eyes dropped at his hand. Suddenly he found his nails very interesting.

Akash had turned his laptop off by then. He sat with a notebook and pen. Sometimes he preferred to be old fashioned. Ray used a spiral A6 notebook for the purpose of taking notes.

'Samir had a video of my daughter.' Finally Tejas brought himself to meet Ray's eyes. His helpless stare smudged his arrogance a little. 'He made a porn video.'

'Okay,' Ray said, just to push him further into the conversation.

'He not only made the video. He blackmailed her too.'

'Money?' Ray asked.

'Money.' Tejas said. The he added in a quiet voice. 'And sex.'

Akash exchanged a quick glace with Ray. Their eyes met for a brief second. Then they looked back at the old man.

'Can I speak to your daughter?' Ray asked. 'I don't want to hurt her. But her testimony might be important.'

Before his eyes Prakash Tejas resigned. He shrank like a crumple piece of paper. Exposing his beloved daughter to a couple of strangers would be the last thing a father would do. Yet, truth demanded that they pushed forward.

'We will do it at your home,' Akash said. 'At your presence.'

Tejas did not look convinced. 'You will use her testimony in the court when time comes?'

Akash paused, not knowing what to say. Yes, they would drag her to the court and make her testify. If she did not come, they might use legal threats to make her appear to the court. And Prakash knew all these. In his eyes Ray saw the knowledge. Lying to this man would not work. 'Yes, we will,' Ray said. 'If her testimony convicts the man who killed Samir, we will call her to court.'

'Then I am sorry Mr. Ray, I cannot let you talk to my daughter. I came here to request you to destroy the video Samir made of her.' He finally brought himself to blurt out the truth.

Destroy evidence, Ray thought in disbelief. Not that he hadn't destroyed evidence to convict criminals before. But right at the moment, this man needed to be stiff-armed. 'I am sorry Mr. Tejas, I cannot do it. The videos are all legal evidence now. I cannot destroy them. I will not even if I can.'

Prakash made a face which told that he had heard this before. 'I will pay you money.'

Akash gave a small chuckle at the statement. He had heard this before too. People came here offering them money to do a lot of illegal things.

'How much?' Ray asked just for the sake of a good laugh.

But being wealthy and powerful, Tejas did not get this. He took Ray's question as his triumph. 'Ten lakh.'

'Thank you,' Ray said. 'Now, you can leave. We have loads of work to do.'

'Think it over Mr. Ray.' Tejas did not budge from his chair. 'No one will give you ten lakh to destroy a video of no importance.'

This time Ray laughed. 'Had it been a video of no importance, you would not have offered ten lakh to destroy it, right?'

It silenced Tejas. But the quiet lasted only for half a minute. 'Fifty lakh,' he said, unfazed by the refusal.

'I am sorry,' Ray said. 'My answer remains the same.'

The man got up to his feet. He stared at Ray, seething in anger. For a while, time stood still. Ray had created a fresh enemy for his lifetime and he knew it. After what it seemed like a lifetime, Tejas turned and thundered out of the office, pushing a stunned Chirag out of his way.

'Whoa,' Chirag said. 'Angry man.' He laughed. Then his face became serious. 'I got a call from AKD.' AKD was Alok Kumar Dasgupta, a famous public prosecutor.

'What happened?' Akash asked. 'New case?'

'Yeah,' Chirag said. He chose to sit facing his employers. 'It's that Beemer hit and run case.'

'Beemer hit and run?' Ray asked.

'11th December a Beemer zoomed through Park Street area at dawn. It hit six people on the way. Two died on the spot. Three died later in the hospital.' He looked at Ray with a puzzled expression. 'Don't you read papers or watch television?'

Rudransh Ray shook his head in reply. He did not get the time to look at the newspaper or watch the television. 'What AKD wants?' he asked.

'I don't have all the details. But the driver belongs to a rich family. His father has friends in high places and also in some low places. AKD wants assistance.' Chirag's young face looked flushed in excitement. Ray felt happy for the boy. But there was something which needed to be done first.

Ray pondered the scenario for a minute. 'AKD is gonna pay us for the service right?'

Chirag shrugged. 'Of course, I am not working pro bono.'

This Ray knew. Chirag had honed his negotiation talent while working on tough cases. He never settled for less and earned what he deserved. 'What about the driver? The cop got him?' Ray asked.

'The driver is a business merchant's son.' Akash said. 'He is absconding.'

That surprised Ray. 'What the fuck was he doing so early in the morning?'

'Drunk driving I guess.'

'Name?' Ray asked.

'Ashutosh Khemka,' Chirag said. 'The only son of the great Arman Khemka.'

Arman Khemka, the name startled Ray. This man held power in the high places. No wonder AKD wanted assistance of Rayon Corporation. This could get nasty.

'Meet AKD,' Ray said, trying to decide whether to encourage Chirag or ask him to drop the case. 'Talk about everything. Have a discussion.' He paused, groping for the right word. 'But be careful when you are trying to stiff arm a powerful man. These people don't play fair. The game could get real dirty, real fast.' Saying this, He looked at Chirag's surprised face. Never before Ray had attempted to scare his team. But sometimes fear worked like miracle in saving lives.

Chirag got up to his feet. Despite the warning, his face remained bright with excitement. Each time a case came along he exploded with energy. 'I will report EOD.'

'Call me,' Ray said.

'I will drop by,' he said. This was a bad habit of both Karan and Chirag. They both dropped by to report their progress.

'You are always welcome.' Ray waved his hand and sent Chirag off.

Chapter - 8

Clank of heels reverberated as Shraddha walked inside her office building. It was seven thirty in the morning, no one had arrived yet. She liked it this way, empty office, without interference of unwanted chatter, utter silence, and prolonged peace. She loved to start early.

After booting her computer, she went to fetch coffee. This she drank in gallons. Coffee to her was what patrol to vehicles. Approaching footsteps got her attention as she began pouring steaming coffee in her red floral printed ceramic mug. She turned to find Kevin walking in with a big grin on his unshaven face. A charmer, thought Shraddha with affection.

'Are you following the Beemer case?' he asked.

No she hadn't. She poured all her attention into finding Raghav. 'Nope,' she said. 'What happened?'

'A Beemer grazed six people on 11th December early morning. Two died on the spot. Three died in the hospital. The driver is a rich guy.' Kevin stopped to take a deep breath. 'One is hanging by the thin thread of life. Barely alive and all.'

'Rich guy?' Shraddha asked, not paying attention to what Kevin said. Her mind was on The Ripper case and Rudransh Ray.

'Yeah, Arman Khemka's son.' Kevin came to stand in front of the coffee machine. He too had a coffee addiction. After pressing the coffee vending button, he looked at Shraddha. 'You will get the latest update if you get online. It's trending.'

Shraddha gaped at the mention of the name. Arman Khemka, the great industrialist with political connection throughout the world. 'Ashutosh Khemka was driving the car?' she asked.

'Ditto,' Kevin said. He took a cautious sip from his coffee mug. 'The son of a rich bitch and asshole.'

'Don't these rich people teach their children to value life?' Shraddha asked, though she already knew the answer.

Kevin laughed. 'Oh, these people do value life. Their own.' He turned to leave, but something stopped him. 'By the way Rayon Corporation is working with the prosecutor.'

'Rudransh Ray?' Shraddha asked surprised at the news.

'Not Ray. He is not a lawyer. But his company has a legal department,' said Kevin. 'The senior lawyer Chirag Malhotra has taken over the case himself.'

'Wow.' Ray's hard, expressionless face popped in her mind. She felt a sense of warmth inside her heart which took her by surprise. Ray seemed to her like an entity from another planet, alive yet dead. She recalled the last day at the Ranaghat resort when Ray stood in the middle of the room and revealed the identity of Lisa Brown's killer.

'You can arrange for another interview with this man.' Kevin suggested after taking another careful sip from his coffee mug.

'I am going to visit Samir's office later today.' Shraddha looked behind her back to make sure that no one heard her saying this.

'Let the boss know before going anywhere.' Kevin too looked behind his back.

Shraddha winked at her friend. 'I will, I will.'

By eleven, Kolkata sky filled with thick angry looking clouds again and the hope of a sunny day vanished. It seemed sun had decided to stay behind the veil all winter long. Wind followed the clouds and now blew to slam walkers off their feet.

Shraddha pulled her red trench coat tightly around her slender body. She felt proud of the fact that now she fitted into the small size of any brand. A few years ago she could not even think of wearing anything beyond large.

Her heart kept beating against her chest. The closer she got to Samir's office building, the jumpier she got. Yet, she had to see the building with her own eyes. The yellow building materialized after she took a sharp turn. Even from a distance it was apparent that something bad had happened there. Police, both plain clothed and uniformed roamed the area. Shraddha could tell them apart from body language. She congratulated herself for learning to study people's body language.

Like a local she walked ahead. The key, as Kevin said, was to keep a nonchalant face. Two more steps and she could take a sneak peek of the interior. If she was lucky, she could take a few photos of the murder room as well. Cops in uniform loitered like ants around a grain of sugar. They would not allow her in. She knew that much. Still, it was worth a try.

'Where do you think you are going?' asked someone from behind.

She turned to see a middle aged man with a bulging stomach stood just inches away from her. She took a step back to create some distance between them.

'I was just looking,' she said in a low voice. This made the man smile. The sudden lift of the mouth sent a sharp sensation of unease through her veins.

'I am the investigating officer of the case,' he said. 'You cannot look without my permission.'

His attitude did say cop. She considered showing her ID but then decided to allow the officer to have a blast. She could always pop the balloon later on.

Before conversation could proceed, a slender man huddled in a thick woolen jacket appeared from behind. He had a baseball cap on his head which hid most of his face. What remained was covered by thick facial hair. Shraddha could only see a long throat and a sharp nose.

'This is a crime scene,' said the cop. 'Where do you think you are going?'

The question stopped the man. It seemed he became aware of the surrounding for the first time. 'I…I am looking for this address.' He extended a piece of paper. 'Can you tell me where it is?'

'I don't have time for all these,' said the cop. His voice rose high enough to attract attention.

Time? Shraddha chuckled at the statement. What the fuck were you doing anyways? She wanted to blurt the question.

The cop whirled around to look at her. 'You laughed?' he asked, astonished at the audacity. Didn't she know he could arrest her right there?

'Nope,' Shraddha said, grinning at the fat man. 'How can I laugh?'

The police officer took a step towards her. This time Shraddha did not move. Instead she dug into her purse and retrieved her press card.

'Shraddha Basu, Kolkata Breaking,' she said with all the sweetness she could muster for an ugly man. 'I just want to have a discussion with you. Can you spare me some time?'

In a fraction, a smile spread on the face of the police officer. His eyes brightened. Without even looking at the man he had detained, he nodded. 'Sure,' he said. 'I will be glad to talk. You are dealing with the case?'

She felt a pang of pride for a fraction of second. 'Yeah, I wrote the piece on the killer and the mutilation that made it to the front page.'

'Sir, the address?' asked the man with baseball cap.

'Go, find it yourself,' barked the officer.

'Where have you been?' Akshaj's voice boomed in the hall, the moment she stepped inside.

She looked around, everyone stared at her, waiting for an answer. Kevin beamed from the corner. His face reflected an amused watchfulness.

'I went to visit Samir's office.'

Akshaj's face broke into a surprised gape. 'Samir's office?' Displeasure tightened his facial muscles. 'Alone. Don't you know it's risky?'

'I just wanted a glimpse,' Shraddha said. Her hands raised in mock surrender.

'That's ok.' Akshaj came to stand near her. 'But you should have taken Kevin with you. And more importantly, you should have informed me before going there.'

Shraddha nodded. Kevin winked from the furthest corner of the hall. 'I have interviewed the supervising officer. Can we talk after typing the report?' she asked her boss.

Akshaj opened his mouth to say something. Then he stopped. 'Yeah, go ahead.'

As Shraddha passed by, her eyes fell on Shivani. The girl glared at her with such malice that she had to look away.

'My, my princess, you have scored a sixer again,' said Kevin when she came to sit beside him.

'Sixer?' she made a face. 'The cop was leering at me.'

Kevin gave her an once over through the corner of his eyes. 'Don't take it to your heart, but, you are looking good enough to eat today.' She glared at the comment and he laughed. 'Let's go down for a cup of coffee.'

It was after ten thirty in the night when Shraddha finally snuggled under a thick blanket with a sigh. In her hand she held a thick paperback. The mystery thriller had her glued to the pages for the last couple of days. She closed the book and laid her head on her arms, dreaming of writing a fast-paced psychopath thriller someday. The day's ordeal had exhausted her enough to make her sleepy.

She had been dozing off when her cell phone vibrated. Shraddha straightened to check the number. Must be Trisha, she thought hopefully. But it was an unknown number. She pondered for a second whether to answer the call. It was her official number anyways. In the state of indecision, the call got disconnected.

As she was about to toss the phone away, it started to ring again. The same number. For reason unknown to her, Shraddha's spine turned cold as she looked at the device screen. This time she answered the call.

'Hello.'

'Shraddha Basu?' asked a male voice.

Goosebumps erupted all over her body at the sound. She did not even know why she felt that way. 'Yes,' she said.

'You write well,' said the caller.

'Who...who is on the line?' she asked. Driven by her instinct she reached out and parted the curtain of her bedroom window to look at the street. It was dark outside. Empty street stared back at her. No one. She almost cursed herself for her overactive imagination. 'May I know your name?'

This question made him laugh. 'Name?' he asked. Then went quiet. A thick silence materialized. Fraction of second later, the caller asked. 'What's there in a name?' His lazy tone made Shraddha think of predators, patiently stalking their preys.

Inside her stomach Shraddha felt a twist. Her past experience had taught her to listen to the feeling. Something did not strike right. 'May I know what's this call is regarding?' she asked finally.

Another pause, longer this time, took place. Shraddha started at the emptiness of the street, fully aware of her isolation. Her right hand rested on a thick notepad which she kept by her pillow all the time. Somehow she knew the call was a bad omen.

'You wrote about my work of art. But you did not write about me.' Finally, the caller broke the silence. He spoke out in a low, gentle voice which sent a sharp sense of fear through her veins.

'I…wrote about you?' she asked, frantically looking for a pencil. 'Who are you?'

For a full minute she heard heavy breath rising up and down from the other side. Then the male voice spoke in a low whisper, 'I am The Ripper.'

Chapter – 9

It was 11.30pm. The temperature had dropped to the point of making knuckles numb. Wind hissed with ferocity. Once again, Ray marveled at the cold. Kolkata was not used to this type of winter. It usually get moderate cold with a few gusts of frosty wind. But this year, winter really came to freeze.

Ray retired early that night to write his book. It had been pending for years. Would anyone want to read his story? The question loomed over him like a dark shadow. Was his life important enough to write a book on it? Probably not. But he needed to get everything out of his system to feel lighter. It was a kind of therapy which could keep him sane when night turned too dark and air breathed loneliness.

His fingers flew on the keyboard of his desktop computer. To write Ray preferred desktop. Laptops seemed too fancy to use his own way. Funny, in the last three years he solved more than ten murder cases alongside the CID and only wrote six chapters of his book.

In the trance of writing, he missed the first vibration of the phone. It trembled and then screamed for his attention. Ray almost jumped as the silence shattered.

Like it was his habit, he checked the time before answering.

'Sid,' Ray greeted with no enthusiasm at all.

'The killer called,' Sid said without wasting a moment. In Sid's case he screamed over the phone. Ray pulled his ear away to escape the brutal assault.

'Called who?' Ray asked, already on his feet, moving towards his bedroom.

'That Kolkata Breaking reporter.' Sid paused. Ray could see him groping for a name. 'Shraddha Basu.'

Shraddha, Ray breathed. He had not anticipated this move. When he had given her the scoop, he had thought of rattling the unsub. He thought the media attention would make him come out of his rathole. But he had not expected her to get a call from the killer.

'How did he get her phone number?' Ray asked, pulling open his closet.

Sid was quiet for a fraction of second. Then he said. 'He called her official number. Probably someone from her office has tipped him.'

'I will be there in thirty minutes,' Ray said, feeling a healthy bout of anger rising.

It took him ten minutes to get ready and ten more to reach her house. A tall boyishly good looking young man opened the door. Ray identified this guy from various crime scene coverage, Kevin Gray. Kevin looked genuinely worried. He nodded at Ray and stepped back to offer space to enter.

The house had a sense of welcoming comfort which embraced him the moment he stepped inside. Home coming, the phrase sprang in his mind. Only it was not him home. Probably home was not a place. Home was a person to whom people went back to. Ray thought as he followed Kevin.

Inside he found her sitting on a single leather couch. Her face revealed no trace of emotion. In another single couch sat a tall, lean man in his early thirties, another journalist from Kolkata Breaking. But Ray failed to attach a name to the face.

'Rudransh Ray.' The greeting or the question made Ray turn. By the only window of the room, just across the couch Shraddha sat, stood a man in his late sixties. He commanded more than respect. He commanded the soul. A man who came to this world with the divine urge to be the God. Ray studied him. He did the same.

The dislike was mutual & immediate.

'I am,' Ray said. None of them made any attempt to shake hands. After this Ray saw no need to further the conversation with the old man. He turned to look at Shraddha. 'What happened?' he asked. She looked up. In her expressionless eyes, Ray saw a hint of fear. He felt the fear it in his soul. Flood of emotion did not greet him. They came to assault him. He wanted to go forward to hold her in his arms. Maybe he could even promise to keep her safe from the world. But with three men watching him, he could do neither.

'I received a call from someone who claimed to be the killer.' In her voice Ray heard a void. It showed nothing, fear, anxiety or even curiosity. To the others it might seem like courage that the girl displayed. But from years of experience Ray knew that she suffered from extreme fear. He had unchained this on her. He should have stopped himself from giving her the information.

'How can he trace you?' Ray asked. 'Your name was there but not your phone number.' He chose to sit on a couch across her. It gave him the full view of her face. He did not want to miss a single frown or touch of fear which would cross her eyes. 'Also, why he contacted you two days after the murder?' he looked at Shraddha. 'What have you done to tick him off?''

'I…' She started with hesitation. Her eyes turned towards her boss who stood frowning like a father who caught his teenage daughter in bed with her lover. 'I went to visit Samir's office.' Ray did not let his emotion show on his face. Yet, Shraddha seemed to feel it. 'I just wanted a glimpse of the office. That's it.' Her defensive tone told him that she had felt his rising anger. But instead of allowing the rage to come out, Ray focused on the case.

This could lead to something. 'Did you talk to anyone?'

She thought for a moment as if trying to decide whether she should reveal anything to him without her boss' permission. 'Yes,' she said finally after a lengthy pause. 'Met a cop…the investigating officer…'

'What nonsense,' Ray snapped despite his resolve to remain calm. 'What investigating officer? Siddhant Thakur is investigating the murder and he is not in the town right now.'

'Well the cop said…' She shrugged.

'You know what?' Ray asked, letting his voice turn cold and cruel. She swallowed before raising her eye brows. 'You are not a journalist material. You should sit back at home and write romance or fantasy,' he said. The cruelty of the words he lashed out at her turned her eyes soft. Ray could feel that he had hit her where it hurt the most and he regretted it immediately. Before he could say something to mend the damage, she nodded. Her head bobbed up and down in agreement. Ray wanted to slap himself for hurling those words towards her in front of her boss and colleagues. But he could not control himself from speaking his mind out. It took him a long time to calm his racing heart down.

'Mr. Ray,' her Kevin said in a calm voice. 'You are here to catch the killer. Not to assess her capability.' The young man looked straight into his eyes and held the stare. 'So, please focus more on the case and less on her.' A calculative pause then a smirk materialized. 'I know that will be difficult.'

Ray heard a low chuckle coming from Shraddha's boss. It surprised him to think that the situation actually struck the old man funny. Shraddha might be a newbie who lacked experience, but, Akshaj Mukharjee was not a kid. He did not lack experience. 'I am not assessing her capability. I don't do that.' Ray knew he had crossed his limit. 'But she is not cut out to handle something as dangerous as this case. Her involvement might jeopardize the progress.' He paused to look at her tired eyes. Dark shadows had formed around them to give her a haunted look. Getting a call from a psychopath could be traumatizing. Getting a call from a man who sliced people after killing them could be dangerous to mental health. He did not want her to get in the line when he finally clashed with the killer.

Shraddha rolled her head to give her neck a little relief. Then she drew a deep breath before looking at Ray. 'You think I don't know my weaknesses?' She did not raise her voice. Yet, in her tone Ray heard madness. No, it was not the kind of madness which made people go biting others, or, murder someone with a single slash. It was the kind of madness which pushed people ahead. Often such madness made miracles happen. 'I do it every day. I question my capability every day. I know I am not the right person to handle such a high profile case. I know what I can do.' She paused. 'But Mr. Ray, you like it or not, I am already involved in this case. I am knee deep in the shit right now.' She flashed a smile then. 'You knew this would happen. Didn't you?' she asked. 'You wanted the killer to come out of the lair so that you can catch him.' Ray expected her to be bitter but she only sounded tired. 'You used me as a bait and I fell for the trap. Now, you have to deal with me until you kill the man or he killed me.'

The grim silence of the room turned even grimmer as she spoke this in a calm and serene voice. Ray sat frozen in his seat, agreeing with everything she had accused him of doing and cursing himself for being an asshole. But the damage had been done. The killer had come out of his lair. He got what he wished for. Would anyone congratulate him for being so fortunate? He doubted it. But he had not expected the offender to be bold enough to call a journalist.

He had been wrong to question her capability. It was the time to call for a truce. 'I am sorry. I did not mean to say you are incapable. I am just saying you should not have gone there alone. You have exposed yourself. Now, you cannot work on this case anymore.' Taking her off the case would not help much if the killer had identified her. But he kept the information to himself. She did not need to be scared any more than she already had been.

'Quitting won't help much,' she said with a smile. 'Will it Mr. Ray. He knows me now. He has called me. I am now the thread which can lead you all to the right person.'

'Shraddha,' said her boss, suddenly coming out of the zombie land he had drifted off to. 'You cannot work on this case. I am taking you off.'

She laughed at that. 'As if that's gonna help,' she said. 'You guys like it or not. I am already nose deep into this. He will call me again.'

'How do you know?' Ray asked surprised to hear his own thought coming out of her mouth.

She gave him a pitying glance. 'The guy is looking for fame.' Her smile widened at his expression. 'Or else he would not have called me knowing I am working for a newspaper.'

'Okay,' Ray said, not wanting to interrupt her. 'So, what do you want to do?'

'Let's continue as if nothing has happened,' she said. 'I will write a piece about the conversation tomorrow.'

'What exactly has he said?' he asked, finally remembering the main reason of his coming here.

Shraddha closed her eyes, thinking. He could see her mind racing back to the time when the man had called. He could sense fear. But along with it he could sense something else, a touch of excitement which she felt deep down inside.

'He said he liked the article. He said I write well.' She paused to look at Ray. In that fraction of moment when their eyes met, he saw fear. It passed quickly. 'He said to tell the world that the reign has just begun.'

The reign, Ray stopped short, almost open mouth. It confirmed his initial suspicion of thirst for fame. But the claim of reign changed it all. The guy gotta be suffering from some kind of God complex.

'Reign of terror,' said Shraddha's colleague whose name Ray was yet to know. 'This is getting better every moment.'

'And this gonna get better with time,' Ray said. 'What about his speech? What can you say about it?'

She licked her lips, staring hard at the floor. 'He had a low, lazy tone which...which you normally hear in the movies. You know the assassin badass sort?'

What she meant was a cold, low voice which sent creeps down the stomach. 'Yeah, I guess, I do.' Ray nodded.

She rubbed her eyes, sleepy, tired and definitely scared. 'His accent is good. I think it is UK accent,' she said.

'British accent,' said her boss, surprised.

'Guess we are dealing with a call center guy, flaunting cheap accent.' She flashed a smile that did not reach her eyes. She rolled her head again to release tension from her neck.

Feeling her exhaustion, Ray said, 'You cannot stay here alone. It is not safe.'

Before she spoke, Ray knew what she would say. 'I am not going anywhere.'

Ray chuckled. 'You won't have to go anywhere. I will arrange for security.'

'Or, you can stay at my place,' said Akshaj Mukherjee. His face contorted with worry. Ray detected a strong fatherly protectiveness. If Akshaj was so protective about Shraddha, why did he allow her to get involved in this case? Probably, he did not predict the turn of the event.

Ray would have shaken his head in dismay had Sid not called at the very moment. 'Yeah,' he greeted.

'What's up there?' he asked. 'Anything useful?'

By that he meant did Ray get the killer handcuffed. Well, nope, he was sorry to disappoint his best friend. Nothing in life offered solution that easy. 'Well, not really. I think Ms. Basu needs protection.'

'She does,' Sid agreed. 'But as always we are short of man power.' Ray could hear his smile. He did not care who died as long as he got his target. Sadistic, but, they were trained to deliver justice by catching criminals, not by protecting civilians. Yet, there was something about the woman sitting across. Ray could not just walk away.

'So?' asked Akshaj Mukherjee the moment Ray disconnected the call. 'They are sending in guys?'

Which planet was this man from? 'Yeah, they are. You guys can go home and all. I will wait outside till they come.' Ray got up to his feet. 'You should take a day or two off.' Before anyone could react, he lifted his shoulders. 'Just stay out of the sight for a few days.'

To his surprise, she did not jump at the suggestion. Instead, she nodded. 'I think that will be better.'

Akshaj readily agreed to allow her to cover some useless fashion updates which she could do from her home. Since no one was coming to guard her, Ray himself had to patrol by her door. Since it was him who had put her in the direct line of fire, he should be the one to take her out too. So, he walked out, got into his car, and got comfortable. Akshaj and his sidekicks disappeared into the darkness. Ray stared at the tail lights till they vanished. Once alone, he rested his head on the seat and let his mind drift.

Samir in his mutilated state came to visit. The guy who had knifed his way through Samir's body had more than a cruel mind. He had a sort of distortion which could qualify him in the league of wild animals. He loved the sight of blood. He loved to inflict fear. And he loved to be known for the terror he could spread. This was the guy he had let loose on an innocent girl.

Ray felt guilty for being the bad guy here. If something happened to her because of him, he would not be able to forgive himself, not this time. With his eyes closed, he went back to the crime scene. But he did not see Samir lying lifeless on a blood splattered room. In situations like these, only one vision always managed to intrude into his mind – the lifeless body of his wife, lying in a dark pool of blood. Today it was no exception. Rusha came and stayed. Ray tried to push the image away. But it did not fade. It did not budge. It remained like the scars which refused to heal, no matter how hard one tried. Scars like these had an advantage. They never let one forget or heal. They never allowed you to drift from the path that fate had set for you. Ray was tired of this scar. But since there was no cure for the pain, he embraced it with open arms.

A knock on the window forced him to open his eyes. Shraddha stood with a smile on her face. Ray rolled the glass down to hear what she had to say.

'Come inside,' she said. Her smile did not fade. 'I will hate to write the news of you freezing at my door step while waiting for the cops to come.' She paused to scan her neighborhood area. 'Who I doubt will make it tonight or any other night.'

Back inside her apartment, Ray found a couch pushed against the window which was not there earlier. 'You have pushed it here?' he asked.

'Yeah I wanted to read.' She carried two cups of steaming coffee and sandwiches. 'Going to sleep would have been a task tonight.'

'You are scared?' Ray asked though was a foolish question. Under this situation, any civilian would have been frightened.

She handed him a red ceramic mug before settling across him with her own pink one. 'Yes, I am.' She nodded. 'But I am not scared to die. I am scared that I will die without making it. I am scared that I will go away and no one will ever know that I ever existed.'

Creeps down his stomach rose. He felt each hair of his body standing up. He had heard it before. He had seen this passion before. He had witnessed this fire. It had burned him to ashes once. 'Immortality huh?' Ray asked unable to take his eyes off her.

'Yeah, I want to live forever.'

Because he had nothing to say to this he kept his mouth shut. She appeared to be someone who would hear you out because you said it and then would go her own way. He had a chance to come across a personality like that. His wife, his late wife to be exact, Rusha, had been a writer. She displayed every single character flaws that this young woman enjoyed living with. In the end, Rusha's passion had ruined her. How Shraddha managed to deal with hers was a question.

Initially, Rusha's passion, her love for writing and her never to give up attitude attracted Ray. With time…he closed his eyes and let loose a deep breath. Don't even go there, he said to myself. Don't even think about it.

Buzz of his cell phone made him open his eyes and focus. Shraddha looked at him. On her was a practiced detachment which made Ray smile. It was near two in the morning, who would be calling so late? Must be her boyfriend, he thought with no apparent pleasure.

'Oli, hi,' she cooed over the phone. 'How are you doing?' Her pause turned long as she listened. 'Oli my love, you gotta hold on to yourself. I found nothing on Raghav. Let me sit on it for a day. Then I will run a missing person ad, if that gets me to him.'

She paused to listen again. 'Yes baby, I know. I understand.' Her gaze found Ray. For the first time since they met, Ray saw helplessness in her eyes. She truly felt powerless to change whatever was happening to Oli.

Once she disconnected the call, Ray raised his brows in curiosity. 'That's my friend Oliva. Her husband Raghav is missing for the last six months. She is frantic and…' Shraddha bit her lower lip before speaking out in low tone. 'Pregnant.'

'Raghav has a last name?' Ray asked.

'Yeah, Ahuja.'

'Raghav Ahuja…' Ray narrowed his eyes, thinking. 'By any chance he works for Delhi Chronicle?' He asked.

'You know him?' Shraddha all but jumped to her feet.

Her enthusiasm hit Ray hard. He hated to tell her when someone of Raghav's profession went missing for six months, it usually meant bad news. 'I don't exactly know him. But we brushed shoulders a couple of times. A daring reporter,' he said. 'He limped?' he asked just to confirm the fact that they talked about the same person.

'Yeah, his right leg does not work well.'

'Hmm.' His hand snaked inside his pocket. He fished out his cigarette packet. It surprised him to think that he had spent the last three hours without smoking. 'Do you realize that the chances of finding him alive might be slim?'

'I do,' she said. 'I had a talk with the Delhi Chronicle's chief editor, Faisal Iqbal. He sent me the last emails of Raghav. I found nothing in them. Nothing that might lead to something at least. He expressed fear for his life in last few of his emails.'

Fear, Ray understood fear. He understood the feeling of not knowing what the next moment would bring. It might be a bullet in the chest. It might be something else. But then again crossing a road brought the same type of uncertainty. It might be a bus it might be something else. Better to die in the line of duty than to die in a road accident.

'Forward me his emails. Had he been to Kolkata?' Ray asked.

'According to Oliva and Faisal, yes,' she said.

'Any idea what he chased?' he asked, already strategizing his move to find Raghav, even though he have not been hired to do it and he should not get himself involved in unsolicited cases..

'No.'

'Fantastic.' He leaned his head back to get a few moments rest. Before long he drifted to sleep and dreamed of being chased by a shadow with a knife.

Chapter – 10

Chirag walked into AKD's office. The man had been in prosecution for a long time. He had his office set up in one of his two garages at his house. Smell of dirt and old book hung in the air. Chirag looked around expecting the old prosecutor to be in his seat. But he found the old recliner of the public prosecutor empty.

'AKD,' Chirag called. 'You there?' he asked when no one answered.

Chirag decided to wait for five minutes and then push off. But he did not have to wait that long for the prosecutor to arrive.

'Chirag,' said the small man in his late fifties. His eyes bore signs of sleepless night.

A wide grin which was the signature of the young lawyer spread across his face. 'Hey, already staying up the night?' Chirag asked.

The old man let out a deep breath. It sounded as if coming out of the deepest part of his soul. 'This case…' he began, dropping his growing weight on the recliner. It shirked in horror as the bum of the public prosecutor hit its leathery surface. 'It's pretty dangerous.'

'Yeah I know,' Chirag dropped his own weight on one of the chairs, resisting this urge to pop his legs on the table in front of him. Not my office, his mind warned him. 'That's why we are here.' He picked up a cheap ball point pen lying on the table. To focus his hands needed to hold something. This had been a subject to inside joke in Rayon Corporation. Outside no one dared to mess up with him. With time his reputation as an asshole had spread. Everyone knew Chirag went after what he wanted until he got it. 'Tell me about the hit and run.' He invited after a long pause, which promised to stretch longer. AKD could sit in silence all day long. Chirag Malhotra did not have that time. He had things to do. He sat back and fixed his cold stare on the prosecutor.

'It happened very early in the morning of 11th Dec,' started AKD. 'Even before the dawn broke free.' His eyes looked shadowy already. Something had gone wrong, Chirag thought. Something had gone really wrong. 'Everything was calm in the Park Street area. Everything. Not a single person loitered in the street, given the weather and the darkness. A team of four constables and two of their common friends stood in front of Oxford book store. They were speaking and having a good time. Even though the street was empty, they were standing on the pavement.' AKD pulled a thin file out of one of his drawers. He sighed again and looked into it. 'Out of nowhere came a BMW. A black one. It grazed them. Two died on the spot. Four lay bleeding on the pavement. One of them took a picture of the zooming car. It captured the license plate number.'

'And it's registered under Ashutosh Khemka's name?' Chirag asked.

'His father Arman Khemka,' said AKD.

'How do you know that Ashutosh was driving the car?' Chirag pulled out his notebook from his pocket. Time to get down to the paperwork he thought.

'The only survivor of the accident Mukhesh Jha saw him behind the wheel.' AKD looked helpless all of a sudden.

Akash jotted down the name and made a note to tell Fiona to run a BGB of the man. 'Except…' he prompted. AKD was getting old and slow by the day, he thought with irritation.

'Except… a defense lawyer will tear the case apart saying that Ashutosh Khemka was not driving the car. That the victim does not remember what he saw. That trauma had made him hallucinate.' AKD raised his eyebrows. 'Besides…'

'Besides…' Chirag shifted his weight in the chair, already feeling uncomfortable in the hard backed recliner which must be hundred years old. He did not like the guessing game. AKD had to speak faster or else he would be outta here in five seconds. To expedite the slow moving information presentation, he checked his watch.

'Ashutosh Khemka's driver has already come forward and confessed being behind the wheel.' AKD dropped the bomb.

'Ouch.' Chirag sat straight. 'When?' he asked. He had no information of a confession or arrest being made.

'I just received a call from the police department.' AKD let his head hang. His chin touched his chest and a brooding silence filled the room.

Finally, Chirag asked. 'Do you have any other evidence apart from the victim's testimony?'

'Yeah, the accident has been captured by a security camera…' AKD said slowly. The advocate looked pale. Chirag could see tiredness in AKD's eyes. The old man needed sleep.

'Security camera?' Chirag asked. 'In Kolkata those things work?'

'It belongs to Oxford.' AKD's face darkened.

'My bad.' Chirag flashed a smile.

'The camera captured the accident in full motion. But it did not capture the driver's face properly.' He gave a thin smile. 'It could be anyone.'

'Can I see it?' Chirag asked, already strategizing his next move.

'I will send you everything.' AKD said.

'What do we have to do?' Chirag fished a recorder out of his pocket and set it on the table. He preferred to record his work related discussions in multiple ways. Sometimes he failed to read his own handwriting.

'Evidence collection.' AKD cracked his knuckles. 'This is a big case. A lot of media attention will be on us.'

'And you don't want to look like a fool…' Laughed Chirag. 'Right?'

'Sort of.'

'So where can I find this Ashutosh character?' asked Chirag.

AKD sighed. 'He is absconding. There is simply no sign of him.'

'Wow. Things get better as it gets deeper,' said Chirag. 'I will speak to Mukesh Jha. That will be the start.' He checked his watch. Almost three in the afternoon, the visiting hour of the hospital would be two hours from now. He decided to take care of some pressing matters, including getting a bite.

Outside, he called Fiona. 'Hey love, do some digging for me.' His looked around the road, people walked huddled into their warmest clothes. He himself made sure to wrap himself in his thickest coat to stay warm. Ray's hard feature flashed in his mind. The guy roamed without much cold protection. The man must inject supplements to erase any kind of human feeling from his nerves.

'Whatta you want?' Fiona asked in a cheery voice. Her usual.

'The Khemka family report.'

Fiona paused. Chirag heard some keys being rattled. 'Which aspect you are focusing on?'

'You know me babes don't ya?' Chirag side stepped an old lady to avoid collision.

'You are looking for dirt,' said the field assistant in a calm tone.

'Ditto. You get me the dirt. We gotta give this guy a royal ass fucking.' Before Fiona had a chance to say anything, Chirag disconnected the phone. His mind raced trying to locate any possible way to break the case. From where he stood, everything looked bleak and dark.

Mukesh Jah was in bad shape. Chirag frowned at the bandages and swollen eyes. It was hard to say how the young man looked before the Beemer found him standing in the street. He inquired whether it would be safe to talk before approaching Mukesh.

'Mr. Jha,' Chirag said leaning forward so that the guy could make out what he said. 'I am Chirag Malhotra from Rayon Corporation. We are investigating the accident.'

Mukesh stirred at the mention of accident. His eye lids fluttered for a moment then he pulled his eyes open. He had pitch black eyes which stared hard at Chirag.

'I need to ask you a few questions. Are you up to it?' Chirag asked, leaning closer.

Mukesh nodded. He opened his mouth and tried to strike a smile. But the movement cost him. A grimace formed on his bandaged face as pain shot up. 'Sure,' he mumbled.

'What were you guys doing out in the street that early?' Chirag asked. A pointless question, but it would give him an idea about Mukesh's state of mind.

'We…we were on duty. Decided to catch up.' In slow and slurred tone said Mukesh.

'Did you see the man who had been driving the car?'

'Had a quick glimpse,' again Mukesh said using the same slurred tone.

'Can you recognize him if we show you some pictures?' Chirag had his doubt about it.

To this question, Mukesh thawed. His eyes drifted and he almost made a face, thinking hard. 'I guess.'

'Hmm, get well soon buddy. We gotta nail this motherfucker.' While he said this he thought of the absurdity of the case. There was Ashutosh Khemka already on flight. And his driver took the responsibility of the hit and run.

He called Ray. 'Khemka's driver has taken the responsibility of the crime. Ashutosh is absconding. I don't see any way to penetrate the case.'

'Ashutosh cannot get out of the country until he gets permission from the law,' said Ray. 'We will get to know if he tries to get out of the country. What do you think, is it worth spending time on?'

'The only witness of the case and the only survivor Mukesh Jha is under medication and I doubt he will be able to identify Khemka. The security camera which captured the accident does not show the face of the driver clearly. It could be anyone.'

'So, what AKD wants from us?' Ray asked.

'Assistance in evidence collection.'

'Hmm…how much will he pay?' Ray asked.

'Our usual fee.'

'I guess we could work a couple of days and see what materialized. We gotta find Khemka, if we want to get anywhere near breaking it open.' Ray said in a voice which did not sound too hopeful.

Chapter – 11

He stood in the darkness, hiding. Hiding from the world. Hiding from himself. He looked up and stared at the stars. So many of them, he tilted his head to embrace the sight. One would not be able to distinguish one from another. They just existed. They happened by. Some day one of them would fall from the sky and no one would miss the absence. He leaned his back against a tall tree, thinking. He did not want to exist for the heck of it. He did not want to be just there. No ways. He wanted people to know that he existed. He wanted to leave his mark in the history. He wanted attention, a heave of sigh hissed out of his mouth.

Today he made it to the front page. Yeah, true people did not know him by his name or face. That did not bother him much. People don't know the identity of The Ripper either. Yet, they still talk about the murders. There was something about unsolved mysteries. He wanted to do something similar as well. He wanted people to talk about him long after he departed the world.

Faint sound of a music system came from a distance. Someone listened to songs this late. Passion would get people to do anything. Passion, he thought of the cute journalist. The girl had fire inside her heart. She needed a real man to get it out. One look at her and he knew she was a star in making. Her words laden with passion and excitement got his attention. Yes, he wanted someone like her to write about him. Every Alexander the Great needed an Aryan to sing the praise. The fact that she looked good made the selection easy.

He pulled out his cell phone from the back pocket of his faded denim. He needed to make a call. Tonight he needed time for himself. There were things he needed to come to terms with. When the call went unanswered, he headed back home.

Like always his house reflected lifelessness. He loitered aimlessly for a couple of minutes. Then he settled down on a couch in his living room. Everywhere they talked about him. They sang his praise. They tried to guess his next move. Stardom, he chuckled. That young girl had given him his due fame. Now, it was him who would return the favor. She worked hard for fame too. He would give her the next scoop. This one would surpass the previous one. He promised to himself.

He switched on the television which sat across the sofa set and flipped channels while humming an old Bollywood song under his breath. Fame came at a price. And he was ready to pay. He was ready to make the sacrifices required for something so big.

His phone rattled. The vibration made him look at the device with irritation. 'I called you,' he said after hitting the receive button.

'I was working. Do you know Rudransh Ray is investigating Samir's murder?' asked the caller.

'Who?'

'Rudransh Ray,' said the caller louder this time. 'You don't want to mess up with this man. He shoots first asks questions later.'

He chuckled at the sound of fear. 'Really?' he asked. 'That bad?'

'Really that bad.' There was a pause. 'Why did you do it? You could have killed Samir and walked away. Why did you have to rip him apart?' The frantic question made him chuckle. 'Why did you have to be The Ripper? It jeopardized everything. Ray knows about our business. In due time, he will know about us as well.'

He listened to the whining without saying anything. On the television screen, he saw the headline The Ripper strikes in Kolkata. He liked it. The name befitted him. The Ripper. He had always been fascinated by Jack's MO. He had spent countless hours thinking about Jack the ripper and his killing methods. Fascinating. What would these people know? He thought flipping to another channel.

'You need to back out for a while. They will not be able to link us to Samir. I made sure that there is no thread of connection. You just have to stay put. Control that desire for fame. There will be time for that,' the caller continued to rant on the phone.

'Yeah, yeah.' He disconnected the phone before the call stretched any longer. The name Rudransh Ray remained in his mind, hung like heavy clouds which covered the sunlight and reflected darkness. Rudransh Ray, he pulled himself up on his feet and went to his laptop. Did search engine know this Ray character? He banged a few words down in the search box and hit go. It took a second for the search engine to come up with its search result.

Rudransh Ray was a famous guy. Too famous for this own good, he thought. Such a guy would never be able to become a shadow or hide in the darkness. Not, that Ray needed hiding. A widower, Ray went into depression after the death of his wife. He worked with CID crime division for eight years then drifted away when depression hit hard. But eventually he made a comeback and now for the last seven years he ran Rayon Corporation. Ray employed only talented people with some spark to speak for.

Impressive, he leaned back staring at the screen. Pretty awesome guy, would Ray hire him for a job, he chuckled at the question. It made him feel slightly proud that such a man had been brought to investigate his deed. Shoots first, talks later, the description flooded back to his mind. Hmm…Ray could be dangerous. But then again, he liked danger.

He reached out and hit the image tab. Always look the enemy into the eyes, his father said. He took his father seriously and that one liner stuck to his mind. He thought of looking for the image of the man who would put a bullet into his head if he could.

A hard looking, square jawed man with cold eyes started back at him few seconds later. Unknowingly he flinched at the stare. Now, this was an enemy you would not leave loitering by. He had two options now. He could retire, leave his art and go on living the life of an ordinary man. Or, he could take Ray down and claim the ultimate victory. He could see flashes of lights. He could hear buzz of media. They would be hovering over Ray's mutilated body.

He straightened. Blood began to rush into his veins. He could feel his pulse throbbing. Heart thudded against his ribs. With each beat, the vision became more vivid. He could smell blood. He could hear a loud thump as his cricket bat hit Ray's skull. Beads of perspiration formed on his forehead as his breath quickened. A snake climbed down his spine. It made him shiver a little.

Without knowing his hand reached for his crotch. With a long drag of breath he began to massage himself. Before his unblinking eyes was the image of Rudransh Ray lying dead at his feet. Should he expose the dick of the criminologist after killing him? That would be the ultimate humiliation to a man so dignified. Before, the climax took him over, he made a sudden decision.

Sometimes you gotta do what you gotta do, he thought philosophically. A moan of pleasure escaped him mouth as he thought of the kill. He leaned back stretching his legs as far as he could move in that state. Hiss of quick breath echoed in the room. He threw his head back, his vision blurred as the feeling captured all his senses.

Chapter – 12

Ray entered his office premise, thinking about Samir's murder scene. His head felt strangely light even after staying up the whole night discussing the case with Shraddha. In five years, she had learned a great deal about criminal profiling and crime scene reconstruction. It was Shraddha who pointed out that the blood splatter in Samir's murder scene did not look natural. It seemed like someone had deliberately splattered blood on the wall. Ray knew that the blood they had seen on the wall did not come from stabbing only. The offender had decorated the room with Samir's blood. It was not a dilutional, disorganized offender they were dealing with. Even though the unsolved murder loomed over him like a dark spot, Ray felt at peace that morning.

'In great mood skip?' asked Karan, eyeing Ray with an amused smile. 'Cracked the case wide open huh?'

'Fallen in love,' said Chirag, the love guru of the premise. 'Who is the lucky girl boss?'

Lavanya turned to look at Ray with eyes wide enough to swallow his whole existence. 'Really, who is she?'

'Guys grow up, you don't have to be in love to be calm,' Ray said. Shraddha's face formed in his mind.

He had manipulated her to stay back at home today. But whether those four walls could keep her safe was a question. It did not matter, he would be back guarding her door when the sun went down. He would do so till this mad killer got caught or killed. 'Fi in my office right now.'

Fiona displayed every sign of a girl who needed to eat healthy food. 'You don't eat right?' Ray asked.

Fi cocked her head and considered this. 'That's the saddest part boss. I do eat. Only people cannot see it on me.'

'Okay cool,' Ray said, already moving on to the murder. 'I want you to dig into the background of a man named Raghav Ahuja.'

'Okay,' Fiona said. It sounded a lot like Hokay to him. Fiona had started to work on her accent and lately sounded like an Indian trying to imitate foreign accent. The effect was funny but no one had the heart to tell her that. She wrote the name down on a paper and looked up with a smile. 'Anything else boss?'

'Anything else on Samir?'

'His neighbors are glad that he is dead. He brought women to his home. He beat his mother.' Fiona looked bored as she narrated the details. 'Oh, here is a possible suspect.' She smiled. 'A guy named Nicholas Jones came to Samir's home one night with a couple of guys and screamed at him for trying to rape his sister. This Nicholas guy had vowed to kill Samir.' Ray nodded. He did not think an angry brother had killed Samir and then called Shraddha to hit a sixer. The murderer was a classic asshole. He might have killed Samir for some personal reason, but, he had ripped the body open for pleasure and now after the front page news, he would do it for fame next time. 'So Samir caught this guy later. They had a little fight. You know the guy thing. In the chaos, Nicholas lost his right eye.'

'Worth looking up,' Ray said. 'But…'

'Don't just stop there.' Fiona laughed as she finished what Ray was about to say.

'Send Chirag in.'

'So, what's the latest update?' Ray asked once Chirag took a seat across him.

'Does not look too promising.' He cracked his knuckles. 'We don't have any evidence to tie Ashutosh to the accident. His driver had already confessed. What we have is an injured witness who would not be able to identify his own mother with both eyes open. Added to this Ashutosh is absconding.'

'Wow. I guess that does it. AKD will have to take the fall this time.' To be frank Ray was not too concerned about the whole thing. Yes, his sympathy was with the families of the dead people. But other than that he had nothing else to give them.

Chirag shrugged. 'I guess, I will go chase some ambulances now. Or, else you will have to justify my salary this month.'

'Why should I justify your salary?' Ray asked, knowing he would hear the most bizarre answer.

Chirag shrugged. 'Because, you have hired me. It's that simple.'

'Of course.' Ray nodded. 'Makes sense.'

Since he had nothing else to do and nowhere else to look at, Ray went in search of Nicholas Jones. He ran a coffee shop near Dalhousie. The shop is named The Coffee. Ray was appreciating the creative insight of choosing such an abstract name for a coffee shop when Nicholas came to take his order. Ray identified him from the sightless right eye. Even if he was conscious of the shortfall, he did not show it.

Though Ray did not go there to have coffee, the aroma of the caffeine made him yearn for a cup. 'Vanilla Latte,' Ray said. 'You are Nicholas?' he asked.

Automatically his right hand shot up and touched the right cheekbone. 'Yes, I am.' He looked down at Ray with a mixture of awe and suspicion.

'Rudransh Ray, can I have a minute?' The tonality of his voice left no space for a denial. Ray wanted to talk and Nicholas would have to obey. This dominion never failed to work in professional life. But when it came to personal life…he wondered whether his marriage fell apart because of this dominating nature of his.

Nicholas pulled a chair to sit across him. He placed his elbows on the table and leaned forward to look Ray into the eyes. 'Is it about Samir Shrivastav?' he asked.

Rather than answering immediately Ray looked him into the eyes for a second longer than required. 'Yes, it is.'

'I knew cops will come looking for me.' Nicholas flashed a smile. 'I did not kill him. I would have.' He admitted.

'I can understand.' Ray nodded. 'So, what happened?'

'You don't know?' he asked.

'Not a lot.' Ray shook his head. His hand touched the pocket of his jeans where he kept his cigarette. The café had a clear No Smoking sign hanging from the wall. So, he did not fish it out, not that he was afraid of Nicholas. But Ray firmly believed in following rules as long as rules paid.

'Samir ran an advertising agency. He produced short films…or so he said. He auditioned young girls, filmed them and then blackmailed them for sex and prostitution,' said Nicholas. 'Have you checked his studio?'

'No, we are not aware of any studio.' Ray leaned forward for a better view of Nicholas' eye that could see.

'It's in Lake Town. An apartment in third floor.' He pulled out his cell phone, punched some keys. 'Here is the address.'

Ray took the cell phone and looked down. 'What he did there?'

'Took girls, raped them and filmed the act,' Nicholas said with as much disdain as he could master. 'Nasty guy. He damaged my sister forever. She does not want to come out of her room or meet anyone. It's been more than a year.' He paused. 'I am not sorry he died.'

With the way the things proceeded. Ray could not deny that he felt a little delight in the death too. Such a human being did not have any right to stay alive.

'But you know what?' Nicholas said. 'Samir's death will not solve the problem. It might delay the business. But there are other people attached with him. They all are together in this. You need to break the racket, if you want to stop it.'

'How old were your sister when she went for the audition in Samir's office?' Ray asked.

'Seventeen.'

'How can you be so sure that there were other people?' Ray asked.

'My sister told me. She…' Nicholas stopped as if trying to decide how to tell him or not. Ray leaned back in the chair and waited for Nicholas to come to a decision. 'Off the record,' said Nicholas after a long pause.

'Sure,' Ray said, for now, he added silently.

'There were two more of them with Samir.' Reading Ray's mind, he added in haste. 'She was drugged and could not remember much.'

'I understand,' I said. 'Thanks for the information.'

'I am gonna bring that latte now.' With that he left Ray with disturbing thoughts. Three men…he could not even bring himself to imagine what she had gone through.

The apartment in Lake Town looked nothing like a studio from the outside. The caretaker knew Samir and was glad that he died.

'Everyone seems happy that the guy is dead,' said Vivan.

'Some cause happiness wherever they go; others whenever they go,' Akash commented as he climbed the stairs after Vivan.

'Hey well said.' Vivan beamed at the quote. 'Very well said.'

Akash beamed back. 'Intelligence is my natural talent,' he said with a straight face.

Ray turned to look at Vivan. 'Don't you read anything but porn?'

'I don't even read that. I watch. It's more fun, you know,' he said. 'Keeps your hands free for…'

'Spare us,' Ray said, before it went any further than that.

'Yeah sure,' Vivan said, happily looking at his hands. 'In the college days, we used to call them hand happy movies.'

Akash snorted at this. 'Too long and not crisp enough.'

Vivan made a face at this. 'Really?' he asked. 'Why don't you come up with a crispy name?'

Akash looked up, thinking as he unlocked the apartment. 'Dick ride video.'

Vivan clapped in mock appreciation. 'So crispy that I am gonna munch it now.'

Smell of rose room freshner floated in the air as Ray opened the door. His traced the floor for any tale-tell sign of recent entering. A series of fading footprints came to view. To take a close look he squatted. Hmm could not be older than a couple of days. Someone had come here after Samir's death. To clean off evidence? Ray pulled himself up on his feet.

'Who else came here other than Samir?' He asked.

'A lot of people,' said the caretaker. 'But I don't stay here all the time. So, I have no way of knowing.'

'Hmm.' Ray looked around. The living room was painted pink. A psychological thing, he thought. Pink tended to make people feel comfortable. It had none of the high intensity of red. So, you bring a person, a girl especially in a pink room, you win half her trust.

Lavishly furnished with wrought iron furniture, it depicted signs of money being spent for the decoration.

'Who else lives in the building?' Ray asked.

'No one,' said the caretaker. 'This is the only rented flat.'

'Great.'

Vivan went for the bedroom which was also painted pink. Akash went for the other room. Ray did not hope to find anything in either of the rooms, so he remained in the hall, scanning with a calculating expression. Whoever had come to visit this apartment had wiped it clean. Yet, they always missed something. He had seen this in numerous occasions. Before he could start digging, his phone vibrated. It was Sid, informing him that the autopsy of Samir's body had not been done due to some technical issues. But the ME would perform it within two days. Ray's brows furrowed at the delay. Each moment was important in a serial killing case. He knew that one brutal murder did not make an offender a serial killer. But the dagger marks, the hit against the skull, and the blood splatter pointed towards a practiced killer. This guy had done it before, countless times, Ray was ready to bet his life on this claim.

A showcase made from shiny wood stood in the corner of the room. It was loaded with show pieces. Marble men and women in various poses stood inside it. Driven by a whim, Ray started to move the showpieces around. Maybe he would find something, he told himself. Maybe whoever had come here to wipe the room clean had missed something, he hoped.

Hope keeps the world alive, his late wife used to say. But sometimes there is no hope to adhere to. Right now they all stood at the point of dusk breaking free. The night had just started. Ray thought of Shraddha and the man he had knowingly let loose after her. The offender would tear her apart if he got the chance. Though he tried hard to control his imagination and worry, she remained in his mind like a stubborn scar. Ray let out a deep breath before he started to search the showcase with animosity he did not know he possessed.

To keep his mind busy he took the showpieces out. Someone had wiped them clean too. Trying to hide fingerprints? Of course, they were. He put the things back, nothing. Did he just waste half a day coming here? He wondered. Maybe he should take a look at the back of the showcase. Something from within asked what he hoped to recover from there. Might be nothing. Might be everything. In his line of work, anything could break a case. So, he got down to work. Using both of his hands he pulled the showcase away from the wall. Nothing only pink wall came to view at the back of it. No one had…his eyes narrowed. He could distinguish a color difference on the surface of the wall. For a better view he pushed the showcase further away and moved closer. He could detect a faint mismatch on the wall. Though the same shade of pink had been used to patch up a particular area, time played a big role in displaying the difference. Ray could make out the dusty layer which bordered a square, newly painted.

With his knuckles he tapped the square area. It sounded hollow. He tapped again. Yes, he got the same unmistaken echo coming from inside.

'Vivan,' Ray called.

'Yes boss.' Vivan rushed out of the room he had disappeared to.

'First, don't call me that. Second, you gotta break this thing.' Ray pointed his index finger at the chunk which looked mismatched to him.

'As you wish boss.'

It took thirty minutes and a lot of mess to get the piece down. Inside was a shelf, a vault actually which housed a metal box. Ray removed it with his latex gloved hands. What could be inside? He had already come across a bag full of money, a closet full of porn movie and a ripped apart dead body. What else remained? He questioned himself as his fingers struggled to open the metal lock.

The box opened unceremoniously, revealing a cherry velvety interior. Ray's throat went dry at the sight of the content of the box. Vivan drew a sharp breath as he stared, wide eyed. Akash looked away for a moment then shook his head.

The metal box was loaded with bones, cut into small pieces. It looked like someone had neatly sliced human fingers and then put the bones after the flesh had decayed. Ray narrowed his eyes. His initial deduction was wrong. Whoever had come to visit the apartment had not come to take away evidence. The individual had come to hide this box. He rubbed his gloved hand over the lid. Not a speck of dust existed on the surface. It had been placed inside the vault recently. So, the offender collected mementos from his victims.

'It confirms two of my theories,' said Ray. 'One Samir knew his killer. Otherwise the offender would not have the access to the house key.' He paused to look down at the stack of bones, wondering how many people had died to contribute to this collection. 'And the offender has killed before.' He drew a deep breath. 'Many times.'

Chapter – 13

Shraddha paced the length of her living room space. She could not get herself to focus. Being under house arrest could be maddening. But Akshaj would not allow her to come to office. He said it would be better to work from home. Once long ago, she had been fascinated by the prospect of working from home. But now…well she was ready to tear down every single drape around the room.

Akshaj was bad enough and now Rudransh Ray…

She ran her hand through her thick hair. The man spent the entire night at her apartment. He finished four steaming mugs of coffee before dawn. At the sight of sun ray he decided to finally go home.

In the empty living room, with the silence echoing, she fought hard to keep the memory of Ray being in her apartment at bay. It would lead to nothing, she told herself. At this stage of life, when the ground under her feet was finally getting solid, she did not need any emotional complication. Her last relationship was poisonous enough to make her cringe at the thought of another one.

To calm her beating heart she crossed the living room and headed for her study. It was a large attic in rectangle shape. At the corner sat her writing desk and her laptop. A comfortable recliner was placed snugly against the table. She had bought this after much debate. It did cost her big bucks, but the expenditure had been worth it. At the opposite corner was a leather couch placed near a massive wooden bookcase. Some of the shelves were empty. Soon she planned to fill them out. Both of the furnishings had been bought from a second hand furniture store, though by the look of them no one would say that.

She dropped on the couch and looked at the bookcase. It calmed her to take inventory of her collection. She liked to look at the shiny covers and feel proud to own so many titles. Her heart slowly calmed and she could gather her thought.

Her main concern was not the murderer right now. Selfishly, she thought about Oliva and the unborn child. Raghav would not come home, Shraddha knew that. Someone had ended the young life. She would have to find out who and why.

His last emails were all she had and there was nothing to indicate a mission, an antagonist or some perilous road to follow. She reached out and pulled a book. It was her favorite title, a hardcover novel with a beautiful book jacket. She was yet to read this book. For some reason she could not get to it. Maybe later sometime. She thought brushing her hand on the smooth cover.

A couple of hours later, after her tenth attempt to read and find clues from Raghav's emails, Shraddha decided to quit for the day. Her eyes throbbed due to lack of sleep and stress. Even though she acted nonchalant and showed no reaction over the killer's call, in the seclusion she admitted her fright. Yes, the man scared her. Yes, she feared for her life, but only for a moment. Then once it vanished she felt a sense of excitement. This could be big, she told herself. But another voice which seemed a lot like common sense told her that this could be nasty too.

Shraddha drew a deep breath before switching off her laptop. As she started to get up from her chair, her cell phone vibrated. Shraddha stiffened immediately. Her eyes turned towards the window which gave a clear view of the street. Only casual passers-by she saw no suspicious entity loitering there. Her phone continued to vibrate, a little insistent this time. Shraddha picked up the device finally. Her heart raced as she looked at the unknown number flashing on her screen.

'Hello,' she said uncertainly.

'Hi,' replied a cheerful male voice. 'You won't remember me. I am Akash Bajaj, Rudransh Ray's business partner.'

A sigh of relief escaped Shraddha's heart. 'I do remember you,' she said, wondering about the reason of this call. She remembered Akash Bajaj's boyish good looks and charm.

'I am preparing a case report and need your side of the story,' said Akash. 'It will be great if you can spare me some time and sit with me.'

The prospect of speaking about the last night experience once again made Shraddha's stomach roll. She let out a long breath, considering. Rayon Corp was assisting the police force profiling the murderer. Therefore, they held the power to force her to cooperate. She did not want to drag the matter to the stretching level. 'Sure,' she said. 'I am working from home for a few days.' Meeting people would do her good, she thought. 'So, you can come down anytime.'

'Working from home will keep you safe?' asked Akash. Shraddha heard suppressed sarcasm in his voice.

She had to admit that working from home would not keep her or anyone safe. It was true that she lived in the heart of the city. It was also true that no one could enter her house without waking up the entire neighborhood. But it was also true that the man who had ripped a criminal like Samir apart could find a way to get to her. 'People seem to think so,' she said.

Akash laughed a humorless laughter. 'I will be down there with Ray this evening,' he said. 'After office.' With that the line got silent.

Shraddha sat back pressed her index finger against her temple and began to massage. She detected a faint promise of a headache. As a child she had experienced frequent bouts of headaches. It kept her from school most of the days. Her father was afraid that she would lose her eyesight. But fortunately with adolescence the problem subsided slowly. Today, after a long time she got the feel of the same ache. A lot had happened since the last bout of ache and this one. A lot had changed.

She sighed. Her phone vibrated again. She picked up the device without looking at the number.

'Hello,' said Shraddha, keeping her eyes closed. The familiar drum inside her head began to beat. Right now the rhythm was slow. It would increase as the day passed. If she was fortunate, she would be able to get away with a single day old spell. She rolled her head and waited for the caller to answer. When no one did, she greeted again, a little louder this time. 'Hello.'

Silence echoed on the other side of the phone. But it was a different type of silence. Shraddha felt a presence on the other side even though the caller had decided to keep quiet. She could hear light rustle of leaves in the background along with the sound of passing cars. Whoever was there on the other side was silent on a purpose.

Shraddha opened her eyes and looked at the screen. She found a landline number flashing there. 'Hello,' she said with irritation. Then she heard it. The caller began to breath in the receiver. The breath sounded like gasps. Goosebumps rippled all over Shraddha's body at the sound. The drum which was beating slowly inside her head even a minute ago, picked up pace as her agitation increased. 'Who is it?' she asked, noting with irritation that her voice trembled a little. In reply the caller breathed in the receiver again then only a doom like silence rose from the other side. Shraddha got up to her feet. Her stomach twisted. Bile formed in her throat. She had not expected this type of a reaction upon getting a blank call. But her overactive nerves began to work double time and forced Shraddha to toss the phone on her table and run for the washroom.

After getting the bile out of her system, she stood still, clutching the wash basin with her trembling hands. In front of her was a small vanity mirror which reflected her pale face. She looked tired, and frightened. Shraddha shook her head in dismay, a little ashamed now that the worst was over. If she kept throwing up at the slightest trouble, what the fuck would she do when the going would get really tough? That made her press her lips together in consideration. Of course, she could not tell anyone about her reaction to the blank call. But she would have to report the call, so that cops could try to trace the caller.

Outside, she took a couple of minutes to gather herself before dialing Akshaj's number. Last night cops tried to trace the number from which the killer had made the call. But they found the phone switched off and thus untraceable. The number was registered under the name of a man who died two years ago.

'Yes,' Akshaj's deep voice boomed through the phone. It calmed Shraddha down a little. The fatherly affection which Akshaj showered upon her made her feel secured. 'Any problem?' Even though the question sounded impatient, Shraddha could hear concern in Akshaj's voice.

She narrated the story of the blank call quickly, wondering what good her staying back at home did. The killer knew her number. Probably the guy knew her address as well. Rudransh Ray had failed to arranged for security to guard her. Even though the killer seemed unlikely to make any move in the day time, one should always be prepared for the worst.

Akshaj listened with patient. 'He only breathed in the phone?' he asked at last.

'Yes,' Shraddha said, thinking about the raspy breathing and wondering what the caller was trying to indicate.

'You called Ray?' asked Akshaj.

Shraddha had considered calling Ray right after coming out of the washroom. But then she decided to call Akshaj instead. 'No, not yet.'

'Call him. Report it,' said Akshaj. 'I don't think it is safe for you to stay there all alone.'

Before Akshaj could ask her to move to his house, Shraddha hurriedly said, 'He has arranged for people to guard my house. I am completely safe here.' She heard slight tremor in her voice. It made her doubt her decision to try criminal journalism. Probably she should try writing celebrity gossips. Tired and stressed her eyes began to burn. 'I am calling Ray right now.'

Akshaj was quiet for a while. Then he spoke in a low voice. 'I am sorry Shraddha.'

The apology startled Shraddha. She blinked twice before finding her voice. 'For what sir?' she asked.

'For putting you through this,' said Akshaj. 'I thought you would not be able to break the case. I just wanted you to have a hang of a high profile case and build your reputation in this industry.' A deep sigh echoed from the other side. 'I had no idea that you would come back with those images and write a piece so compelling that the killer would crawl out of his rabbit hole.'

The concern in Akshaj's voice touched Shraddha. She swallowed a big lump which threatened to come out in the form of a sob. 'It's not your fault sir. It's my hunger for fame and acceptance which brought me in this situation. I could have said no to the case. I did not. I could have stayed back in the office and watch the news updates on television. But I had to go to Samir's office to impress people.' She paused, feeling like a fool, and being grateful that Trisha was not in the town. Shraddha did not want her sister to be in any kind of trouble.

A long silence materialized. Shraddha heard Akshaj's deep breathing from the other side. Then her boss said, 'We all are hungry for something Shraddha. Don't ever beat yourself for going after what you want.' He blew a breath which sounded like a hiss. 'Call Ray and see what that arrogant asshole has to say about this. If you feel insecure, you can always come and stay at my place. I live in a six bedroom, double story house.'

After the conversation with Akshaj, Shraddha sat for a couple of minutes. Then as she reached for her phone, it vibrated. Shraddha's hand froze in mid-air immediately. Then she let out a sigh of relief as Ray's name flashed on the screen.

'You received a strange blank call?' Ray asked without bothering to come with any greeting.

Shraddha blinked in surprise. 'How do you know?' she asked. Then the answer formed in her mind by itself. Ray was watching her calls. His team had their eyes on her phone and movements now. She was the thread which could lead cops to the killer. Before bitterness could form to make her retort, she reminded herself that everyone who worked on the case wanted to solve the murder. Therefore, she should not expect special treatment from anyone.

'Yes, from another unknown number,' replied Shraddha.

'We have traced it,' said Ray. 'It came from a telephone booth near Sonarpur.' He paused, waiting for some reaction. When Shraddha gave none, he asked, 'You know someone from this area?'

No she did not. 'No, I don't believe I do.' She knew that the answer did not satisfy Ray. But she was powerless to help him here.

'Ok, cool,' said Ray. 'Don't go outside until I come back. I need to sit with you and do a proper interview. My partner Akash and CID senior investigator Siddhant Thakur will be with me.'

Shraddha did not know why Ray told her all these. He did not have to inform her who he was bringing for questioning. 'Should I call for backup?' she asked to make the situation light. 'Otherwise it is going to be three on one.'

Ray chuckled. 'Don't worry,' he said. 'We are perfect gentlemen. But if you feel insecure, you can always call someone to be with you.' The last statement was made in utter seriousness. 'You have the right to be wary of three unknow men.'

One of whom had spent a night on her living room couch, thought Shraddha. But aloud she said, 'Oh, I am not afraid. I was only joking.'

'I know,' Ray said. 'But you should always be aware of your rights.' He paused for a brief moment. 'And never trust anyone.' With that the line went dead.

Chapter – 14

His head buzzed as he forced himself to think. Events, words, and even people jumbled in Ray's mind like mash of energies. In front of his eyes his team moved, worked, spoke. But he could not relate to them. Guilt, he understood that it was guilt. He should not have dragged Shraddha in this mess. He should not have given her the photos.

'Don't.' Akash's voice penetrated in his mind. He tore his glance away from the front door where he was staring and looked at his partner.

'What?' he asked, confused.

Akash chuckled at his expression. 'You look sexy when you look bewildered.' His chuckle turned into a sly grin as his face contorted with disgust. 'Don't look so guilty. You have done what you thought was good for everyone. Of course, you have been an asshole to do it. But it has been done already. You cannot undo it.' Akash whistled as Ray shook his head. 'You have dragged that woman into this fucking mess. You have completely fucked up with the evidence. You have placed your ass on the direct line where you may get the burn no matter what.'

Ray licked his lips, staring at Akash. Even though his business partner was in his mid-thirties, he still looked to be in his late twenties. Fair, slender, and tall, Akash had the charm to pose for any clothing brand. But he chose to be a true crime story writer. At times, Akash could be a real pain in the ass, especially when he sat reading every expression which crosses Ray's face.

'I wanted to drag the asshole out of his hiding place,' Ray said after measuring his words carefully. 'But I did not want to put a civilian's life on the line to do that.'

Akash played with a pen for a couple of minutes with a grin on his face. Ray did not like the grin. But then again, he did not like a lot about Akash's face. 'Especially a good looking civilian's life.' His smile widened when he noted a touch of displeasure of Ray's face. 'You think this guy will physically attack Shraddha?' The smile on Akash's face vanished as he asked this.

Since the moment Ray heard about the killer calling her, he had been asking myself this question. Could she be physically attacked? Could this man do something unthinkable just to gain fame? Unfortunately, the answer always came in positive. Yes, the guy could hurt her just to be in limelight for a while. He could give her the same treatment he had given Samir Shrivastav to prove his superiority.

'Yes,' Ray said after a long pause and not without regret. 'He can and he will.' Even to his own ears that sounded like a warning. 'I think I should go and check on her. You come over after office to prepare the report.'

Akash nodded. He did not crack any of his usual wise jokes. Akash had written enough true crime stories and interviewed enough criminals to understand the situation. 'Fine, I will bring Sid along.'

'We have to arrange for security,' Ray said. 'We are lucky that Akshaj Mukherjee hasn't yet written a piece on us for failing his star reporter.'

'It is not only about getting the burn from the media,' said Akash. 'If we fail to crack the case soon enough, the special force will take it over.'

Ray shook his head. 'That's the least of our concern,' he said as he made his way towards the door. He would speak to Sid about Shraddha's security tonight, he decided as he got into his car. Though he did not mind spending time at her place, he could not guard her forever. So, either he arranged for people to keep her safe. Or, he found this bastard and put a bullet into his skull. Whatever came or happened first...

Twenty minutes and a long traffic battle later he pulled his Honda City in front of Shraddha's house. From a distance the two story, yellow pained building looked like any other houses of the neighborhood. But the tension which pulsated her home made it stood apart from the others. Ray scanned the area after getting out of the car. It had been a habit to look for trouble wherever he went. Old habit, he sighed with remorse. Probably this one would never die. He scratched his chin looking for something, at least someone. Finding none, he crossed the road to reach her front door. His cell phone vibrated before he could get a chance to ring her door bell.

'Sid,' Ray greeted with as much pleasure as a cancer patient showed on getting a call from their doctor. 'What's up?'

'I am in the town,' said Sid. 'I gotta speak to this journo. We need to move fast. Chetan is under pressure thanks to you.' His voice sounded amused. 'Before the task force comes, we need to get our asses cleared.'

Ray licked his lower lip. The matter was getting out of hand. They needed to get closure on this case and they needed it fast. 'Anything on Samir and his associates?' Ray asked.

'Samir's business partner Ishant Trivedi is returning to Kolkata tomorrow,' said Sid. 'He has denied having any information about Samir's wrong doing. Together they used to run a health insurance business.' Sid paused for a moment, probably to catch his breath. He had been speaking without a break. 'So, I ran a quick check on this Ishant guy. He looks to be a clean one. But then again, every criminal looks clean.'

Ray gathered it all quietly. 'Great let's talk to him tomorrow,' he said. 'I want him tired and confused.'

'Drunk?' asked Sid. Amusement crept up in his voice.

Ray shook his head. 'I am not gonna seduce him,' he said. 'I am gonna speak to him.'

'Oh, yeah,' Sid said. 'That tired and confused thing got me turned on.' He laughed and disconnected the call.

Ray put his phone back inside his pocket when something moved behind a bush near Shraddha's home. I turned my gaze to catch a clear view of the movement, but the bush settled in utter stillness by then. For a moment, Ray stood there, considering. He had his gun hidden under my jacket. But in this street where civilian were passing by unloading a gun on a madman would not be a wise idea. He shifted his weight twice from right leg to left and then back, eyeing the bush. Then with slow steps he approached it. When he was just ten steps away, a man covered in a black hoodie rushed out of the hiding place. A black mask covered most of his face. Ray only got a glimpse of a pair of dark eyes. The hooded man pulled his tall and lanky form in a standing position, turned towards the street, crossed the bush in a smooth jump and began to run high-speed. The entire event took place in a fraction of one second.

Ray did not miss a beat and fell after the running figure. The man sprinted through the traffic and people like a cat. Ray followed him in a steady motion, but the distance between us began to increase. The hoodie was a pro runner, Ray realized. Even though he ran every day, he did not have professional touch.

This guy was clearly a professional runner. He pivoted through the traffic without even colliding with anyone. Finally, the hoodie reached an intersection of the street. Ray increased his speed because if the hoodie reached the main road, the chase would end.

The calves of his legs began to burn as Ray ran with all his strength. But before he could even get close to the black hoodie, he reached the main road, and jumped inside a speeding Non AC bus. Even though the chase ended there, Ray continued to go after the bus. Had the driver or the conductor noticed him, he would have tried to stop the bus. But no one saw him. So, finally he accepted with grudge that the man had successfully got away from him.

As Ray walked back home the gravity of the event once again struck him hard. She lived in the heart of the city amidst series of houses and a busy neighborhood. People loitered around in continuous intervals. Yet, someone was there watching her from a distance. How much damage could someone inflict upon another person on a busy street? Ray knew that one could cause a lot of damage to another if one wanted. His stomach rolled for no reason at all. Slowly, a vision took shape in his mind. With bits and pieces the vision formed and protruded itself in vivid horror.

In this distorted version of daydream, he saw Shraddha lying on a wide pool of crimson liquid, her own blood, eyes wide open and accusing. Her long reddish hair gave her pale face a horrific expression. The intensity of the vision delivered a direct blow in his midriff. Ray had to stop walking to let the image fade. It did like all images and visions. But the horror lived deep in his soul. He drew raspy breaths, not from the running, but from the what might happen worry. He had to do something and he had to do it fast.

Ray called Sid to report the incident who listened with patience. But there was an indifference which irritated Ray, though he understood the reason Sid always remained detached from any case or the people involved. If they allowed themselves to feel for every human being entangled in a murder case, they would end up losing their minds. Yet, this time Ray had to swallow his retorts and speak to Sid with outmost decency.

'Sid, she is in danger,' he said again, just to allow the information saturate in Sid's mind. 'You need to arrange for something. At least one cop to guard her house.'

Sid breathed hard, thinking. Ray could hear the whiz of hard exhales in the device he held against his ears. 'I am helpless here,' Sid said finally. 'We are working on skeleton force right now. I cannot spare anyone.' He paused. 'I understand the situation. But she lives in the city, for God's sake. Not in a remote area. What could happen to her if she stays inside her house and does not open the door?'

It made sense to Sid, Ray realized. But to him the situation called for drastic measure. Sid did not know Shraddha. She would not stay imprisoned for a long time. One day soon, she would amble out with or without permission from the law enforcement. They needed to be prepared for that day.

So, the next call went to Akshaj Mukherjee. The old man did not sound too pleased to get a call from Ray, which did not make any difference to the criminal profiler, given the situation. They needed to work together if they wanted to keep Shraddha safe and the case alive.

'So, what do you suggest?' he asked after hearing everything with patience.

'A collaboration,' Ray offered. 'You assign her to work with Rayon Corporation on this case that way we can keep an eye on her.'

A heavy pause materialized. Ray could hear Akshaj thinking, considering, and calculating. The lure was strong and tempting. Kolkata Breaking would get the first scoop of each progress. It would help promote the paper. If he had understood Akshaj Mukherjee well, the old man would not be able to refuse the offer.

'We meant who?' asked Akshaj after a while.

'Me and my team,' Ray replied, not liking the path the conversation was taking.

Again Akshaj went into a silent mode. Ray continued to walk towards Shraddha's house. From a distance, he could see the top of the two story building. It stood with pride, despite its age. He eyed the street, not leaving a single corner unscanned. Everything seemed to be normal now. The wide porch of Shraddha's house basked in the dim light of the sun. The shy sunlight could not diminish the chill though. But it had a bright effect on his darkening mood. Every time Ray worked a case, he experienced this mood darkening moments. Things dulled and life slowed. He usually felt like screaming at someone and he always did. Mostly Akash took the burn. Becoming a vicious offender and thinking like them was not easy. People might think he relished his job. But mostly he did not. Most of the cases made him wish to retire forever and go somewhere isolated.

'You and your team?' asked Akshaj. 'Or you alone?'

Ray foresaw this question. He knew one day, Akshaj would pop this question. But knowing something and facing it in reality were two different aspects. Knowing did not lessen the fury which rose inside him just then.

'If you wanna play fucking dirty Akshaj, then be it,' he said, through gritted teeth. 'All I am trying to do here is – protect a valuable resource of my case. But since you don't want your employee to be safe, I am not going to get my ass involved.' He paused to allow the coldness to sink in the heart of the old man. 'I will get the fucker one way or another. I don't need your paper or your journos.'

Despite the attack, Akshaj did not burst in rage. He went quiet again. Then when he spoke, his voice sounded low and tired. 'I am not married, you know Mr. Ray?' he asked. Ray took it, not knowing where the conversation went. 'I never had a child. I thought I did not have the fatherly affection in me. I was wrong.' Akshaj's voice mellowed down. He lost a lot of his usual coldness. 'That girl proved me wrong. She walked in with her resume and a desperate expression on her face and I felt the father in me waking up.' Ray remained quiet, letting Akshaj speak. The old man sounded better when he was not trying to be an asshole. 'I can ask her to stay at my apartment. But people will not understand. What I can take at the age of sixty seven and being a man, she will not be able to tolerate. So, please be careful and keep your agenda under control' A warning, Ray chuckled. Any other time he would have showed Akshaj the right place. But right now, he just felt glad that Shraddha had someone to check on her.

'I perfectly understand Mr. Mukherjee,' said Ray. 'I will not allow any harm to come her way.' He closed his eyes, remembering another time, another promise, and a death. The memory of Rusha's lifeless body, wide open, accusing eyes formed in his mind. He had failed her. He had failed to keep her alive. Would he be able to protect Shraddha when death would come knocking on her door?

'I am sure you will keep her safe Mr. Ray,' said Akshaj. 'Please let me know if your force fails to guard her home. I will arrange for special security force.'

'You don't have to do that,' Ray said. 'I will take care of these things.'

The next call he made to Akash and arranged for a security officer to guard Shraddha's house. He would not be able to stay with her every night. Akshaj was right. What he could take as a man, Shraddha would not be able to tolerate as a woman. Ray rang her door bell, after making the arrangements. Something in him told him to be on alert all the time. The case had reached the point from where things would begin to slide further down. When it happened, he wanted Shraddha to be out of the firing line.

She opened the door with a broken expression. Ray detected the glassy look which spoke of crying hard. 'Is something wrong?'

She stepped aside to let me in. 'I hate being under house arrest.'

Ray laughed at her expression. 'You are not under house arrest. You are staying home and working from there.'

Shraddha looked up at me with wide eyes, tears formed in the deep depth, then she blinked them back. 'But I need a life outside.' Her whispered in a thick voice. 'Staying inside all day long is going to kill me. I need a life.'

Ray did not feel least bit sympathetic towards her. 'It's just a single day Shraddha. Don't act like a child.' Then he understood her agitation. She wanted to be in the middle of the action. She thought she was missing important scoops. 'I am sure your boss will come up with something good for you.'

She led him to her living room and pointed at a couch. 'Have you eaten anything?' she asked. 'I am going to make chicken salad.'

His stomach, his treacherous stomach, growled just then, telling the world how hungry he was. She smiled at the sound. 'Let's have something to eat then. I am starving.'

Instead of sitting to the appointed couch, he followed her to the kitchen. It was a wide, old fashioned cooking space with modern utilities. She brought cucumbers, tomatoes, onions, and lettuce out of the fridge. 'You like salad dressing?' she asked.

Ray shook my head. 'Not too much meyo.'

She nodded and turned back to work. Ray watched her slicing fruits and vegetables like an expert. 'So, did he fire you?' Ray asked, keeping his tone carefully normal. I did not want to laugh and make her feel awkward.

'No,' she said sharply, keeping her back firmly towards him. 'He has not fired me.' She was quiet for a long time. The steady tapping of her knife filled the silence of the kitchen. Then she asked him in a low voice. 'Has the autopsy report arrived yet?'

Ray should not discuss the case with her. But then again, she had been dragged in the case already and he saw no harm in telling her about the status of autopsy report. 'Not yet,' he said. 'The ME is taking his sweet time to look at Samir.' He made a mental note to ask Vivan about the autopsy report. It should have arrived by now.

'Okay,' she said and then gone quiet.

Ray watched her for a while and then asked. 'You wanted to be a novelist, didn't you?'

She turned to look at him with a smile. 'You remember?' she asked.

Ray nodded. 'Yeah, I do,' he said. 'I hope all these grooming and polishing up haven't killed that dream.' He was surprised at the bitterness in his voice. Why was he angry with her? He wondered. Was it because she was too good looking now and he found it difficult to take his mind off her? Or, did he really mourn the loss of the simplicity which she carried so confidently in the past?

Shraddha tilted her head to regard him for a while. 'All these grooming and polishing up?' she asked, her voice filled with amusement. Even her eyes danced as she asked.

Shame flooded all over him and he looked down. 'I am sorry,' Ray said, shaking my head. 'But you have changed.'

She nodded. 'I make effort to look good now,' she said. Then shrugged. 'If you don't like it, fine. I like myself this way.'

Ray stared at her, feeling the rush blood again. She had no idea how much he liked her. Before he could stop himself, he reached out and tucked a silky strand of hair behind her ear, making her jump. 'I like you,' he said. His voice had thickened, he noticed it. But he did not care. He was tired of being alone. Tired of avoiding people he liked. He was tired of the life he had given himself. 'I like you a lot.' His hand slid down and cupped her face. With his other hand he held her arm and drew her close, giving her time to pull away. She did not. He heard her drawing a deep breath as her slender body pressed against his chest. It broke the resolve he had in him. The world vanished, leaving only the two of them there in the silent kitchen.

He lowered his head to take her mouth in his, softly in the beginning, then he deepened the kiss. He had imagined it in his mind so many times in the past few years. He had felt it in his heart even. But reality always came with a surprise. She moaned in his mouth, rewarding him with the pleasure of knowing her desire for him. He pulled her tighter against his chest and kissed deeper. She accepted his aggressive approach and matched it with her own. They breathed hard like two runners struggling to suck air in their lungs. Their chests rose and fell. He felt her heart beating against his own, matching his rhythm. Then before he lost complete control over his resolve, he pulled his head away from her. But his arms refused to release her just then. So, he continued to hold her tight, remembering the mousy little girl who had walked in his interrogation room clutching a copy of The Count Of Monte Cristo.

'Write your novels,' he said to her, looking down into her eyes. 'Write them fast.' Her deep eyes turned soft as she looked at him. 'Make me proud.'

Chapter - 15

It was dusk when Shraddha finally stirred from her writing desk. Her story-fogged mind protested but she forced herself to move away from her laptop. If she did not get herself a cup of coffee, she would have a massive headache. So, she switched off the laptop and turned to look at Rudransh Ray who was sleeping on her couch, wrapped in a woolen blanked. Funny, how it took someone else to come and rekindle a fading passion. She had always wanted to be a writer. Her only dream had been to write bestselling novels. But then life began to move too fast and somehow she forgot all about her dreams and her half-finished books. Then out of the blue came Rudransh Ray. She was surprised that he remembered her passion. *Make me proud*, he had said. It had gone straight inside her heart. *Make me proud*, no had ever said to her. Without warning, her eyes moistened. She would try her best to make him proud of her. Ray's eyes fluttered but before he could come to a full wakefulness the doorbell chimed.

'Fuck,' said Ray. 'Must be Akash and Sid.' He sprinted up from the couch. 'Get ready. I will get the door.' He started to walk towards the door then stopped and turned. 'I…' He began, then let the sentence trail. Shraddha braced herself for a serious. Instead, Ray flashed her a smile. 'I see that you have started writing already.' He peered at her laptop, the lid was still open. 'I would like to hear the storyline while we eat dinner.' With that Ray stormed out of her writing room, leaving a bewildered Shraddha staring after him.

Downstairs, Shraddha found Siddhant Thakur, Akash Bajaj, and Rudransh Ray sitting comfortably. They turned to look at her the moment she entered. Siddhant Thakur looked the same as she remembered him, tall, lean, stunning with golden brown eyes and matching hair. Sid looked at her with a smile.

'You have changed a lot,' said Sid. 'Polished up well.'

It made Shraddha smile back. 'Yeah, had to follow the trend.'

Sid shook his head. 'You don't have to ma'am. You were amazing without polishing up.' That came as a surprise. But before Shraddha could say anything, Sid proceeded. 'I am sorry I could not arrange anyone to guard your house.' He paused to look at her with genuine regret. 'But I don't think a single guard will do anything special for you.'

Shraddha nodded. She knew that a guard will not be able to keep her safe from the man who had killed Samir Shrivastav. 'I know.' Her voice did not tremble. But she knew that Sid could read her feeling.

'You gotta stay home until we catch the killer,' said Sid. 'It will not be safe for you to go out right now.'

Before Shraddha could say anything, Ray's phone rang. He checked the number and then looked at her with a smile. 'It is your friend, Shivani.'

'Who?' asked Akash, puzzled. He had been quiet till now, writing something in a thick notebook.

'Another reporter from Kolkata Breaking,' said Ray. He let the phone continue to ring.

'I know her,' said Sid. 'She is a kind of vulture. Does not hesitate to sleep around for a scoop.'

Shraddha had heard this about Shivani. But until now, she had her doubt. 'Is it for real?' she asked.

A crooked smile flashed on Sid's face. He looked even more handsome smiling. 'I know for sure.' He winked at her. Akash cleared his throat. Ray coughed. Shraddha flushed at the dirty men talk.

'When did you fuck her?' asked Akash.

Sid shook his head. 'I don't sleep and tell.'

'Yeah, right,' said Ray. 'He does not sleep and tell.'

Sid shrugged. 'I don't give out details at least.'

'Can we talk about the murder?' ask Shraddha in a hurry. She did not want to sit here and listen to them talk about their rendezvous.

Sid chuckled. 'Gladly ma'am,' he said. Then his face turned serious. 'Look, this is a serious business. This guy is a lunatic who is looking for fame and he will not hesitate to kill you, if he thinks it will earn him some footage.' He stopped for a breath. 'It was a mistake to go and visit the crime scene. But you had no way of knowing that the fucker would be there.' He looked at Ray with a worried glance. 'What bothers me is the fact that he has your number.'

Shraddha nodded. She waited for the next bit of warning. Goosebumps spread across her arms as she drew a deep breath. 'I am also baffled to find that he has my phone number.'

'It is easy to get,' said Ray. 'He must have called your office and asked for you.'

'Yeah,' said Shraddha. 'But still.'

'He might even have your address,' said Sid. 'I don't want to scare you. But it could be a possibility.'

'What do you suggest me to do?' asked Shraddha. 'My boss is not allowing me to go to office. I need to stay home.' She looked at Ray helplessly. 'I have nowhere else to go.'

Ray grinned at her as she said this. 'Maybe you should speak to your boss about letting you start working.' He winked. 'Go ahead give him a call.'

Shraddha narrowed her eyes at this encouragement. 'You have spoken to him about me?'

Ray did not deny. 'Yes, I did. I told him that we can go for a collaboration. You can work with me and cover the murder story.' Shraddha started to protest. But Ray held up his hand. 'We need media coverage to keep people updated about the murder. So, I am not doing anything special for you.'

'You can come to office,' said Akash. 'You can come with Ray and leave with him.'

'Impossible,' said Shraddha. 'I can travel this short distance without anyone accompanying me.'

'If you come, I could use your expertise a bit,' said Akash as if she had not spoken. 'I will pay you to help me work on my book. I always pay my employees.' Sid rolled his eyes at the comment. Ray shook his head. Akash lost his smile and his amused expression. 'My upcoming book is not going anywhere. A few more days and the publisher will start screaming at me.'

Sid ignored Akash. 'That's settled then. You are going with Ray to his office and coming home with him.' He too raised his hand when Shraddha started to protest. 'It's our only way till I can arrange for manpower.'

Shraddha was quiet for a while. She stared at her hand, considering the whole matter. If Akshaj had agreed to Ray's terms then she would have to obey it. Otherwise, Akshaj would make her sit at home and write fashion. If she sat back at home, she would go crazy. Outside leaves began to rustle as wind picked up pace. Shraddha looked outside. The darkness had gone deeper somehow. Within a moment an ear piercing sound echoed. Everything trembled under the pressure and then rain drops began to beat against the rooftop.

Sid looked at the window with an expression of dismay. 'You don't have beer or whiskey at your home, do you?' he asked.

'No, I don't booze,' said Shraddha in a low voice. Rainfall had a way of making her feel lonely. It made her think of her father. He loved rain and sound of storms. She still remembered each rainfall that she had enjoyed with her father and Trisha. They used to dance and sing each time it rained. And then one day, everything silenced, the dances, the songs, the laughter. Rain still came, but it was only Trisha and her now. So, they did not dance, did not sing, did not even speak about rain. When the mist of memories passed, she became aware of three pair of eyes staring at her. She opened her mouth to say something, to make the sudden feeling of heaviness go away. But nothing came out of her mouth, other than a deep sigh. 'I…I am sorry.' She lowered her eyes in embarrassment.

'No issues,' said Akash. 'We all think about our first love when it rains.' He winked at Shraddha and she found herself smiling at him.

'I have chicken nuggets and coffee though,' she said. 'If anyone wants it…' Sid raised his hand. Akash followed. 'Let's discuss the case once again and see what we can come up with.' Shraddha said over her shoulder as she walked towards her kitchen.

Chapter - 16

An amalgamation of medicine, room freshener, and decayed flesh attacked Ray the moment he walked inside the autopsy room with Sid and Akash at his toe. Vivan was already present in the room. Standing by the motionless body of Samir Shrivastav. Vivan continued to take notes. His bowed head could not conceal his bewildered expression. Ray stopped for a while to take in the scene. The ME Dr. Gaurav Roychoudhary stood a little distance away from Vivan. The young doctor was studying some notes from a thick writing pad. Hearing the approaching footsteps, Gaurav looked up with a smile.

'Hey,' he said, extending his hand towards Ray. 'Nice to see you.'

Ray shook the young doctor's hand heartily. 'Same here.' Then he looked at Samir Shrivastav. 'Blunt object?'

Gaurav nodded. 'Yes, of course. That and something else.'

Sid whistled at the comment. 'As in?' he asked.

'Poison.'

'He had been poisoned?' asked Vivan. 'Then why go to this length? Just for show off?' he asked.

'Probably, his first attempt did not work,' said Akash. 'Even after poisoning Samir must have been alive. Hence the blunt object.'

'Right,' said Gaurav. 'The dose of poison does not seem too high.' He extended his notes towards Ray. 'Take a look.'

Ray took the thick notebook from Gaurav's hands. For a while everything quietened and hum of an ancient air conditioning machine stirred the silence of the room. Ray's blank face turned thoughtful as he read the notes. 'Pro poisoner,' he said after reading it. 'What's this poison?' He mumbled the name, trying to pronounce it with effort. But then he shook his head and gave up. With a sly smile, Ray looked up to meet Gaurav's eyes. 'What's this poison called?'

Gaurav met Ray's gaze with a knowing expression. He knew that poisons could come in various forms. People usually did not understand how poisons work and which could work as a poison. 'Cerbera odollam,' he said. 'Looks pretty decent when you look at it. But acts as a deadly assassin when given to somebody.'

'What made Samir take it?' asked Ray. 'I don't think he was a man who could be forced to take anything.'

Gaurav looked at Samir's dead body. He lay under a white sheet which had been pulled up to his chin for which Ray was grateful. He did not want to look at Samir's torn body so early in the morning. It was not even 7 am yet. Shraddha was waiting outside in his car. He felt bad for dragging her out so early. But leaving her alone at home would make him feel restless throughout the day. He would not be able to focus on his work. It would be deadly for the case. With CID special task force breathing down on his neck, he needed to get to the killer fast.

'I think he had been given it with something edible,' said Gaurav. 'We found traces of chocolate syrup in his blood. Because of the bitter taste of chocolate Samir must have missed the tangy taste of the plant extract.'

'So, this is an Ayurvedic specialist we are looking for?' asked Ray.

Gaurav nodded. 'That and an amateur surgeon.'

Ray's eyebrows shot up at the statement. 'And what the fuck does that mean?'

The outburst made Gaurav laugh. 'Those slashes look like the handy work of an experienced surgeon.'

'Fuck man,' said Ray as he looked at Samir's body. Even though it was hidden under the white sheet, he knew what lay under the cover. A surgeon with the knowledge of Ayurvedic was so bizarre that he did not even want to consider the fact just yet. It had solidified the entire killer profile he had built from Samir's MO. It was not a disorganized killer they were dealing with. Ray drew a deep breath to make himself think slow. Life had taught him to be calm and serene. *'Calm and quiet, you win the race, my boy,' his grandfather used to tell him. 'There is power in silence.'* Impatience brought nothing but failure. Ray pushed a thick lock of hair which fell on his forehead out of his eyes. 'Great. Send me the report,' he said. 'I need to sit and think about it a little.' He turned to look at Vivan. 'What happened to Samir's business partner?'

'Ishant Mallick is not back from Mumbai yet,' said Vivan. 'In fact, we are not getting any trace of the guy. He has disappeared.'

Ray froze at the news. 'When have you come to know that Ishant Mallick has disappeared?' His voice had turned cold enough to give the chilled autopsy room a run for its freezing air.

Vivan held up his phone. 'Right now,' he said. 'I have contacted their police department on the day of the murder,' he said. 'They had been keeping an eye on Ishant. But since this morning, the guy has completely disappeared.'

'Fuck,' said Sid. 'I think I will have to go and check.'

'No, you are not running away,' snapped Ray. 'You will stay here and assist me. I need you man.'

Siddhant Thakur stood in utter silence for a long time, staring at Ray. Then his face cracked in a tired smile. 'No, man you don't need me. You are enough without anyone.'

'Fuck, your philosophy,' said Ray. 'You cannot just run away every time. At least not this time.' His voice echoed around the corner of the room, elevating the vibration a few level higher.

Sid raised his hands in surrender. 'Got it man,' he said. 'Don't blow on my face. I am gonna stay put.'

'You fuck do that,' said Ray.

When they came out of the forlorn building, the sky had started to darken again. Thick, dark clouds had shrouded the sun. Everything looked unnaturally gloomy. 'It's gonna rain,' said Shraddha once Ray got into the car.

Ray looked at the sky and gave a shrug. 'Does not matter by the time rain comes, we will be safe at my home,' he said.

'Your home?' asked Shraddha.

'Yeah, I gotta get some papers before going to office.' Ray turned the key and the Honda City Zx came to life.

'Drop me at my home,' said Shraddha. The desperation in her voice made Ray laugh.

'No ways,' he said. 'You are under my protection now.'

The car zoomed past thickening traffic. Sleepy faces, huddled in thick coats ambled down the street. The cold had taken the city by surprise. Kolkata had never seen such winter before. Ray looked at the rear view mirror to check on Akash's red Beemer. It drove carefully through the passing cars and followed Ray close. They were going to Ray's home to summarize the case and then to office.

Ray could feel Shraddha's restlessness. Even though she sat quietly, she kept fidgeting. Her eyes looked wide and worried. Ray wanted to take her in his arms and tell her some gentle words of assurance. He wanted to tell her that he would be there for her, no matter what.

But he stopped himself from doing any such thing. He did not want Shraddha to weaken down, not even for him. She would have to stand on her own and keep going with or without him. Ray had been a protective wall for his wife Rusha. But he could not save her. This time, he would not try to become a human shield for every problem Shraddha went through. Some she would have to solve on her own.

'After reaching home, you can write down the case report, from beginning to end, including everything,' Ray said when she appeared to be too distracted and unfocused. 'I will need the report at office today. It will help write your own report as well.'

She turned to look at him with a surprised expression. She had not thought of getting any work while she waited for her life to get back to normal. 'Sure,' she said beaming. 'I will do it.' For a while neither of them spoke. Then Shraddha looked at Ray with a smile. 'Thanks for understanding.'

Ray chuckled. 'Anytime writer,' he said. 'Make me proud.' That earned him the smile he had been looking for since the morning. Shraddha's face bloomed like a fresh flower.

'I will,' she said, happily. 'Sir called when you were inside the autopsy room. He told me to stick to you and monitor all your moves.'

Ray chuckled. 'I will gladly allow you to monitor all my moves.' The undertone made her flush and look away. Ray found himself laughing at her embarrassment.

Rain started to pour hard when Ray drove to his office with a nervous Shraddha by his side. He looked up at the sky with irritation. 'What's with this year's winter?' he asked. 'It seems someone does not want the sun to appear even for a moment.' Shraddha followed Ray's gaze but she said nothing. Her silence made Ray want to hold her hand. But again he controlled his urge to try to protect her from the hardship of life. If she faced adversity in his office, which he knew she would, let her deal with it alone. 'Have you mailed the report to Akash?' asked Ray.

'Yes,' said Shraddha. 'I have.'

Akash pulled his car just beside Ray's shiny Honda City a moment later. Shraddha sat still in her seat. She did not move, nor did she speak. Ray could understand her anxiety. He did not try to pry her out of the reverie she had drifted into. Instead he killed the engine and got out of the car. Akash was waiting for Ray to catch up. He had a disturbing grin plastered on his face.

'What?' asked Ray, narrowing his eyes. 'What the fuck are you laughing at?'

Akash cleared his throat before speaking. Then with a cheerful tone he said, 'I am excited.'

Ray did not smile back. 'Care to explain?' he asked.

'I will love to see how your Lavanya reacts to your Shraddha.' His grin widened as he said this.

A moment passed, before Ray spoke in a harsh tone. 'She is not my Lavanya.'

Akash nodded. 'You are admitting that she is your Shraddha.' Saying this Akash turned and walked over to Ray's car. He opened the passenger's door and waited for Shraddha to get out. 'Don't look so scared,' said Akash. 'We are not bad people here.' He chuckled. 'You are going to give us the fame we deserve. So, we are gonna be real nice to you.'

Ray left them standing in the front yard and went inside to fetch his team for an early morning stand-in meeting which was a custom of Rayon Corp. Everyone was already there on the floor, behind their assigned laptops, working. Looking at their focused and determined faces Ray felt a bout of nostalgia. He remembered his childhood when he had been this focused and determined. Focused on his work and determined to impress his grandfather who had been the first one to introduce Ray to the world of crime.

Fiona looked up from her laptop screen as Ray approached the stairway which led to the conference room. 'Hey boss, good morning,' she called. Her voice grabbed others' attention and one by one everyone greeted him.

Ray motioned them to follow him upstairs. Because they all were accustomed to this routine none were startled at being called up this early in the morning. 'Let's go up and discuss the case,' said Ray. 'We are losing a hell lot of time. We need a break through fast.'

Karan took his notepad and led the team behind Ray. Once settled inside the large conference room, Ray stood at the head of the table, waiting for Akash and

Shraddha to join them. He cut a quick glance at Lavanya. She looked pretty in a bloody red V-Neck sweater and a pair of tight blue jeans. Her feet were stuck inside a pair of camel skin ankle boots. She had left her hair loose and wavy this morning. Without moving his head, Ray took in her makeup, red painted lips, perfectly lined eyes, and properly blushed cheeks. A deep philosophical breath escaped Ray's mouth, he was heading for a disaster, he thought with remorse.

Then the door of the conference room opened and Akash walked in with his usual grin. His eyes automatically fell on Lavanya upon walking inside. 'Good morning, guys,' he said gleefully and Ray winced. Before anyone could respond Shraddha appeared behind him. Her loose hair rested over her shoulders in lazy waves. She had chosen to wear a white knitted top and a pair of blue jeans beneath a red sports coat. White sneakers, a pale green backpack and red framed glasses completed her looks. Thankfully she did not have much taste for makeup. Ray liked her bare lips and naked cheeks.

Everyone stared at her, waiting for an introduction, which Akash did not offer. He led her to the head of the table, pulled a chair and motioned her to sit near Ray. 'Guys this is Shraddha Basu, she will…' before he could finish the sentence, Fiona spoke up.

'She wrote the piece on Samir murder case and named the killer The Ripper,' she said with a grin of appreciation. 'I liked the name. Fitting.' She nodded her approval.

Shraddha gave a ceremonious bow at that. 'Guilty,' she said.

'You ruined the entire case,' said Lavanya. 'Why did you have to visit the crime scene?' Her face contorted with a perfect blend of fury and hatred. She creased her forehead and squinted her eyes and fixed her gaze on Shraddha. 'Did you think you would be able to solve the crime, single handedly?'

For a moment, nothing moved, no one spoke, only the chirping of a group of unknown birds held the conference room hostage until Fiona cleared her voice. She cleared her throat to get everyone's attention. Then she looked at Shraddha with a grin. 'You want something to drink?' she asked, in an amused tone.

To her credit, Shraddha caught the underlying joke immediately. 'Yeah, something sweet and delicious please. Had enough of bitterness for the morning.' Her face bloomed in a bright smile which made everyone smile back at her, everyone but Lavanya.

Fiona pushed herself up on her feet. 'You want anything boss?' she asked.

'I want what's she is having,' said Chirag, pointing at Shraddha. 'Something sweet and delicious.' He rolled his neck with a grin.

Fiona made a face. 'We don't feed ambulance chasers here at Rayon Corp,' saying this she turned and walked away, leaving a cursing Chirag behind.

Ray dragged a deep breath. He had promised himself not to come between Shraddha and the hardship she would face here. But Lavanya's behavior irked him a little. 'Lavanya,' he said. 'You need to speak to Akash after the meeting. I don't tolerate unnecessary rudeness on my floor.'

Lavanya's face blanked in a moment's gap. She looked down at her perfectly manicured hands to collect herself. Then she moved her gaze at Shraddha. 'I did not mean to belittle you or anything. But you have been wrong in acting like a sleuth when you know nothing about crime investigation. Otherwise,' she paused for an impact. Ray braced himself for a hard blow. 'You would not have become a burden on us, right?'

That hit the mark. Shraddha flinched and drew a sharp breath. Her hands moved to grab the thick notebook she had laid open in front of her. Again that old silence fell like a shroud around the room. Then Akash spoke in an unusually cold voice. 'Lavanya,' he said. 'I think you should take a day off.' Before Lavanya could protest, he proceeded. 'Go home. Give yourself a nice hot bath, have coffee, and come back tomorrow to work in a fresh mind.' Then he flashed her a beautiful smile. 'Thank you.'

After Lavanya left, everyone turned to look at Ray, who was waiting for the drama to settle, so that he could begin with his latest update. 'What's taking Fiona so long?' he asked.

'Right here boss,' said Fiona, walking in with a tray loaded with steaming ceramic mugs and sandwiches.

'Got a little bite for the lady.' She gazed sympathetically at Shraddha. Then her eyes moved around the table. 'Where is Lavanya?' she asked.

'She got lucky and got a day off,' said Chirag.

'So,' Ray said. 'What do we have to show the Chief?'

Karan shook his head at that. 'Nothing boss.'

'What about Samir's computers and laptop?' asked Ray.

It was Nilesh's turn to shake his head. 'Nothing boss. Everything is tightly encrypted. I am still working on it.'

Ray looked at Fiona. 'Anything else on Samir?'

Fiona shrugged. 'I checked your gym instructor's bank account details,' she said. 'She used to make regular money transfer to Samir's bank account.'

Ray pinched his lips at that. 'I will speak to Ekta officially. Anything else?'

Fiona nodded. 'I don't know whether it is relevant or not,' she said. 'But Samir was writing a book on Jack The Ripper. He was also developing a Ripper game.'

'What's a Ripper game?' asked Ray.

'Nilesh broke into his private drive to get the file,' said Fiona. 'He was developing the storyline of a game which allows gamers to get into the guise of Jack and stalk females to kill and mutilate them.'

'Wow,' said Shraddha. 'Is that legal?' she asked.

'Nope,' replied Chirag. 'Not legal. So, he would have launched it on some private platform.'

'That or on Dark Web,' said Shraddha. 'Have you checked the Dark Web by the way?' she asked. 'The murders might be there circulating on the web.'

Everyone went quiet at that. Ray exchanged a quick glance with Akash. Ray did not think the offender would release the videos of murders on the Dark Web, mainly because he earlier had little idea about the fame he could get from his act.

'The murder seems too disorganized,' Karan said in a patient voice as if he was speaking to a child. 'Will a disorganized killer be on the Dark Web?' he asked.

Shraddha did not speak for a long time, then she said. 'He might be a disorganized killer. But someone very organized is working closely with him. Either that or he is layering his act by leaving the murder weapon behind. A disorganized offender will not take the knife he used to cut his victims with him.'

'How do you know that?' Challenged Karan. 'How could you say that he has an ally? Taking the knife does not prove anything.'

'How else has he walked out unseen after killing Samir?' Shraddha asked. 'How else has he succeeded in staying low for so long?' She asked. 'A disorganized killer would have struck again by now.' She paused to scan the room with her usual watchful eyes. Then she spoke in a practiced patient tone. 'I don't think having someone to check the Dark Web will hurt the case or jeopardize it. There is nothing to go on with anyways, right?' Her smile made Karan blink. His jaw tightened and Ray knew that Shraddha had made an enemy for life, that as long as she lived, Karan would begrudge her for this opposition today. 'Also, it will let allow me to write something about the murder case.'

Chapter - 17

Ishant Mallick sat in his plush Lonavala cottage, by a French window which overlooked a picturesque hill standing by the edge of the town. The sky had taken the shade of a starling blue today. It made Ishant think of an Italian girl he met years ago on a month long vacation. A patch of fluffy cloud passed the sky in leisurely pace. Any other time Ishant would have smiled at the sight, he would have fished his phone out and taken a photo. But this morning, he felt a little edgy. Nothing made him remotely pleased this morning, not even the group of birds dotting the Lapiz blue of the sky. In his college days, he had been an enthusiastic bird watcher. He had taken countless photos of birds and hung them on his Kolkata apartment's living room walls.

The thought of his hometown conjured an uneasy twist down his stomach. He swallowed hard, wondering what was going on there. With Samir dead, he felt strangely exposed. For years, he had run his extortion business with Samir and made huge money from it. But he had made the mistake of thinking that he was Samir's only partner. Apparently there were others and one of them had slashed Samir up for good or bad, Ishant had no idea. But before going back he needed to collect his thought and be prepared for the cops because they would come to meet him, of course, if they did not shoot him first.

He closed his eyes and tried to recall all the faces he had come across through Samir. One of them must have committed the murder. For a moment, he shuffled the faces, staring at each one of them with careful consideration. One by one, he began to eliminate those he regarded as innocent. By the information he had gathered on Samir's murder, he understood that the man who had committed the murder had medical expertise. Probably a surgeon or a medical student. Or maybe someone…

With a startled gasp he sprang to his feet. A face, a long forgotten face appeared in his mind. He looked at it for a while. Yes, a smile played on his face. Yes, this could be the one. Now, all he had to do was, make a call and wait for the killer to find him with a bag loaded with money.

He bent forward to check the plant which he had been nurturing for the last few months. It had come out well. Better than he had anticipated. With his gloved hand he touched its skinny green stem. The plant moved at his touch. A smile played on his mouth. Had the plant been a little stronger, a little more grown up, Samir would have died from its overdose. He had miscalculated the poisonous strength of the plant. Due to which the poison did not kill Samir. His smile widened as he began to caress the plant. But what this little baby failed to do, his cricket bat did for him. It battered Samir so nice, that now he came to love the blunt weapon even more. He liked the thump which the cricket bat caused each time it fell against a skull. Happily he looked over his shoulders. On the wall across his planting table were showcased his knives. There were total ten knives. He had forged each one of them. Eight of the knives had copper red stains on the stainless steel blade. Blood. He liked the sight of blood on his knives. It reminded him of the murders he had committed with so much effort. He was not a person who took mementoes. But at times, he felt the need to remember his victims and then only he sliced their fingers to keep in his collection. His face fell as he remembered his box of bones. He had to stash it in Samir's studio after police got involved in the case. His boss had already given him a good piece of his mind for slicing Samir up. But what could he have done. Sometimes passion turned into obsession and people just acted. He too just acted that day and things started to happen.

Outside rain began to pour. He straightened to admire the view which the expanse of the glass wall of his work room provided. Hard wind made the trees dance with the raindrops. Scrawny branches, and freshly washed leaves fluttered like dying animals. The sight reminded him of the puppy he had cut open when he was a kid. It wreathed in pain as he tied the plump furball to the fence and used his father's dagger to cut the little thing into pieces. The taste of warm blood, he closed his eyes, remembering the moment when a shrill sound echoed from downstairs, making him jump slightly.

Within a moment he recovered and turned to head downstairs, who the fuck was calling him at this hour?

He took three flights at a time to go down to the ground floor. The phone was on its seventh ring when he picked it up. 'Hello,' he said in a casually composed voice, one he used to calm people, to sooth them. They trusted him. They always did. Would Rudransh Ray trust him too? The thought froze in his mind when the caller from the opposite side spoke.

'Well, hello,' said a deep male voice. He stiffened at the practiced cheerfulness of the tone. 'How are you doing?' Not even an introduction, he noted.

'Cannot say doing bad,' he replied, playing along. 'What about you?' he asked, desperately trying to attach a face to the voice. Who was it? From experience he knew that the caller wanted something from him. Something which would make the matter very complicated. He rolled his head to work on the tension building on his neck muscles.

The caller on the opposite side laughed at the question. 'Good, very good,' he said. 'So, the thing is, I was wondering did Samir mentioned my name when you killed him?'

Even though he knew it was coming, the reality hit him hard in his stomach. It took a lot of strength to hold himself straight and upright. 'I am not sure I get you,' he said.

'Oh you get me right,' said the caller. 'Samir called me on the night of his death and told me that you were going down to the office to meet him.' The last part had been said in a sing song voice.

He swallowed hard. With extreme self-composure, he controlled his urge to tell the caller to fuck off. Instead, he remained quiet. Whatever had made the guy call him, would eventually come out. He was willing to bet his freedom on the fact that the caller wanted money. But he was not about to go ahead and pry the want out.

'What has the chick called you?' came the question in an amused voice. 'The Ripper?' The question was followed by a hearty bout of laughter which made him want to rip the asshole apart. But he would have to be patient, like a vulture. 'So, Mr. Ripper, how about parting with some of the money you have been extorting from those porn movies you make?'

The urge to burst elated in his heart just then. But he forced himself to remain calm. He would not give this man the satisfaction of knowing that he had succeeded in creating a ripple. 'May I know who I am talking to?'

'Of course,' said the caller. 'I am Ishant Mallick, Samir's business partner. We had a small business of cheat fund running, nothing as fancy as the one you have been running with Samir. I had no idea.' The familiar laughter, mingled with sarcasm boomed in the phone again. 'Truly,' said Ishant. 'Very clever of you.' Then he paused. 'You see with Samir dead and exposed down to his dick, it will be fucking hard for me to make my living. Police has already ceased our business accounts and holding all the files we had. So, I will have to go undercover for a while now.' He listened without saying a single word. Ishant continued with the same amused tone which he had been using since he had answered the call. 'Will ten crore be too much for you?' asked Ishant. 'I believe not.' When he said nothing in reply, Ishant continued. 'Okay I will settle for eight crore. I believe that's not too much for you.'

'How do I transfer the money?' he finally asked. 'Your bank accounts are ceased, right?'

Ishant laughed at that. 'Of course, you will have to come down to Lonavala to give me the money in hard cash. After that I will disappear, and you will never hear from me again.'

'Gimme the place, date, and time.' He was not someone to bargain. People like Ishant did not believe in controlling their greed, he knew that. He also knew that Ishant would return for more money and keep returning until the day…

'I will call you back tonight,' Ishant said, shattering his train of thought. 'I will tell you where to come and when.'

'Very well,' he said. 'I will wait for your call.'

After the call with Ishant Mallick, he made a call of his own. It went straight to the police department. His line of business would never see success without assistance from the authority. So, he had befriended cops with low salary and big family, preferably a mistress to take care of. The burly cop who answered the call was the one he had been looking for. 'I just received a call,' he said with firm authority. 'Trace the location and let me know where it came from.' He knew that Ishant had called from Lonavala. But he needed the exact location. If Ishant was foolish enough, he had made the call from his hiding place.

'You will get it by EOD,' said the burly cop.

'I will be waiting,' said The Ripper. His eyes moved towards the wall across the telephone set. It was adorned by another set of knives of different shapes and sizes. The blades, carefully forged from the finest steel, shone even in the gloomy morning. He watched in fascination for a while. His grandfather had been the one to start this work of art. Then his father took over, and him. Who would take it over from him? He tilted his head and gave it a thought. Who would be his perfect wife? Someone with a zeal for success. Someone passionate. Someone like...he rolled his head, blood began to rush down his body. Within a moment, he felt the familiar tightness between his legs. A long breath escaped his mouth, he needed to rip someone apart, someone unsuspecting, someone trusting, someone who would do anything to please you.

A small puppy barked somewhere in the distance. The sound crept inside followed by a crack of thunder. The poor thing must be frightened to death, he thought looking out the wide window intently. Without waiting another moment, he stalked outside to fetch the little thing, the unsuspecting thing, the trusting thing. Given a chance it would do anything to please him. Given a chance…

Chapter – 18

Everything about Ray's office spoke of wealth and effort. Shraddha sat hunched in her chair, trying hard to conjure a report from the flimsy thread of information. People of Rayon Corp, barring Fiona, were distant, unfriendly, and downright rude. The big guy Karan had a permanent blankness imprinted on his face. The silver rimmed glasses which he wore must have costed a lot. Shraddha had little idea about these things. Her own red plastic frame was below 2000. She made it look expensive because she had been gifted with an uncanny ability to make anything look expensive. Thus, her online store bought clothes looked out of the showroom of some famous fashion designer.

Ray and Akash had locked their office door, probably discussion something important. She did not expect Ray to baby sit her throughout the day. But somehow this all seemed to be like his fault. She sighed, thinking about her old office, her colleagues, Kevin, and even Shivani. A loud thunder rambled outside. Shraddha flinched at the sound.

'You are scared of thunder?' the question came from the opposite table. Chirag sat with his back stretched, head in the cup of his interlinked hands, and legs apart in a lazy manner. He was watching her with a serious expression. Shraddha's skin crawled at the stare. Karan turned to throw her a disgusted glance. For the first time, she had had the luxury of seeing his expression. 'You flinched.' Chirag added when she did not speak. 'I saw it. You cannot deny.' Everyone laughed at the amused tone which Chirag used.

'So, the tigress, who was about to crack the entire ripper case alone, is scared of thunder,' said Nilesh. Again everyone laughed.

Shraddha took the jabs without a single word. It reminded her of the first day of her school. After her father left her inside the locked gate of the enormous building, she had broken down crying. It attracted the attention of some senior girls who bullied her for years. She had been a lonely child. Friendship never happened easily, small talks never took place with ease, people seemed to be like monsters ready to swallow her. It still remained the same. She still could not make conversation easily. She still felt ill at ease with strangers. Kevin helped her a lot in the previous company. They created a strong bond with each other. She had been building a place for herself there in the print media. But now the killer was after her and Akshaj wanted the first scoop before anyone else. All those years, she let out a deep breath.

'Give her a break guys,' said Fiona. 'Let her work.' The scrawny girl threw a kind glance at Shraddha. 'Don't pay them any attention. They are like this always.'

Shraddha forced a smile when her phone vibrated. It was her office number. Automatically she stiffened at the vibration. Someone had sent her a text message. She opened it and gasped in horror. Four high resolution images of a muddy ground came to view. On the mud was a mutilated body of a puppy. A deep cut ran from his chin to naval. All its internal organs had been taken out, so that the hollow carcass gawked at her. Below she could read a caption – I am getting better at ripping babes. At the end of the message just before the period, a grinning emoji sat comfortably.

Trembling, Shraddha pulled herself up on her feet. She glanced around the floor, at the heads bent over laptop screens, oblivious to the surrounding. Nausea rose in a form of a bitter bile in her throat. With effort, Shraddha swallowed it. Then she untangled herself from her chair and desk. A couple of deep breaths later, she hastened upstairs, a moment later, she found herself running to Ray's office. The entire floor looked up from their computer screens to stare at her, horrified. She heard Karan's irritated voice, 'Now, what?'

Ray's office upstairs, which he shared with Akash, was perched at the furthest corner of the first floor. She found its door tightly shut. Without stopping to knock on the door, she just walked inside, panting. Ray was in a deep conversation with Akash. Her footsteps made them turn. Ray scowled, Akash raised his brows in surprise. Before they could say anything, Shraddha pushed her phone towards them, screen unlocked, the mutilated little puppy stared at them with unmoving eyes.

'What the fuck?' asked Akash, already reaching for the phone.

Shraddha opened her mouth to speak but then she closed it shut again, unable to form a single word. She had not anticipated the extent of shock which she had experienced at the sight of the torn carcass of the animal. Strangely enough it was more shocking than the sight of Samir's dead body. Twice she tried to speak. But when nothing came out of her trembling lips, she simply gave up and dropped on a leather back chair.

Ray took the phone from Akash's hand. 'The Ripper,' he said, leaning forward to examine the slashes. 'Fuck,' he cursed after a while. 'This guy is getting better at it.'

Akash leaned back to stare out the window, at the cloudy sky. 'Apparently, he knows it and boasting about it.'

'Yeah,' Ray agreed. 'Also, he is enjoying it now.' He pointed at the cuts on the dog's little's body. 'These slashes are done in leisurely pleasure. He had taken his time to cut it apart.' Akash made no attempt to lean forward for a better look at the cuts. Ray continued in his habitual tone, grim and cold. 'The kill has probably gave him an orgasm.' With a thud he place the phone on the table. 'I just hope he had his climax.'

'Or else?' asked Akash.

'Or, else he will be out on the street hunting down humans to reach the height,' said Ray. 'Need to call Sid. We should put everyone on high alert.' Without another word, he rose from his chair and walked out the room. His footsteps left no echo behind. Apparent, Ray was a man accustomed to disappear without a trace, Shraddha noted with rising panic.

'You okay?' asked Akash, embarrassed at Ray's careless manner. His face despite its casual mask showed a tinge of guilt and apology. 'I know this is tough for you.'

A thunder rambled just then. The sound found its way inside the office through the tightly shut windows. Shraddha did not flinch this time. The sound, seemed to her, was an echo coming from a distance, from another planet, probably. To gather her strength, she looked down at her hands. They were trembling, she noted. In the stillness of the room, everything appeared to be unreal to her, as if she had been placed in a tightly scripted movie which would end in a tragedy.

'You okay,' Akash asked again. He reached for her hands this time. The touch of his cool, strong fingers against her trembling cold ones made Shraddha blink. She cleared her throat twice.

'I am fine,' she said. He gave her hands a brotherly squeeze or maybe it was a friendly one, Shraddha could not detect the approach just then. 'I think, I am a little shocked.' She mumbled. Her tone barely above a whisper. But Akash caught it easily. His mouth turned up in a cheerful smile.

'I guess, you have a right to be shocked,' said Akash. 'If that does not shock you, then you have a serious psychological problem.' Before the conversation got the chance to proceed further, the glass door of the office flew open. Ray stormed inside with a frown. His forehead had creased and his mouth was set in a tight thin line. With cold, hard eyes he looked at Shraddha and then at Akash.

'I spoke to Sid,' he said in a voice which would have sliced thick tree trunks had it materialized in the form of an object. 'We need to run a location check on the number from which the image had come from. I don't believe we will find anything. But it's worth a try.' He lowered his head to look at his shiny leather loafers. It seemed that the pair of shoes had turned into a crystal ball and now was showing the future to him. For a moment none spoke. Then Ray looked up and turned his eyes stare at Shraddha. 'You need protection, my lady,' he said, finally. 'I need to watch you 24/7.' His voice suddenly sounded tired and defeated. 'I had been only misleading myself by downplaying the risk you are in.'

Akash cleared his throat. 'I think we should pressurize Sid to arrange…'

Ray shook his. 'I have a hunch that this guy has informers within the department. Or else he would not have found Shraddha's number.' Saying this, he paused to crack the knuckles of his fingers, one by one, a bad habit noted Shraddha. But she said nothing to point it out. 'If so, then he knows where she lives, when she goes to office, and when she comes back.'

A cold snake uncoiled itself and rose to slide down her spine. Shraddha began to shiver then. It came suddenly and unannounced. Trauma of the series of unexpected events hit her then. She hugged herself tight with both of her arms and attempted to control the shudders which wrecked her slender body. Ray looked at Akash, who nodded and rose to leave the room. He pulled the door shut behind him.

Ray got up to his feet and went over to Shraddha. Without speaking a word, he scooped her up in his arms like a child, cradling her shaking body against his hard chest. Then Ray sat down on the chair where Shraddha had been sitting a moment ago.

Outside thunder rambled, rain fall hardened its assault on the earth, trees began a wild dance which only nature could provoke, a thick curtain of mist rose to smudge the world, robbing off its vividness and making it look like a fading portrait from the ancient time. Inside two damaged souls clung to each other, seeking solace from each other's warmth.

It could have been bad, thought Shraddha as she prepared dinner in her kitchen. Animated voices drifted in from her living room. Ray sat with Sid, Akash, and Kevin, and they all were engaged in an agitated discussion about how to catch The Ripper. The conversation soon turned into a debate about why ripper, the original one, stopped killing. Because the debate would never find its inclusion, Shraddha did not want to be a part of it. Instead, she decided to prepare dinner. Feeding four grown up hungry men was a task she never wanted to undertake. But here they all were, none wanted to leave. She knew what they were doing. They were guarding the turf. A long breath escaped through her mouth. How long would they do it, she wondered. As long as this man walked free, she would be in threat.

'What's for dinner?' Ray's deep voice breathed into her ears. In her trance, she did not hear him entering the kitchen. Now, she felt his warmth against her back. His solid chest brushed against her back. She remembered the kiss they shared standing in this kitchen only a day ago.

'Steamed rice with chicken curry, and salad,' she said. 'Nothing fancy.'

Ray placed his hands on her shoulders. 'I like fancy cooks preparing bland meals.' He leaned forward and touched her neck with his lips. Shraddha shivered at the touch. Ray stood there for a moment just resting his lips against her heating flesh. Then he moved back, drawing a deep breath. 'Woman, you are a bigger threat than The Ripper.' He said before disappearing from the kitchen. Shraddha stood rooted for a long time, savoring the warmth of Ray's touch. Her flesh burned as she fought her craving to have this man completely.

'Take care of our star reporter,' said Kevin. They all gathered around a coffee table to eat their dinner.

Shraddha had tried to cajole them to use the dining room, but no one wanted to leave their seats.

'We will keep her safe, don't worry,' said Ray. His voice held no malice for Kevin. Somehow the tension of the first meeting had dissolved. Now, they all seemed like old friends sharing a meal.

Kevin's face turned grim. 'If you guys fail to catch this asshole, she will be forever in danger,' he said.

'No, she won't be,' said Ray. 'We will get this guy.'

Sid leaned back to look at Ray. 'I am not getting a simple point. Why the fuck is he sending all these photos to her?'

'He is looking for fame,' said Ray. 'He thinks that each one of his acts will be featured on the front page through Shraddha.'

'I think we should make it clear that she does not hold the authority to write exciting pieces,' said Akash. 'That he should go and find someone else for his fame campaign.'

They all considered this while eating. A deep silence fell in the room. It brought a touch of deep peace which felt like a warm blanket. A sense of gratitude embraced Shraddha. She said a silent thanks for this moment. But it lasted only for a second. Then her phone vibrated. This time it was her personal number.

She looked at the screen and then at Ray. The call came from an unknown number.

'Answer,' Sid said.

'Hello,' said Shraddha in a hesitant voice. Deep down inside she knew who was the caller.

'Hey sweety, this is The Ripper,' said a voice which smiled over the phone.

Chapter - 19

Ray's heart skipped a beat as he noted Shraddha's expression. She held the phone in her hand and turned to look at him with eyes which spoke of fear and agitation. The blend was intense enough to make him straighten. Within a second he went to sit beside her. With his eyes, he encouraged her to continue to speak. Then he turned his gaze at Sid, who had already started to text furiously to alert his team. If she could hold on to the conversation for long enough, they would know the location of the caller.

'Yes, tell me,' said Shraddha. Even though her eyes spitted fear, her voice had no trace of the emotion she showed on her face. Ray admired that ability. Since his childhood days, he had come to admire courage and strength. His grandfather was a strong man who stood by and watched his son in law disappear, then bade adios to his loving wife, and then burned the body of his only daughter. Yet, he stood strong and raised Rudransh singlehandedly. Shraddha put the call on speaker, so that everyone could hear the conversation.

'Did you like the photos?' asked The Ripper.

Shraddha's eyes flashed in that instant. 'You did not have to kill that helpless animal just for the sake of fame, you know.' The fear from eyes faded then and gave way to anger which made her face flush as blood rushed to color her cheeks.

'Yes, I have to,' said The Ripper. 'Exactly the same way, you have to write. I have to kill and continue to kill.' He paused, probably for a breath. His voice appeared to be calm and well rested. It made Ray doubtful. The man was not afraid of being traced. 'Have you ever drank blood sweety?' The question startled Ray. He raised his eyes to meet Sid's cold gaze. They exchanged a silent message before turning their attention back to the conversation.

Shraddha's mouth dropped at the question. She swallowed before replying. 'Never tasted it,' saying this, she threw a helpless look at Ray. He placed his hand on her shoulder, to provide his support.

'Would you like to taste some?' The Ripper asked.

Why was he calling? Wondered Ray. The conversation had no purpose. It seemed like the man felt a sudden desire to make contact with the world and to him Shraddha was the world. It unnerved Ray. He did not want another man to regard her as his world. Especially not a man who ripped people apart.

Shraddha drew a deep breath. She looked at Ray with hard eyes. He nodded, they had 60 seconds. She could disconnect the call now. Without another word, she disconnected the call and before anyone could react, switched off the cell phone.

Sid made a call to his team then. 'Trace the location of the call and report back to me ASAP.' He looked at

Ray with a half smile. 'If this guy is as clever as he acts, we will not be able to track him down.'

Shraddha raised her brows questioningly. 'Didn't I stick around for 60 seconds?' she asked.

'You did,' Akash said. 'But sometimes that's not enough. Tele soaps make it look too easy.'

Shraddha looked down at her hand. Ray could detect a slight tremor. Only a slight tremor, he noted with regret. Soon, she would feel nothing at being harassed by a madman. Her soul would die a slow death. Violence did that to people. Invisible scars told no tale. But they left marks for the world to behold. She too would be a result of violence and cruelty. What it turn her into remained to be seen. Ray reached inside his pocket and retrieved a fresh packet of cigarette. After lighting one, he finally relaxed. 'We are not going to track this guy,' he said, blowing a thick cloud of gray smoke in the air. 'At least not tonight.'

'I think you should switch your phone on,' Kevin said. He had been typing furiously on his iPad. It was too good a scoop to ignore. 'He might call again.'

'I hope you guys understand that I am a human being,' she said in a tight voice. Her angry eyes found Ray's calm ones. 'I am not an animal who you will use as a bait.'

Akash chuckled. 'I am sorry sweety. But you are already a bait. Playing along is staying alive for you now.'

It made Sid frown with irritation. 'Do you have to make your fucking wisecracks all the times?'

Akash grinned, tilting his head. 'Yes, I do.'

'Shraddha,' Ray began in his calmest and most serene voice.

'Don't fucking use that voice to me,' snapped Shraddha. 'I am not a child.'

Ray laughed. He reached for her hand and before she could pull it back, he grabbed it. 'I know you are not a child and this is a shock to you,' he said. 'But look around yourself, we all are there guarding you. We know the danger you are in.' He paused to look her into her eyes. 'As long as I live, this guy will not get to you. No matter what.' He paused again. 'And those who know me, know that, I am a difficult man to kill.'

The night passed in a non-descriptive way, if shouting at each other all night long while planning to bring down a psychopath could be called non descriptive. Shraddha slept through the entire fiasco with surprisingly ability. When the clock, shy yet sure, struck 3.30 in the morning, Sid pulled himself up on his feet to bid adios.

'I will call you back,' he said. The call from The Ripper went untraced as the killer used a VPN. When someone used Virtual Personal Network, even the most professional hackers got confused while tracing a call. In this case, the killer used onion layering which solidified Shraddha's claim of dark web's involvement. However, they could not say for sure yet. Kevin had left a long time ago. He had a piece to write. Akash was still there and did not show any willingness to leave any time soon.

Finally, after Sid departed, Ray had the time to sit and ponder over the entire scenario. Akash was watching him think. Ray could detect Akash's unblinking eyes upon him. The true crime story writer was waiting for him to speak, Ray knew that. But he had nothing to share just then.

'Why am I feeling that our nuts are being twisted hard?' Akash asked after a long pause.

Ray let out a deep breath. 'Because they are being twisted real hard.' Before he had the chance to say anything else, his phone vibrated. The call came from a landline number. Akash narrowed his eyes and threw a worried glance at Ray.

'Rudransh Ray,' Ray's voice was firm yet muffled. He looked at Shraddha to make sure she slept without disturbance.

'Rudransh Ray?' came the hesitant female voice from the other side of the phone.

'Yes, Rudransh Ray,' said Ray rising from his couch. It was still dark outside. Occasional gust of winter wind howled to remind the world that the storm had not subsided fully yet.

'Please, please save us,' the muffled cry made Ray draw a sharp breath. He stood at the window and scanned street.

'May I know…' Before he could say more, the voice changed.

'Rudransh Ray,' said a male voice. Immediately Ray knew who it was. The Ripper.

Empty road and deem street lights turned Kolkata into a ghost town. It seemed impossible to imagine that the same city bustled with life after day break. Right now while the city slept Ray stormed down the street at 100km speed. His Honda City made no noise as it zoomed ahead towards Samir's home. With the ease of a street car racer, Ray maneuvered his car forward. He could hear The Ripper's amused voice speaking in his mind.

'Come and meet me Rudransh Ray,' the maniac had said. 'Or, I will rip these two oldies apart.'

Even though the oldies had nothing to contribute to the society, Ray ran out of Shraddha's house, instructing Akash to contact Sid without delay. Akash was dialing when Ray started his car and drove out of the deserted parking space. To his relief, Akash did not want to tag along. He stayed behind to keep an eye on Shraddha. The entire scenario could be a ruse to get Ray away from her. So, they did not want to take any chance. When Ray inched close to the narrow lane of Samir's neighborhood, Sid called.

'I am coming,' Sid said without bothering with greetings. 'Don't do anything foolish…' Whizzing wind engulfed the rest of the sentence. Sid was riding his motorcycle which was not a good news, thought

Ray as he parked his car in front of the lane which led directly to Samir's house.

A white Scorpio pulled behind Ray's car. With a swipe of his eyes, Ray checked the rear view mirror. Vivan jumped out of the front seat of the car. Dressed in black trousers and black woolen hoodies, Vivan looked like a college goer. Only the bugle around his waistband gave away his profession. Ray patted his jacket. Secured inside it was his favorite toy Sig Sauer P250. Its' wide grip made it the least favorite gun of the people with small hands. Yet, Ray adored it. Its grip sat perfectly in his long, thick hands. Each time he held it in his hands, a sense of being control washed over him.

'Let's go buddy,' he muttered under his breath. 'We have a skull to scatter apart.'

Vivan eyed Ray with disapproval. 'I heard you love to kill,' he said, bringing his gun out.

Ray opened his mouth to reply but he closed it shut when Sid's motorcycle zoomed in to stand beside Ray's Honda City. Sid gracefully got off the bike and walked over to join the team. He had his service gun snuggly sitting in a holster around his waistband.

'What are the chances of aunt's being alive?' he asked eyeing the street.

'Very less,' said Ray. He looked around to find a way to approach the house unseen. They were all dressed in black. Yet, if someone was perched on a terrace and looked through a binocular, they would be able to see their misty forms.

'There is no place to hide our presence,' said Sid.

'We can always crawl,' said Vivan. 'People usually don't notice crawlers.' No one said anything to this insight. Sid looked down at his feet to avoid Ray's amused gaze. Vivan was like a child who think fast, but never think right.

Ray took a deep breath. He had taken the entire area with a single glance. 'We will have to rely on our speed.' He raised his index finger. Sid nodded. They had worked alongside for too long to miss each other's signals. 'I am going first,' he said.

Without waiting for their approval, Ray ran towards the lane which would take him to Samir's neighborhood. The biggest advantage of the area was its closely knitted architecture. If he managed to find his way unseen to one of the houses, it would be easy to climb up the terrace and then reach Samir's house without being seen or getting shot. But would he be able to sneak past The Ripper's watchful eyes. He had no doubt that the man was perched up on the terrace watching the street. It was a chance, he would have to take, Ray thought.

It took him less than a second to cross the lane and reach the first house. The two story house reflected a combination of tiredness and anxiety. Staple middle class life, Ray thought as he climbed a low brick fence which separated the house from the road. Without making the slightest sound, Ray placed his right foot on one of the three wide windowsills. From there, the climb upward was easy. After reaching the terrace, Ray sat crouched for a moment, gaining momentum. The he sprang up to his feet and began to run. This time he had his gun clutched in his hand, nuzzle pointed down. From the corner of his eyes, he saw Sid, stalking the street in silence. A dark shadow, moving through a dark lane. They had done it countless times. One crept down the terrace. Another went straight for the front door. It worked in the past. But in the past they had not dealt with a killer who ripped people for fame.

Ray halted his progress for a fraction of seconds after reaching the house next to Samir's. Quickly, he scanned the area for any unwanted movement. Other than Sid's fast moving shadow, he found none. Only the slumbering houses stood in silence. It was time to go down, thought Ray.

Samir's house was as silent as a dead body. Nothing moved anywhere. No sound echoed in the darkness. Ray had his doubt that the old women still lived. But he wanted to have a look, bracing himself for a bloody scene. In her bedroom, Samir's mother lay on the floor, lifeless and ripped apart. Beside her was neatly arranged the body of the house keeper. She had gone under the knife of The Ripper as well. A cricket bat rested near the bodies.

Ray did not enter the room. He stood at the threshold, gun down, eyes fixed on the two women he had met just a few days ago. Every muscle of his body vibrated in anger. Moments later Sid came to stand beside him.

'Motherfucker,' said Sid, under his breath. 'He did not have to do this.'

Ray placed his gun back inside his jacket. 'Yes, he had to,' he said, without moving his eyes from the bodies. 'He needed to keep the momentum going.' Then he looked at Sid. 'Call the ME.'

'It won't go down well with the Chief,' Sid said. 'We have completely fucked up.'

'That we have,' Ray said. 'The front door was open?' he asked. 'I did not hear you breaking in.'

'Was hanging wide open.' Sid drew a deep breath. He pulled his cell phone out of his pocket, switched it on and called for an ambulance. 'The Chief is coming himself,' he said. 'It does not look good.'

'This is not for the first time we have fucked up,' said Ray. 'We have been through this path many times before.'

Sid fished out a cigarette from the breast pocket of his shirt and looked down at the two bodies thoughtfully. 'Why is he doing this?' he asked, turning his questioning gaze at Ray. 'Why kill two helpless women?'

Ray shook his head, feeling a bitter bile of nausea rising in his throat. 'Fame,' he said at last. 'It is a game for this man. He is playing to be famous. This guy needs attention. His childhood days have made him long for fame.'

'So, he kills to be famous?' asked Sid. They walked out the front door to get some fresh air. Smell of blood and stale flesh had already impregnated each corner of

Samir's house. They knew it was unrealistic to smell decaying flesh so soon. But something about the house and its setting had them think of rotten bodies and nasty smells. Finally, they decided to wait outside.

There was not much to see. The killer had used the cricket bat to kill the women first. Then he used a sharp object, possibly a long knife, to slice them up. This time, he took their internal organs, heart included along with him. Probably collecting souvenir, thought Ray, or trying to look vicious to make headlines. But he said nothing.

A shrill sound broke the dawning silence. The entire area seemed to stir out of their slumbering state. Police siren had its way of waking people up even from their deepest sleep. People started to mile out as uniformed officers led by Vivan came to seal the front door of Samir.

A tall, lean, and tired figure walked towards Ray and Sid in slow steps. They recognized CID Chief Chetan Bajaj despite the early morning mist. The elderly officer appeared to be in shock. By the frown on his face, it was apparent that something really bad had happened. He came to stand before his two best officers.

'How did you let it happen?' he asked Ray with a kind of malice which spoke of defeat. 'I thought you are able enough to deal with this situation.'

Ray said nothing to contradict Chetan. His face showed no expression. It remained blank and emotionless. No one had anticipated this. But somehow Ray felt responsible for the entire event. It was him who had nudged the desire for fame in The Ripper's heart.

'You have invited this situation,' said Chetan. 'You have showed that man what he can gain from killing people.' His voice rose above the zooms of rushing cars. 'You have dragged him out in the open and now he is killing innocent people.'

Again Ray chose to say nothing. Instead he stared at the space where a thick yellow tape separated Samir's house from the rest of the houses. With passing time, more and people joined the crowd which stood stunned, watching the event unfold. In the gray early morning winter mist, they looked like ghastly shadows to Ray's eyes. He lowered his gaze. One miscalculation had costed two more lives. This man was about to claim more, Ray knew that in his heart. The question was…in his trance he missed what Chetan was saying.

'Are you listening to me?' asked Chetan a little too loud to get Ray's attention. Sid stared down at his feet, choosing not to look anyone in the eyes. together they looked like two teenagers caught masturbating in the corner of the street. Only masturbation did not cost anyone their lives.

Ray let out a deep breath, feeling frustration rising in his veins. Then when he thought he could not tolerate it any longer, a slender figure materialized from the gray thickness of the mist. She had herself wrapped in a red trench coat. A pair of dark blue jean cladded calves peeked beneath the hemline of the coat. Her booted feet were restless, as she tried to find a space to squeeze her slim body through. Ray's eyes met hers and he calmed down a little. Shraddha flashed him a smile from the distance as if to say, no worries we would get the bastard and he believed her.

Chapter - 20

Smell of early winter morning used to make Shraddha want to write poems once. Today, it brought her nothing but a sense of rage. Two innocent old women, who had nothing to do with anything had been ripped apart just to satiate the hunger for fame of a mentally distorted man. She exhaled with force. Days ago when the unsub had fixed his attention on her, she had been taken aback. She feared for her life, and trembled at the thought of crossing path with this man. Now, her blood boiled just to think about the knife which had cut two helpless elderly women without any show of mercy. They had not harmed anyone, they not interrupted anything, they had been living their dismal lives all by themselves. Yet, they could not escape the touch of violence and cruelty.

Pursuit of fame, she let out a deep breath, could be dangerous. Desperately, she tried to find Ray amidst the crowd. Then her eyes found his. He looked a little rattled, she felt his restlessness in her soul rather than see it with her eyes. To the world he appeared to be calm and serene, an emotionless man who felt nothing for anyone or anything. But she knew somehow, that he had been deeply affected by the deaths of the two women. He needed someone to hold him the way he had held her the previous day. A strangely protective and fierce instinct evoked in her then. She wanted to wrap him in her arms and keep him safe forever, if she could. A man who had been standing in her way moved away then and she found her chance. Without stopping to think or looking back to see where Akash was, she slipped through the gap. Before anyone could stop her or say something, she was past the barrier and running towards Ray. Seeing her advance, Ray too left Sid and the elderly man he had been speaking to and rushed to meet her.

'What the hell are you doing here?' he barked the moment they came to stand face to face.

'Making sure that you are alright,' she said with calmness which she did not feel within her heart.

'You fool,' he said, taking her hand in his own. He held tight as if trying hold on to the last threat of life. Shraddha squeezed his hand in reply.

When Ray let her hand go, everyone was staring at them. It was only Sid who had a slight hint of smile on his face. Chetan tried to look stern. But he had a soft tinge in his eyes which said that he was relieved to see his best investigator finding sanity amidst mayhem.

'It was unexpected,' said Ray. 'I did not consider the fact that he could attack Samir's mother.' He exhaled. 'My mistake. It costed two lives.'

Shraddha was quiet. She allowed him to speak, knowing that the more he spoke, the better it would be for him.

'Well, well, well.' A female voice made Shraddha look over her shoulders. She exhaled at the sight of Shivani in a dark red suit. The crime reporter looked oddly bright in the gray Dickensian setting. 'Looks like you have finally understood the deal of this industry. Get squeezed to get scoops.'

Shraddha shook her head at the jab. There was nothing she could say to this. So, she chose to let it pass. But Shivani was on a roll. She came forward and thrust her mike towards Ray. 'So, Mr. Ray,' she said. 'What can you say about today's mishap. Your negligence had costed two more lives.' Before she could say anything else, Vivan materialized from behind.

'Ma'am,' he said in a polite yet firm voice. 'You need to move. Or, else I will have to arrest you.'

That got Shivani spin around to meet Vivan's eyes. 'What the hell huh?' she asked. 'I have to move out and she can stay?' She pointed her finger at Shraddha. 'I am covering a crime news.'

'Yes, she can stay,' said Ray. 'She works with Rayon Corporation, and we are assisting CID to catch the killer. So, we have the authority to be here.'

Suppressing a grin, Vivan said, 'Please ma'am move out.' His voice did not leave any chance of protesting. Shivani did not say a single word. Instead she stomped away to disappear in the crowd.

'She will be back,' said Sid as he came to stand with Ray. 'Why did you hold her hand in the public?'

Ray scanned the crowd. 'Because the bastard is watching us right now. He is there somewhere, keeping an eye. I just wanted him to know that to get to her, he will have to go through me.' In that gray smudged morning, Ray's cold voice sent a chill down Shraddha's spine. For a second, she got the view of the man who lived behind the calm and blank surface. She looked up to meet Ray's eyes. He flashed her a smile before turning towards Chetan. The elderly man hesitated for a second before step forward to meet them.

'This is Shraddha Basu,' Ray introduced Shraddha when Chetan came to stand beside him. 'She works for Kolkata Breaking.'

Chetan nodded. 'I heard. I also read your news clips,' he said. 'It was amazing. You are a gifted journalist.'

Sid chuckled at that. 'Don't take that as a compliment lady.' His golden brown eyes twinkled as he spoke. 'This guy does not like journos.'

'I believe that the son of mine is here somewhere,' said Chetan.

Shraddha craned her neck to scan the crowd. 'He was with me when I arrived. Then he disappeared.'

'Typical Akash,' said Sid. 'I believe we should clear the way.' He flashed a quick glance at his watch. 'There is not much to see.'

Shraddha did not know what to see or what to take notes of. She was already tired of all the blood and gore. Desperately, she wanted to get away from all these. She lived her dream of being a crime reporter, and that turned into a nightmare in a fast forward motion. Now, she wanted out, anyhow.

A couple of minutes later, Akash surfaced. 'I heard the ubsub stole their hearts this time.'

Ray exhaled. 'News travel fast,' he said. 'I don't know what the fuck he will do with their hearts.'

'I just hope he does not make pickles with them,' said Sid in an absent voice. His eyes took a faraway look. 'Why the fuck is he imitating The Ripper?'

'Why the fuck did you play Sherlock Holmes when you were in school?' Akash asked. 'Because he is fascinated.'

Sid dipped his hand inside the front pocket of his jeans and brought a battered packet of cigarette. A couple of lone sticks came to view when he opened it.

'At that rate,' said Akash. 'You will die of cancer within four years.'

Sid lit his fag and cut Akash a strong glance. 'You are saying that for the last ten years.' He paused to take a deep drag. Then he blew thick gray clouds of smoke in the air. 'My point is – I was a kid when I played Sherlock Holmes, fuck I lived the life of Sherlock Holmes.' He paused again to look each of them in the eyes. 'But this is a grown up man.'

'Probably not,' said Ray. 'Probably, he still lives in his childhood days. Something terrible must have distorted his brain in a way that a part of him has been trapped in those days of childhood.'

'But aren't not all these just hypothesis?' asked Shraddha.

Ray nodded. 'Profiling is all about statistic and hypothesis.' He reached inside his pocket and pulled out his phone. 'I forgot to switch it on.' He pressed the side button of his phone to make it come to life.

A melodious sound filled the air. They all turned to look at Chetan. The elderly officer fished his phone out of his breast pocket. He looked at the number and then looked up to meet Ray's eyes. CM, he mouthed before answering the call. Chetan stepped towards an empty space where people did not shout or chatter to speak.

Sid looked at Ray. 'Think our asses are fried crisp.'

Ray nodded, fishing out his cigarette finally. 'Yeah, I can smell the grilled flesh.' He fired his fag and looked down at Shraddha. 'I have a job for you.'

Shraddha was surprised to hear him say that. 'Yeah,' she said.

'I want you to come with me while I speak to a certain female about Samir Shrivastav,' Ray said. 'It's time, I pay her a visit and get the truth out.'

Sid threw Ray a questioning look. 'Ekta Patil?' he asked.

Ray nodded. 'Although I don't expect to find anything from her other than garbage, I am going to speak to her, because it will give us something to do while we wait to get our asses fired from the case.'

Shraddha raised her eyebrows at the comment. 'It does not matter to you?' she asked. 'Getting fired from a case?'

Ray flashed her a toothy smile which erased at least ten years from his hard, tired, and expressionless face. 'Nah, it is part of life. Besides, I don't allow myself to get involved in any case so deep that getting fired will kill me.' He pulled his phone out and called Fiona. He spoke in a low tone so Shraddha could not hear anything but a murmur of his voice.

She turned her focus away from Ray and looked around. Never before she had had the chance to be so close to a murder scene. It fascinated her in a way drugs fascinated an addict. The bustling yellow taped house, the frowning faces of the CSI's, the tensed vibe in the air, and the sense of danger, teamed up to make her feel alive. Since the days of her childhood, she had dreamed of a life like this. As a child she wanted to be a private investigator. But when she grew up, her PI dream faded. It changed into something else which she could not understand just then. It was a few years after her father's death, she finally realized that she wanted to write and become a writer.

A tap on her shoulder brought her out of her trance. Ray was looking down at her. He winked when he got her attention. 'A penny for your thought ma'am.'

Shraddha made a face. 'Make it a million and you will get it sir.' She winked back.

When Ray finally managed to extract himself away from the crime scene, it was 8 am in the morning. Kolkata had come to life by then and the office time traffic jam had already begun to materialized.

'I need to get a few things from my apartment,' he said Shraddha. 'Then we will drive to your house before going to office.' Shraddha was about to ask him to drop her off near a bus stand. But Ray shook his head. 'You cannot be alone right now. That man is not in control anymore.' Ray threw her a quick glance before looking away. 'I cannot let you roam around on your own.'

Shraddha turned her head and looked out of the window, fuming. 'How long will you keep me imprisoned like this?' she asked when Ray made no attempt to speak to her.

'I am just getting started ma'am,' Ray's amused voice made Shraddha smile. 'I cannot take any chance. Samir's mother and care taker died because of my miscalculation.'

'How can you blame yourself for this?' asked Shraddha. 'You cannot go and personally guard everyone,' she said with a force she did not know she possessed. 'You could not have known that he would go after them.'

Ray sighed at her protest. He slapped his hand on the steering wheel to honk at a slow moving yellow taxi. 'I am a profiler. I should have anticipated his moves.'

After a small pause, he said. 'But I could not and they died.'

Shraddha heard a tinge of sadness Ray's voice. It was faint, but it was there. She reached for his hand and held it tight. He linked his fingers through hers and held as they zoomed through the thickening traffic.

'You said you don't know Samir Shrivastav,' said Ray. 'You said he looked like someone you knew.' Shraddha could feel his growing agitation. They were sitting in a café in Southern Avenue with Ekta Patil. The gym trainer had her eyes fixed on the steaming coffee mug in front of her. 'Ekta, I can get a court order and make you speak. But I don't want to do it. I don't want to force you.' He paused to take a quick sip of his coffee. Shraddha did not feel like having anything. Her stomach had already started to twist.

Ekta cleared her throat. She looked up to throw a concerned glance at Shraddha. Then she looked down to stare at her coffee mug again. A thin layer of steam twirled up from her mug of mocha. Soon the coffee would be cold, and bland. But Ekta took no notice of her surroundings. For that moment, her entire world had shrunken down to the size of the ceramic coffee mug. Even though Shraddha could not see Ekta's hands. She knew that they trembled as the gym instructor sat traumatized by their arrival.

Ray had been patient enough. He spoke very little and sat watching the slender girl opposite him. Occasionally, he moved to take sips from his coffee. But other than that he did not move at all. He waited for Ekta to speak, to shed some light on the darkness which threatened to engulf his city, to get him a morsel of information to build a world upon it.

Finally, probably sensing Ray's growing anger, Ekta began speaking. 'I met Samir one year ago in Mumbai. I had been there for a body building show. Samir came and introduced himself to me as the talent manager of a production house. He offered me a job. He wanted me to train his actors and actresses.' She placed her hands on the table and leaned forward. Shraddha could see her nervous fingers playing with each other. 'I went to his studio, at Rajarhat.' She looked down at her coffee mug again.

'Was he alone?' Ray asked.

Ekta shook her head. 'No, he had a team with him.'

'How many?' asked Ray.

'Four including Samir,' Ekta said. To give her hand something to do, she picked up the coffee mug and took a sip.

'Can you describe them?' asked Ray. He leaned forward to look her into the eyes. For the first time, Shraddha felt his excitement.

Ekta shook her head. 'No, they all had masks on. I only saw Samir's face.'

Ray's shoulders sagged at the statement. He looked at Shraddha for a fraction of second then he looked at Ekta again. 'So, is there anything you can tell me about

Samir and his team, anything that can shed some light upon the murder case?'

Ekta's face cracked then. She gave them a half smile. 'I don't know who killed Samir. But whoever it is has done a great job.'

This made Ray smile. 'I understand your view Ekta,' he said. 'But you must understand that whoever has killed Samir belongs to the same team. He was there behind the mask the day you went to his studio. I don't know what happened to you there. I don't want to know either. But the man who killed Samir is not a modern-day Robin Hood who is out there to avenge ravaged girls.'

Shraddha flinched at Ray's tone. It was sharp and laden with anger. Anyone would shiver at the sound. She bit her lower lip and looked away. Her felt Ekta's pain. Probably Samir deserved to die, thought Shraddha. Then the images of the mutilated body of the little dog came back to her. A shudder forced its' way up her spine. The man who had killed Samir was not an angel, she reminded herself.

Ekta nodded. 'One of them the only one who did not participate in the…' She fumbled for words. 'In the…' Ray nodded, telling her that he understood. 'He had a limp.'

Shraddha's head shot up at that. 'Did he use a steel crutch?' she asked.

'Yes, tall, masculine, and with a limp,' said Ekta. 'I believe his right leg did not work or something.' She leaned back and relaxed for the first time since arriving. 'I think he was with them because he needed money or something. He did not come close to me even for a second.'

Shraddha felt her shoulders sagging. She could see Raghav's tall and masculine feature, trying to balance himself on a steel crutch. How Raghav got mixed in all these? Wondered Shraddha.

'Do you remember anything else about this man with a crutch?' Finally Shraddha asked. Even though not knowing would be better, she needed to find more about this man.

Ekta shook her head. 'It was one year ago and…' she drew a long breath before continuing. 'And I was drugged.'

Chapter - 21

Dark clouds started to gather on the sky. Today, the temperature seemed lower than any other day. Even Ray felt the chill of the winter wind. He shuddered as a strong gust passed by him. It was the first time in years winter wind could make him shiver. Probably, he was not as lost as he feared he was. Probably, there was still hope for him. He maneuvered his car through a narrow lane which led to Shraddha's house. With falling darkness his mood began to take a dip. Soon he would start feeling like an outcast, alone and decaying. In this mood he did not want to be in his apartment all by himself. Earlier he did not know the difference between light and darkness. Now, he looked at the passenger seat just to assure himself that she was there sitting by him. Shraddha rested her head against the window. He could not see her face through her long, dark, and thick hair. But from her relaxed shoulders he understood that she was sleeping.

Without speaking a single word or trying to wake her up, he looked back at the street. It was empty. Once again, he marveled at the isolation of Shraddha's house. Even though she lived in the proper city, and there were other houses around, rarely people loitered on the street after dark.

'We are home,' he said after pulling in front of her house and immediately he stopped. They were not home. She was home. They did not live together. They did not have any tie which would allow them to live together. Probably, he could change that. 'Hey.' He tapped her on the cheek to rouse her from her slumber.

She stirred, turned to look at him, and smiled. Ray's heart began to thump against his chest as he looked at her open and innocent face. It had been years since he had been so close to someone who represented life in its fullest. He dragged a long breath, controlling his urge to pull her in his arms and kiss her deep, till she moaned his name inside his mouth.

'Let's get inside,' he said. 'It's getting colder.'

'Thought you liked cold,' she said. Her face brightened as she tried to suppress a smile. Ray reached out to tuck a lock of her silky hair which had come loose from her ponytail behind her ear. He sat there a moment longer than it was necessary resting his hand on the side of her face. Shraddha closed her eyes and accepted the unsaid promise of being there forever. A shrill ring shattered the moment. Ray flinched, Shraddha jumped. They turned their gazes at the windshield to catch a glimpse of a shadow disappearing into the darkness. Without saying a word, Ray got out of the car and within a blink of an eye he began to run after the shadow.

'Rudra,' screamed Shraddha. Her voice boomed in stillness of the night. But Ray disregarded the call. He continued to follow the man who had been sitting there watching them from a distance. Even though the fog thickened in each passing moment, Ray did not lose sight of the man who raced through the narrow lane. He kept his pace and remained at a comfortable distance. Then the shadow reached the end of the lane where it met the main road.

Ray increased his pace so that the shadow did not get away this time. But the man he chased had stopped running by then. He turned back to look at Ray through a black mask. In the cloud smudged moonlight, Ray saw a metallic glint in the man's hand. A gun, he cursed his thoughtlessness. The man was already raising his gun. Ray calculated his options in a fraction of second. He did not have time to get his gun out. The lane was too narrow to allow him space to make a sidewise move. His fate lied in keeping the momentum alive. So, instead of slowing down or stopping, Ray continued to run. He increased his pace slightly. It was not easy to hit a moving target. But if the gunman had experience of shooting people, the moving target would be history within a few seconds in this lane.

But the man holding the gun was not a pro. The gun trembled as he tried to balance it with both of his hands. Ray needed the confusion. He seized the opportunity to reach for his gun. The masked man sensed the danger and without waiting for a moment longer squeezed the trigger of his gun.

A tremor passed through the narrow lane as the bullet left its home and rushed through the air towards its target. The sound of the gun shot slammed against the walls of the lane, making everything tremble in fear. Had he gone for Ray's chest the bullet would have hit its target. But he went for Ray's head. In the thickening fog, he could not make the right calculation and the bullet zoomed in the air and disappeared in the darkness without touching Ray's head.

By then Ray had successfully pulled his Sig Seur P 250 from the holster. He raised his gun, pointed it at the masked man's leg, and squeezed the trigger. A sharp yell came out of the victim's mouth as he fell face first on the concrete ground, clutching his right leg where Ray had shot.

'Who is he?' Akash asked for the tenth time. His face reflected disbelieve and shock. They had been sitting in Siddhant Thakur's office in the police station. At Ray's insistence, Shraddha remained home.

Ray continued to munch roasted almond his supposedly healthy snacks which Shraddha had frowned upon since the time she had caught him with them. 'Shraddha's ex-boyfriend,' he said patiently.

Sid chuckled. 'The girl has a fetish for the shooters, I see.' His laughing voice forced a frown out of Ray.

'He could have shot her,' Ray said.

'He almost shot your ass,' Akash said. His frown deepened. 'How he got that gun?' The question was thrown at Sid, who shrugged his shoulders in a how the fuck would I know manner.

Vivan walked inside. 'This guy is an ex-army veteran, was in data entry department. Got an dishonorable discharge for high temperament. Apparently he forgot to give one of his guns back and they forgot to check.'

Ray narrowed his eyes. 'That explains.'

'You knew about this hidden treasure?' asked Sid, with an amused expression.

'We are not in a relationship,' said Ray. 'She does not have to tell me anything.'

Sid shrugged and got up to his feet. 'Seems like we are done here,' he said to Ray and Akash. 'Get the fucker a defense lawyer if he does not have one. Make sure he stays inside for the rest of his life.' The last two orders were given to Vivan, who nodded with a grin. 'I need to speak to Shraddha. If we are to lock this guy up, we will have to get some good reasons. He is an army veteran after all.'

'A dishonorably discharged army veteran.' Corrected Akash.

Sid shook his head. 'No one will see that or try to remember. General people don't understand dishonorable discharge or court martial.'

'Lock him up for now,' said Ray. He pulled himself up to get out of the cabin when Chetan walked in. The elderly man had a stern expression on his face which made the trio exchange a quick look.

'Guys, I have bad news,' said Chetan.

'Are we off the case?' asked Ray. He had expected this move after the early morning killing.

'No,' said Chetan. 'They are bringing special force in to join you.'

'What the fuck,' said Sid. 'It has only been five days since Samir Shrivastav's killing.'

Chetan tilted his head and looked straight Sid into his eyes. 'Yes, and in these five days, you have let two elderly women to die the same way.'

Disgusted, Sid threw his right hand to wave the accusation. No one had anticipated this move. Yet, they had been accused of letting the unsub kill those elderly women. 'Who's joining us?' asked Sid.

'Nishant Chauhan,' Chetan said.

'Special task force?' asked Ray.

'The same guy.'

'But he does not know how to think,' Akash said finally.

Chetan threw a calm look at his son. 'Apparently, the authority does not think that way.' He looked at Ray and said in an apologetic voice. 'You need to update Nishant. He is arriving soon.'

Ray grinned at the order. 'Sure.'

Chetan cleared his throat. 'He will want to speak to Shraddha as well.'

A stern silence fell around the room. Between which Ray exchanged a quick glance with Sid. 'Sure, she will speak to Nishant. It is required after all.' He bowed his head. 'She is not my property. Now, I think we should get going.' Before walking out the stuffy cabin he threw a glance at Chetan. 'When will Gaurav perform the autopsy?' he asked.

Chetan checked his phone message to get the date. 'Probably tomorrow. I will let you know.'

Ray gave a quick nod of head. 'Thanks Chief.'

'Nishant is a brute,' said Akash. They had been driving through traffic infected Lance Down Road. 'What will he do?'

'Close the file without solving the case,' supplied Sid from the back seat. 'I just hope Shraddha handles the situation well.'

Ray chuckled. 'She will.'

A lone police patrol car was placed before Shraddha's house. Ray had insisted that the area get checked and thoroughly searched. Two young officers had taken the job and now were combing the entire locality. Though Ray knew that nothing would come out from the search, he did not like the idea of leaving Shraddha alone.

A white cab pulled in front of the house and a female with long reddish gold hair, and a toned body emerged out of it. She stopped near the police patrol car oblivious to Ray's Honda City and the three men watching her from inside the car. After a moment something nagged her and she turned to stare straight at them. Her eyes narrowed immediately and Ray saw Shraddha in this stranger's face. Despite differences, the two women looked almost identical.

'Trisha Basu,' said Ray.

'Who's Trisha?' Akash asked.

'Shraddha's artist sister,' Ray replied. He got out of the car and walked towards Trisha, who took a step backward when she saw Ray approaching. Her face contorted with worry and alertness. The road was empty, the sky was filling out with dark clouds, the houses on the street were all silent and motionless, a lot to worry about.

Ray brought his business card out of his pocket in a swift motion and raised it like a police badge. 'Rudransh Ray, Rayon Corp,' he said as if that mattered. But she relaxed at the introduction for whatever reason and forced a smile on her slender face. What looked like an uncanny resemblance to her sister from a distance, now looked like distinctions from up close. She had dark and calm eyes, almost like a child. Her hair was on the straighter side where as her sister had wavy hair. She was a shade or two fairer than Shraddha. Her straight shoulders and narrow waist spoke of hours spent in gym. The overall effect was striking. Akash and Siddhant came to join them.

'Trisha,' she said. Ray noticed a rich neutral accent, too ladylike. 'Trisha Basu.' She did not offer her hand for a shake. Only a slight dip her of pointed chin said that she approved of them.

'Nice to meet you Trisha.' Ray nodded. 'I am Rudransh Ray, I…'

'I know you,' said Trisha to Ray's surprise. 'I read your book on criminal mind. But that was a long time ago. You have not published anything recently.'

'I am working on a book.' Ray said. A smile formed on his face when she waved her right hand, a polished right hand.

'Good, I am dying to get some good reading material. Keeps my nightmares optimized,' she said and Ray chuckled. 'Joking.' Trish said with a wide smile. 'Where is my sister?' she asked. Her ladylike manner vanished then and appeared a scared woman, looking for the only support she had. It warmed Ray's heart to see her affection for Shraddha.

'She is home,' he said.

'Alone?' the question came out sharp. A little too sharp, in fact.

'No, ma'am,' Sid spoke from behind. He had been standing quietly by them. 'I have placed a police patrol car in front her house.'

Trisha nodded. 'I can see that. An empty police patrol car is pretty effective.'

Sid looked down at her with a smile. Ray was surprised to see Sid smiling. Usually, he did not smile at strangers. 'There he is ma'am, watching everything.' He pointed at a shadow. A tall, lean figure stood there, taking in the scene unfolding before him.

Trisha's face softened at the sight of the guard. 'Thank you. She is all I have.' Her voice dropped as she said it. Sid shifted his weight and looked uncomfortable. Ray thought hmmm. He exchanged a quick glance with Akash who grinned.

'Let's get inside,' Akash said when no one spoke. 'My balls are freezing here.'

'Watch your language,' Sid said.

Chapter – 22

He sat up startled. The dream had returned. He scrubbed his sweat drenched face with both of his hands. The dream had pried him out of his comfortable slumber. How long? He wondered, throwing the blanket away from his body. How long would this continue? With a desperate gasp which spoke of both anger and agony, Ashutosh Khemka got up to his feet. Every nerve of his body screamed in pain as he straightened. He could not be that weak, thought Ashutosh.

In front of him was the only window of his bedroom. It overlooked a major portion of Elgin Road. Even though the city slept at 2.30am in the morning, occasional motorcycles passed with inhuman speed. With no one to monitor the street and no traffic light buzzing, bikers and the drivers had their wings out.

With slow, stealthy steps Ashutosh walked towards the window. He needed fresh air. Despite the winter wind, he felt a disturbing trickle of perspiration on his back. Sweat slid down his flat, masculine abs as well. A gust of icy wind exploded on his face as he leaned forward to look outside. He needed help, Ashutosh knew that. He needed serious help. Something was wrong with him. The dreams that he had been having were not normal. He scrubbed his face with his hands again. His palms felt cold against his face. It evoked a deep sob out of his chest. The horror of the nightmare was still too fresh in his mind. There was no possibilities of going back to sleep now.

Ashutosh returned to his bed, still shivering from the intensity of the dream he had. He sat on the edge of the bed and reached for his phone. Without thinking he started to scroll through his social media feeds. After ten or twenty unmindful scrolling, his hand stopped suddenly, as a strong male face stared at him from the screen. He leaned forward in the darkness and read the post content. Goosebumps rippled all over his body and he began to shake. He must find this man. If anyone could help him, it was the man from the screen, criminal profiler Rudransh Ray, he breathed deep then let it out as noisily as possible. A strange humming sound came out of his mouth which sent a ripple of fear down his spine. Was it his voice, or someone else was down there inside him making the noise? Was he losing his mind? Or had he already lost it?

The walls of his room seemed to be closing in. If he did not get out, he would be choked inside. The realization got Ashutosh moving. He jumped up on his feet, disregarding the freezing floor tiles, and went to his closet. Not for a single moment, he forgot to breath deep. Air, even though invisible, had immense power to hold a human together. It held him together since…

His closet presented a big challenge to him. It was loaded with so many clothes and shoes, that sometimes he got puzzled with what to wear and what to leave behind. After a little ponderation, Ashutosh picked a dark red heavy woolen hoodie, and a pair of black jeans. It would do for now. Before going out of his room, he checked the wall clock once. It was 3 am, almost morning. Without remorse or any feeling for a man who might be getting a well needed night's sleep, Ashutosh drove out of his residential garage. He picked his phone and punched Rudransh Ray's number, found it ringing, and heard a fully alert male voice after the third ring.

'Rudransh Ray.'

Ashutosh Khemka found himself sitting across three stern faced men. They all looked to be alert and widely awake. Did they sleep, he wondered. Rudransh Ray looked more fierce than he did in pictures. His dark eyes seemed to penetrate Ashutosh and got everything out of his soul. After a moment, Ashutosh looked down at the floor just to breathe easy.

'I am Rudransh Ray,' said Ray. 'You wanted to meet me.'

'Yes,' said Ashutosh. 'I am Ashutosh Khemka.' The Southern Avenue apartment where Ray lived had a strange lingering emptiness. It made Ashuthosh think of the hotel rooms which had occasional guests and never residents. 'I saw your social media feeds on criminology and the recent murder.' He paused when his voice echoed in the silence of the wide living room.

Ray nodded, waiting. He made no attempt to introduce him to the other two men. One of them looked like a man just out of Vogue's cover page, too good looking to be working in the law enforcement. His golden brown eyes reflected a strange sadness which Ashutosh had seen in lost puppies. The other one had a spiral notebook open in front of him, with pen in his hand, this guy ignored everyone. He looked like a happy traveler with his expensive tan and sun bleached hair.

'I...I want to speak about the murder case you are investigating,' Ashutosh leaned forward. For the first time since they met, Ray's eyes betrayed any emotion. He looked uneasy for a fraction of second. But then he hid the expression.

'Okay,' Ray said, waiting.

'I see similar type of murder in my dream,' said Ashutosh, after swallowing thrice. It got Ray's attention for he moved a little and straightened his spine. The man with the notebook looked up at him. The man with the puppy eyes, lost his puppy look in an instant. 'I see a man with a crutch getting murdered and ripped by a shadowy man in a construction building on a highway.'

The silence of the room elevated as everyone sat motionless, looking at Ashutosh. Their combined stare made him fidget a little. Did they think he was crazy? Did they think he had made the story up? But why would he do it, wondered Ashutosh.

Ray tapped his index finger on the armrest of his couch before speaking carefully. 'Since when this dream started?'

Ashutosh cleared his throat. He was about to give them a bizarre story which one might find in the pages of thriller novels only. But it was his life and he lived it every day. He lived with the horror of his nightmare which visited him each night, right after he fell asleep.

'It started a week ago,' said Ashutosh. He fell quiet suddenly doubtful about his decision to come here to meet Ray.

'A week ago?' asked Ray, carefully. Ashutosh could see a calculation going on inside the criminologist's head.

'Yes, a week ago,' said Ashutosh. 'Before that I don't remember anything.'

Ray tilted his head and looked at him in a steady stare. 'You don't remember anything?'

Ashutosh leaned forward and buried his face into the palms of his hands. He breathed deep to keep himself calm. 'No, I don't remember. I remember waking up at the doorstep of a large house at Elgine Road. Before I could walk away the gate keeper came out and almost dragged me inside. There I met people who claimed to be my family. But beyond that I remember nothing. I don't even remember the woman I call mom or the man I call dad.' He stopped and looked at Ray's stony expression.

'Are you seeing a doctor?' asked the puppy eyed man.

'You mean a shrink?' Ashutosh asked.

'Yeah. A shrink.'

'They took me to Natasha Mishra,' said Ashutosh. 'She is looking after me.'

'What is her opinion?' asked Ray. He kept tapping his index finger on the armrest.

Ashutosh cleared his throat and then replied. 'She says an intense trauma had taken off my memory.'

'Have you told her about your dream?'

'Yes, I have. She called it a bout of fascination.'

Ray leaned forward. 'And you think it is not?'

Ashutosh smiled a weak smile. 'Fascination cannot be this vivid.'

'Agreed.' Ray got up to his feet. 'You want some coffee and sandwiches?'

Ashutosh's stomach growled just then. 'I would like to have some coffee.'

'On the way,' said Ray before disappearing from the living room.

Chapter - 23

It had been a while since Ashutosh Khemka left. Thunder had started rumbling up on the sky, making Kolkata stop and wait for yet another down pour. Cars zoomed by the street in hope to avoid whatever was coming down. And something big was coming down, Ray could say it from the way everything looked.

'So, what you think is going on?' asked Sid. They had been sipping coffee standing in Ray's balcony.

'Mess,' Ray said.

'You are the shrink, you should have a better explanation,' said Akash. He had a far away look in his eyes. Beneath his calm exterior, Ray could sense a current. He knew this vibe. Writers got it when they smelt a story. Even Akash wrote true crime, he too was a storyteller. Soon The Ripper would find its way out to the bookstores. Akash had written other books on Ray's crime investigations. But none of the cases had received as much footages as this one.

Media was having a field day, blaming Ray for the entire fiasco. They had claimed that any other criminal profiler would have gotten the guy within two days. One of the newspapers ran a long story on

International criminal profilers to establish Rudransh Ray's incompetency. Only Kolkata Breaking stood by Rayon Corp and stated the fact that no one could have guessed that the offender would go after Samir's mother and house keeper. A rivel newspaper had contradicted Kolkata Breaking's educational feature, claiming that due an intimate relationship with a Kolkata Breaking reporter, Ray had gotten away with a subtle jab from the famous newspaper. Overall it was a circus out there. One which had given Rudransh Ray what he had never wanted. Fame.

Ray turned to look at his partner. 'I am not a shrink. I am a criminologist.'

Sid chuckled. 'What's a criminologist?'

'A fake shrink,' said Akash. That made Sid laugh an open laugh which Ray had not heard coming from him for a long time.

'You are laughing a lot since yesterday,' Ray pointed.

'Artistic ecstacy,' Akash countered.

'Fuck it guys,' said Sid, trying hard to suppress a smile. 'Tell me what's going on?'

Ray looked down at the street. From his eleventh floor's balcony, everything appeared to be tiny and toy like. They could make out movements of the passing cars. But it was nearly impossible to identify the models. Ray thought of the event from the beginning. When he received Ashutosh's call, Samir Shrivastav murder was the last thing in his mind. He expected a confession. But what Ashutosh said, completely blew his mind and shattered the entire calculation. The murdered man in Ashuthosh's dream must be Raghav. Ray dreaded to break the news to Shraddha. She had been worrying about the missing journalist since the day her pregnant friend called.

'It confirms my claim that Samir Shrivastav was not the first victim of the unsub,' Ray said. He watched the inky black sky blowing up with light as thunder boomed occasionally. Would it ever stop, thought Ray. It seemed Mother Nature had decided to keep the Sun hidden all winter long.

'And the dream?' asked Sid.

'When did that accident take place?' asked Ray. 'I believe one same day of Samir's murder.'

Aksah straightened a bit. 'Yes, early morning.'

'Right,' said Ray. 'So, my theory is Ashutosh was on the crime scene when the murder took place.' He paused to gather his thought. It was going to be more complicated. 'Or, somehow he came to know about the murder. He got disturbed and went away driving and hit those cops. In the process, he received a terrible emotional trauma which made him forget everything.' Ray raised his hand to stop Sid from commenting. 'But the horror of the murders still remains in his subconscious mind and it causes the nightmare.'

'Makes sense,' said Sid. 'But why an old murder? Why not Samir's murder?'

Ray thought for a moment. 'Probably Raghav's was the first murder Ashutosh has witnessed and like the first breakup, it remains in his mind fresh as blooming flowers.' He ignored Akash's amused face at the description. Yeah, writer effect and all those craps.

'Makes sense,' said Sid. Then he asked. 'What do we do now?'

'We meet his shrink,' said Ray. 'We speak to her about the murder case and Ashutosh's dreams.'

'What if she refuses to speak?' asked Akash.

'We will subpoena her,' said Ray. 'And make her speak in front of a judge.'

Akash tilted his head. 'I believe, we are not disclosing it to the other investigating team.' His grin said he already knew the answer. They had done it numerous times before. They would do it numerous times after this.

Ray whistled at the comment. 'You believe right. We are to keep this to ourselves for now.'

'So, we meet Natasha Mishra today?' asked Sid.

'We do,' said Ray though he debated the wisdom of barging in a woman's office with two of male companions without notice. Yet, he could not wait any longer. He needed to get to the bottom of the matter before Nishant Chauhan arrived. After a quick glance at the sky, he turned to move. 'I will just check on Shraddha once and then we meet Natasha.'

'With her sister back home,' Akash said with an amused look. 'I don't think she needs checking on her now.' The last word he said in voice Italic.

Ray did not reply to the jab. He walked to his bedroom, grabbed a pair of dark blue Levi's and a pale blue woolen sweatshirt with hood. In his mind he kept trying to match the time and the events. After dressing, Ray fished his phone and made a call to Nilesh.

'Nil, do me a favor,' he said walking out of the bedroom. The other two were waiting by the door for him.

'Yes, boss,' said Nil, calling him by the hated word.

'Check Ashutosh Khemka's phone number's locations on the day of Samir Shrivastav's murder.' Sid and Akash raised their eyebrows at the order. 'I need to know whether he had been near New Alipore that night or not.'

'What if he had been?' asked Sid. 'Any good defense lawyer will blow the case saying that the mobile tower failed to detect the right location.'

Ray smiled. 'I am not trying to make an arrest based on mobile location alone. I just want to know whether Ashutosh was anywhere near the crime scene on the night of the murder.'

They fell silent as Ray drove past Dhakuria Lake which looked briming from a distance due to continuous rain. A lone boat came to view. Four people rowed the boat with enthusiasm. Rain drops beat down their fluorescent orange life jackets. Ray remembered his college days when he and Sid used to go rowing. Life was much simpler back then. They both had dreams of saving the world. But little did they know that saviors did not get to save themselves. Either they carried their crucifixes, or they carried the burden of the greatest curse. Either way, it was not easy being a savior.

Ray sped past the bridge connecting Dhakuria Lake to Anwar Shah Road. He did not want to get back to the gloom which had him captivated after Rusha's death. It took him two years to recover completely. Had it not been for Chetan, Siddhant, and Akash, he would not have gotten himself back.

At Shraddha's house, they had been greeted by an enthusiastic Trisha. She had changed into a pair of woolen tights which showed off her strong legs and masculine calves and a black woolen sweatshirt, loose enough to fall around her slender body smoothly and fitting enough to display her curves. It was a girl who spent a lot of time pressing weight Ray decided. In her hand she had a thin brush. Lime green pain dripped from the tip of her brush, smudging the worn out tiles of the floor. She scanned their faces with her dark eyes which looked glazy and moist.

'Well, hello there,' she said, stepping away to let them in. 'Shraddha is in kitchen. She is a lovely cook.' Trisha glanced up at Sid. Their eyes met. But the contact remained only for a fraction of seconds before they both moved inside. 'So, what brings you all here?' she asked.

'I see you have already started panting,' said Sid.

Trisha gave a quick shrug of her narrow shoulders. 'It is therapy for me.' She threw a quick glance over her shoulder before looking back at them. 'That guy is a bad news. He had been since the beginning. I don't want that man anywhere near my sister.'

It took Ray a moment to realize Trisha was speaking about Shraddha's ex. From the way Trisha looked it seemed she was ready to murder the army veteran without thinking twice.

Sid chuckled. 'He will remain behind the bars for a long time. When he comes out he would to be an old man to hunt anyone down. So, don't you worry ma'am.'

'Why do you keep calling me that?' Trisha asked with irritation.

Sid shrugged. 'Should I call you sir?'

Before Trisha could come out with a fitting reply, Shraddha walked in. She had an uncomfortable smile on her face. 'Someone named Nishant Chauhan called,' she said holding up her phone and waving it in the air. 'He wants to speak to me.'

Trisha looked at her sister but said nothing. Ray watched her calm face and the line of her jaw. Something about her nagged Ray deep inside. He could not point it out though. A second passed before Ray could move his eyes from Trisha. With the disturbance still inside his heart, he asked Shraddha. 'Has he mentioned any date?'

Shraddha shook her head. 'No, just that he wants to speaks to me as soon as possible.'

Ray heaved a sigh. 'That will probably be tomorrow morning. He is arriving tonight.'

'Why does he want to speak to me?' Shraddha asked.

Just to intimidate you, Ray wanted to say. But aloud he replied. 'Just preliminaries. Don't worry. You will be fine.'

Even though Shraddha looked doubtful, she did not say anything. Her head bobbed up and down. 'Okay. I believe you.'

Please don't, Ray almost blurted out. Please don't believe me. Rusha did and it got her killed. He found it difficult to meet her eyes. Feeling like an imposter masquerading to be someone else, he got up to his feet. 'Call me as soon as he calls you.'

Shraddha nodded her agreement. Her eyes looked a little too glazy like Trisha's. Probably, they had been crying for some reason. Family reunion, thought Ray. 'I will,' she promised after looking at Ray for a moment. 'Gimme a moment.' She turned and headed for the kitchen.

'I will be gone soon,' said Trisha, watching Shraddha's disappearing back. 'I hope you keep my sister safe.'

'Where are you going?' Sid asked. Ray detected a tinge of panic in his voice.

'I have been offered a job at a Paris museum,' said Trisha.

Sid's handsome face fell at the news. 'Oh,' he said. 'Congratulation.'

Trisha sighed, oblivious to Sid's change of expression. 'I will not be able to go knowing my sis is in danger. She is all I have.' The whisper came with so much pain that Ray looked away.

'I will keep her safe,' Ray said. 'You can be rest assured.'

Whatever was there in his word made Trisha's face soften. She forced a smile. 'It is not easy leaving her behind. But I need to do this for us.' Then she looked straight into Ray's eyes. 'Had it not been for you, I would have refused the job offer.'

'You would have given up on your dream?' asked Ray, touched by closeness of the two sisters. It made him feel all alone in the world suddenly.

The smile which bloomed on Trisha's face brightened up the entire room. Ray heard Sid drawing a sharp breath at the sight. 'I will give up my life for her if it comes down to that.'

Ray cocked his head, smiling. 'You keep your life ma'am. You live your life at the fullest.' His smile widened when Trisha smiled back. 'I will keep that sister of yours safe at any cost.'

'Will you die for her?' asked Trisha.

A deep hush fell in the room. Ray held Trisha's challenging stare. He could feel Akash shifting weight uncomfortably from one leg to another. Then he said in a firm voice. 'No, I will kill for her.'

Trisha rolled her head like a pro martial artist and then got up to her feet. 'I have to go shopping,' she said. 'I need a few essentials before going to Paris.'

Sid spoke up suddenly. 'I will take you ma'am,' he said. 'Right now we are going to attend an important meeting. I will be back in the afternoon to take you wherever you want to go.'

Trisha rolled her eyes at that. 'All three of you are going to attend one meeting?' she asked. 'I hope you are not meeting a lady.'

'As a matter of fact,' Ray said. 'We are.'

'Lucky her,' Trisha said, making a face. Her brush has dried up by then. She looked down at the tip and shook her head in display. Whatever she was painting must be important to her.

Shraddha walked back with a tray loaded with three steaming mug of coffee and a platter of French toasts. She placed the tray on the coffee table. Then she looked at Ray and said, 'I am having a bad feeling about this Nishant Chauhan.'

Ray chuckled. 'Thank God, I am not the only one here.' Then his face fell. 'I need to speak to you about Raghav. But right now, I need to attend an essential business matter.' He turned to leave, then he stopped and looked back at Shraddha. 'Don't leave the house alone.' With the parting instruction Ray left with his entourage.

Chapter - 24

On the way Ray got a call from the ME. 'Gaurav,' Ray greeted. His mouth pulled up in a smile automatically. Gaurav was a charming guy who did not only look good, but brought a lot of positive energy in the gloomy job.

'Ray, I have checked the ladies,' he said. 'It's the usual MO. Poison, blunt force and then sharp object. No sign of any sexual assault.' Somehow Gaurav read Ray's mind who had been waiting for this particular information.

'Which poison?' Ray asked.

'The same,' said Gaurav. 'Guy seems to be fond of double murder weapons.'

'So, he killed them first and then smashed their heads, and then cut them out?' Ray asked.

'In perfect order,' Gaurav said. 'The ladies did not feel the blunt force. They had been already dead when the cricket bat found their skulls.'

'Okay,' said Ray. 'Thanks for the report Gaurav.'

'You owe me. I have taken personal time off to perform this autopsy myself just for you,' Gaurav said.

'Let's go for beer after this case is done,' said Ray. 'We all need a break.'

'The beer will be on you, right?' asked Gaurav, jokingly.

'Of course,' Ray said. He started his car and drove towards Topsia where Natasha had her plush office setup.

Natasha Mishra had a lavish office. It did not exactly look like a chamber of a psychiatrist. Rather, it appeared more like a corporate office which dealt with fashion or lifestyle. A heavily made up woman greeted them at the door with a wide smile. She had worn a cream colored silk top which sat snuggly on her thin body.

'May I have your names please?' she asked, eyeing the three of them in attempt to find who needed her boss' help. In other words, she tried to find who was the crazy one.

'Rudransh Ray,' Ray said. He threw a quick glance at Sid, who presented his ID card to the receptionist. 'We need to see Dr. Mishra, right now.'

For a moment, the woman stared at the card with full intention to refuse their request of meeting her boss without an appointment. But then she changed her mind. With a quick shake of head, she got up to her feet. 'I will see what I can do for you.'

Ray tilted his head and said nothing in reply. Sid was taking a tour of the large reception area. It could accommodate at least fifty people. From a red plush carpet to an enormous crystal chandelier, everything had been chosen with care to adorn this room. On the off white walls, hung colorful and possibly meaningful paintings of distorted people. Natasha earned a lot and she spent money on her office space.

'This a wealthy lady,' muttered Sid.

Akash was busy taking notes. Why he wrote everything down was beyond Ray's understanding, probably a writer thing. He leaned on a wall which was yet to get ornamented with paintings and waited for the receptionist to come back. The woman made an appearance after five minutes with her boss at her toes.

Natasha Mishra was tall, slender, in her early thirties. She had on a stylish navy blue jumpsuit which must have costed her a fortune. Her long hair was down and had a sun kissed beach travelled look. She tilted her head and looked at each one of them carefully as if trying to guess the reason of this visit. Then her eyes turned towards Ray.

'Rudransh Ray,' she said striking a smile. 'May I know the reason of this visit?' she asked, keeping her tone low and formal.

'One of your patients Ashutosh Khemka paid me a visit this morning,' said Ray.

Natasha's face instantly changed and a look of concern appeared on it. 'Ashutosh?' she whispered. 'Is he ok?' Ray detected something more than concern in her eyes as she inquired about Ashutosh. Fear, he realized with satisfaction, she was frightened. But why? Was

Ashutosh suffering from anything other than emotional issues. Or, was she frightened that he had revealed some important details? Either the woman looked guilty as hell to him.

'He is fine,' said Ray. 'At least he was fine when he came to visit me earlier this morning.'

Natasha's straight back relaxed a bit at the news. She bit her lower lip and took a deep breath. 'Glad to know that. The boy is suffering too much.'

Ray looked down at the floor. Ashutosh was more than a boy. He had been accused of grazing six people alive. Only one of them survived the accident. If his suspicion was correct, Ashutosh was also a serial rapist who raped women to make porn movies. The guy was not an innocent child. 'Can we speak in private about this?' he asked after a while.

The question was followed by a sharp intake of breath. Natasha straightened again. The strong spine was back in place. She eyed them before looking over Ray's shoulder towards an artfully decorated glass door. 'Please follow me.'

They waited for Natasha to lead them to her office. The air of the office was heavy with a lemony fragrance. Decorated with a combination of white and off white, her office space reflected success and money. As tasteful as it seemed to some, Ray found the setting a little depressing. Too prime for his taste, he decided.

'Please have a seat,' Natash said, motioning them towards the corner of the room where she had made the sitting arrangement. After they all were seated, she said. 'Coffee and cookies will be here shortly.'

She did not even think of asking them whether they wanted coffee or not, Ray noted. A dominating and irritating trait which he disdained with all his heart. 'Thanks,' he said despite his irritation.

'So, Ashutosh came to visit you this morning?' she asked.

'Yes,' Ray replied. 'Before even the dawn broke free. He is dreaming about a gruesome murder.' Ray stared straight at Natasha's eyes. 'The MO sounded similar to the one we are investigating.'

Natasha nodded. 'I know. Ashutosh's father brought him here when he started to have the nightmares. I believe you know that he has lost his memory.' It was not a question, so Ray did not give any reply.

'We do,' Sid spoke this time. 'But what we cannot understand is – why you did not notify the police when you came to know about Ashutosh's nightmares?' He leaned forward and placed his elbows on his thighs which he did when he wanted to make an impact. But Natasha did not budge under his stare.

'I could not have breached my ethics,' she said, coolly. 'I need to maintain client confidentiality.'

Ray did not allow the conversation to turn into a bitter fight which it would eventually happen if Siddhant continued to speak. So, like a striker who found the perfect gap to score a goal, he moved to steer the conversation back to Ashutosh. 'Do you know he is involved in a car accident which has killed five people and injured one?' he asked.

Natasha tilted her head to look at Ray with calm eyes. 'I believe his driver has already confessed to committing the manslaughter.'

This was a cool lady, who would not break that easily. So, Ray being a pro midfielder sniffed a strong defense line. 'Do you think Ashutosh is involved into some kind of murder which has caused this trauma and forced his memory to fade?'

Ticking of a wall clock filled the room as silence fell at the question. Natasha tapped her freshly painted index finger on the armrest of the couch she had occupied. She took a couple of breaths before speaking. 'I believe he is fascinated by the gruesome aspect of the murder you are investigating and read too much about it that his mind has started to malfunction.' She lifted her shoulders. 'Over data feeding does that, you know.'

Ray looked at her straight. Clearly, she had been lying. But she had a degree which would allow her to write this in her report. Natasha held his gaze. She knew that he knew about her lies. But there was nothing he or anyone could do right now. So, Ray got up to his feet and flashed Natasha a wide smile. 'Thank you so much for your time,' he said.

'Rusha was beautiful,' Natasha said all of a sudden. Ray stiffened at the comment. Sid and Akash looked at her startled. 'She visited me five times before her death.' Ray's face paled at the news. He had no idea about this. His mouth opened but no sound came out. 'She had been writing a book and was looking forward to publish it.' Natasha smiled as she noted Ray's stony face.

'Why she visited you?' Sid asked. 'She did not have any problem.'

Natasha looked at Sid. 'You are Siddhant Thakur, I believe. Rusha's big brother,' she said. It was not a question. Sid did not move to reply. 'There is a lot she had not told you. She suspected that Rudransh Ray's mother had been murdered and was looking for evidence to prove it.'

A frozen silence fell in the room. Everyone stood rooted to their places. Ray heaved a long breath. His heart started to thus against his ribs. 'Is there any evidence which proves this?' he finally asked.

'Rusha maintained diaries,' Natasha said. 'I had asked her to write everything down in there to keep a record.'

Sid had those diaries at his disposal. But he had not read them. Had not dared to even open a single volume. 'But why was she visiting you?' he asked weakly.

Natasha shrugged. 'She felt that Ray was pulling away from her because she could not conceive. So, she visited me for counselling.' A smile, sharp as a slim sword, played on her face. 'She loved him so much that she was afraid to lose him.'

The way back home was tense and silent. Ray kept his gaze fixed on the road and refused to say anything. His heart continued to thud against his ribs. His head continued to ache. Even though he wanted to speak, to get some words through his dry throat, just to see whether he could still speak or not, he failed to make even the faintest sound. Aksah was behind the wheel. He was the least affected one in this entire scenario. Siddhant was on the passenger seat, quiet and thoughtful.

After driving in silence for a long time, Akash spoke. 'I think she was trying to pull your string,' he said.

'Why would she want to do that?' Sid asked. His deep voice sounded low and grim. His fair face looked ashen.

Ray heard Sid's voice, he heard them arguing about what Natasha had claimed but all of a sudden his mind had stopped reacting. It had come to a complete stop. He looked out at the semi fogged road. Even though it was midmorning, the muted sunray had created a type of gloom which made people remember all the heartbreaks. Thick mist had engulfed most of the street. Cars had the headlights on just to make others know that they were there. It was dismal, unbearable, and cruel. Ray looked down at his hands. They were shaking. The tremble came years later.

'What do you remember about your mother's death?' Sid asked, looking at the rear view mirror to catch Ray's eyes.

What did he remember? Ray closed his eyes and slumped against the backseat. His back began to hurt. The problem was – he remembered everything. He remembered coming home from school with his grandfather, and finding his mother lying on the ground with her wrists slit open. It was too late to save her as she had lost too much blood. Years later, he walked home to find his wife lying on the ground with her wrists slit open. With a firm shake of his head he pushed the two scenes away. If he allowed himself, he would go downhill fast and would never come back again.

His phone, thankfully, rang just then. It was Shraddha. Her beautiful face flashed on the smart phone screen. Ray drew a deep a breath, then let it out. Slowly, his old self crept back. 'Yes, tell me.' He answered the call, nothing of the gloom he felt remained as he saw her face flashing on the screen.

'Nishant called,' said Shraddha. Her voice trembled a little when she spoke. Ray's jaw tightened. He knew that Nishant could be rude sometimes. Ray himself was not a soft spoken man. But at least he did not roughen up those he spoke to during a crime investigation.

'What did he say?' Ray asked. He longed for a cigarette.

Shraddha drew an audible breath. 'He said that I am to appear at the station at exactly 11am tomorrow. I must bring with me everything related to the case and be prepared to answer all his questions.'

Ray clenched and unclenched his right hand. It itched to hold Nishant by his throat and squeeze real tight. 'Fine, you will appear at exactly 11am tomorrow,' he said.

'Nishant called?' Akash asked after Ray disconnected the call.

'Yeah,' Ray said.

'Asshole,' said Sid. 'He has always been after us for one reason or another.'

'And now he has joined the circus to create more spectacles,' Akash said. Nishant hated Ray and Siddhant. He also hated everyone connected to the duo. The reason of his hatred was unknown to Ray and he never tried to go beyond giving Nishant the finger. But even though Ray did not pay any attention to Nishant, the other cop made it his life's mission to keep track of everything Ray did.

'Why does he hate us so much?' asked Akash.

'Fuck if I know,' Ray said. 'Frankly I don't care.'

'Where are we going?' asked Sid.

'Where do you want to go?' asked Akash. 'Should I drop you at Shraddha's?' He flashed Sid a grin.

'Drop at me at home,' said Ray. 'Then take the car and do whatever you want.'

'How will you go to the police station tomorrow?' Akash asked.

Ray cut him a quick glance. 'I am not going to the police station. I will come to office.'

'Oh come on,' Akash said. 'You are not going to ditch her with Nishant, are you?'

Ray, finally grinned. But his grin lacked the usual humor. It took a lot of effort to make his mind function. 'A strong man is not someone who always protects his woman and keeps her weak. A strong man will step back and allow her to take over, so that she can overcome her fear.'

Sid pulled the car at the side of the road, near Ruby Hospital, careful to be away from the racing cars. Then he look at Ray. 'I am glad to know that she is your woman.'

Ray leaned his head back on the head rest, suddenly feeling exhausted, suddenly yearning for someone to hold him and say that life would get better again. 'I hope she is my woman. I hope I can keep her safe.' Then he looked at Sid through the rear view mirror. 'I need Rusha's diaries.' He knew reading them would drag him back to the dark and murky lane where he had lost himself.

Akash stiffened at the request. Siddhant looked out of the window at the foggy street. Neither spoke for a long time. Then Siddhant said. 'I will give the diaries to Shraddha. I believe she is the best person to read and extract data from them. We both are too burned out to read any of the diaries.' When Ray started to protest, Sid shook his head. 'No, Rudra. We cannot. We cannot let ourselves be carried away again. If Rusha had been murdered, we need to find the killer. If she had killed herself, we need to know why Natasha has tried to mislead us. Either way getting caught in the mazes of the past will not serve any of us.'

Ray cursed. He hated to admit that Sid was right that reading those diaries would only tear him apart from the reality and push him once again to the road which led to the realm of death.

Back at his home, Ray sat with a large mug of steaming dark coffee and his notebook in the balcony. He needed to think. The offender had brought the murder weapon with him but then he left it behind. But he had not left the sharp object, possibly a knife to the scene. Ray wrote down the fact in the middle of a blank page and circled it. The offender, Ray was ready to bet, had forged this particular piece of weapon with his own hand. It was in a way, memento collection to the unsub.

He remembered an offender who used wooden sticks to batter down his victims. The guy brought his weapon with him and took it away. Later they found that the young man worked in a furniture store. He made his weapon and thus was attached to it. Ray sensed something similar in this case as well. He let out a breath to allow himself a little space to relax. So, he was looking for a man who was tall, strong, in his late twenties, educated, came from a medical background, dealt in medicine, and forged knives. The offender had a disturbing childhood which had left him yearning for attention. This was a man who spoke well and had charm to mislead people. A dangerous predator who would strike over and over again, until he was stopped.

Someone had trained the guy to rip people apart. Every serial killer learn their craft from somewhere. This guy too had his training. Ray needed to find out from where.

Chapter - 25

Shraddha tapped her index finger on the keyboard of her laptop. Words started to jumble up. Thoughts started to mash with each other. Suddenly everything appeared blurry and unreal. She felt a surprising twist inside her stomach. Outside clouds had begun to part. A slice of the sun peeked through the gap. Dull sunlight hesitatingly touched the window pane of her attic room. She wanted to work on her novel after Ray departed because there was nothing else to do that morning. She could not go to office. Akshaj had strictly instructed her to come back with something solid on the case or else he would place her in the local municipal department. She could not write about open manholes and confetti covered walls. So, she decided to stay back home and follow the leads she had.

'You wanna eat something?' Trisha appeared at the door. She looked like the untidy artist she had always been. 'You have not eaten anything since that Nishant character called.'

Shraddha rubbed her eyes with the heels of her palms. 'That Nishant character is the investigating officer of The Ripper case. He will work alongside Rudra.'

Trisha walked inside the room. 'I like him. Ray.' She leaned her back against Shraddha's writing table. 'I really liked the way he holds himself and cares for you.'

Shraddha reached out and held Trisha's hand. 'Sis, don't think so much,' she said. 'Just go. Live your life.'

Trisha gave her a bright smile. 'You think I care about painting more than I care about you?' she asked.

Shraddha knew Trisha well enough to know that she might decline her job offer without even thinking twice. 'I know you love me. Too much.' She added after a bit. 'But sis you need to go. You need to make it big. So that we can live in comfort. So that we can settle down, finally.' The last sentence came out in a whisper.

Trisha's face changed. The warrior came out all of a sudden. She rolled her shoulders twice. 'Okay, I will go.' She took a couple of breaths. 'You be careful. Even with Ray ganging up to protect you, I want you to stay low. Don't try to do anything smart.'

Shraddha nodded. She knew what Trisha was speaking about the rash decision of visiting Samir Shrivastav's house. 'I won't do anything to risk myself.'

For a moment neither of them spoke. Trisha looked down at her sneakered feet. Shraddha watched her younger sister. There was something different about Trisha. Something which went beyond the surface level. From outside it was the same Trisha, Shraddha knew. But on the deeper level, Trisha seemed like someone else, a completely different person.

'You seem different,' Shraddha said.

Trisha's head snapped up. 'Different as in?'

Shraddha shrugged. 'I don't know.' She paused and groped for the right word which did not come. 'I feel something has changed. Your body language is different.' Then it struck Shraddha. 'You are a lot calmer now. Earlier you would have been anxious about me being in this mess. But you are not.'

A smile flashed on Trisha's face. 'Ikigai,' she said. 'I am practicing meditation now.' With that Trisha straightened and before Shraddha could say anything else, she was gone.

For a long time after Trisha hurriedly retreated from the attic, Shraddha sat savoring the moment and the chilly air, knowing it would not last for long. Kolkata did not get to see winter that much. It was a summer city, hot and sunny most of the year. People got tuned to the heat and did their best to stay away from the sun. Most Kolkatans wait all year long for two events. Durga puja and the arrival of winter when the fun began.

Shraddha leaned back and closed her eyes. In just one week her entire life had changed. She had been leading a comfortable life writing crime stories of the world. Her research and information platform had been internet. Then Samir Shrivastav died and things took a different turn. Her carefully constructed life turned upside down. With a deep breath which did nothing to calm her raw nerves down, she pushed away from her writing table. Being able to sit and work only on her book was a privilege which she could not take. She needed to do something productive which would help her keep the job. Her cell phone vibrated then. It was Ray.

'Hi,' she said.

'Hey.' Ray sounded tired. 'Are you free?' he asked.

It made Shraddha laugh. 'Yes, I am free.' She had nothing to do. No job to go to. Suddenly she had all the free time to do anything she wanted. Earlier she had to snatch moments to work on her book. But now that she had so much time, the worry about the future captivated her. If she failed to supply continuous scoops, she would have to give up crime reporting. It sent a disturbing twist down to her stomach.

'Hey, you there?' asked Ray. 'You sound worried.'

'So do you,' Shraddha said.

Ray sounded drained. His long breath echoed from the other end of the phone. 'Yes, I am worried. I am worried and tired.' He paused, then began to speak again. 'I need to speak to you about Raghav. I need to speak to you about me.' Shraddha heard a slight tremor in Ray's voice. Something was terribly wrong, she thought. 'I am coming to pick you up.' With that Ray disconnected the call.

On the way to Ray's apartment neither of them spoke. Shraddha remained glued to a thick crime novel she had been reading. Ray had his eyes fixed on the street ahead. With the promise of a clear winter evening ahead, foot traffic had streamed out of their homes. Cheerful faces had replaced the gloomy worried ones. For the first time since the first winter wind, Kolkata had bloomed like a fresh flower. People had chosen to wear colorful winter clothes. Suddenly the gloomy looking gray rain coats had disappeared, giving the city its natural vigor back.

But Shraddha noticed none of these. Her mind whirled around the past week's event one by one, even though she had her eyes on the pages of the new crime novel. Beside her Ray kept shifting gears like a robot. Something was bothering him, Shraddha noted for the first time and all of a sudden she wanted to run away. Whatever had Rudransh Ray frozen to the core, must be cruel and dreadful enough and she had no intention of prying. But it seemed, regardless of her wish, she would be a possessor of the secret which the criminologist now carried alone.

'You want coffee?' asked Ray after they settled in his living room. Then he said without waiting for her to reply. 'I am ordering pizza and beer.'

'I don't booze,' said Shraddha. 'I will be happy with pizza and soda.'

Ray arched his eyebrows. 'Soda?' he said as if she had uttered an unacceptable slang.

Shraddha grinned. 'Cold drink.'

'You read the British writers and speak like the Americans.' Ray pointed.

Shraddha lifted her shoulders in reply. 'Well, I am a global citizen.'

After their pizza arrived, and they went to sit in Ray's balcony, Ray finally spoke. 'Raghav is dead.'

The unceremonious revelation startled Shraddha to the extent that she choked on a chunk of chicken. Ray reached out and affectionately rubbed her back. 'How…' Shraddha managed to get the word out with effort. Then she coughed again in attempt to spit out the tiny piece which had caused so much nuisance. 'How do you know that?' she asked finally when the cough subsided. Even though she had guessed it already, the news made her heart drum against her ribs with the ferocity of a mad drummer.

Ray took a long sip from his beer can before turning to face her. 'I had a visit from Ashutosh Khemka this morning.'

Shraddha swallowed a large piece of sausage carefully, before speaking. 'Ashutosh Khemka as in the cop grazing guy?'

Despite the gloom which the conversation brought Ray chuckled. 'Yeah the cop grazing guy. He came here this morning.' Ray paused. 'At the dawn to tell me that he is dreaming of a murder. The MO is very similar to the way Samir Shrivastav has been killed. But the victim in Ashutosh's dream used a crutch.'

The last word exploded like a tire of a speeding car. Shraddha leaned her back against the wall just to provide herself some kind of support. She thought of

Oliva. She thought of the baby Oliva was carrying. Then she saw herself breaking the news to her best friend. It was not possible. 'Just because this guy used a crutch…' she said for the sake of argument.

Ray raised his hand and nodded. 'I know.' He rolled his neck and took a couple of deep, whizzing breaths. 'But my best guess is Raghav is dead and Ashutosh Khemka has witnessed his murder.'

Before Shraddha could speak, Ray's phone vibrated. It was Nilesh. 'Hey boss, I broke into Samir's laptop. It is loaded with videos of Samir Shrivastav and a three other guys doing those nasty things.'

'One of them used a crutch?' Ray asked.

'Yeah,' Nilesh said. If Ray's knowledge had surprised him, he did not say. 'But the guy with the crutch does not do the mean things to the girls. It is Samir and the other two.'

'Cool,' Ray said. 'I want to have a look at the videos.'

'Also, it contains details of bank accounts,' Nilesh said. 'Samir had hidden money in these accounts.'

'Get print outs,' Ray said. 'We will have to hand over the details to Nishant.'

'That prick?' asked Nilesh.

Ray's lips turned upwards. 'The same.'

After Nilesh hung up, Ray turned towards Shraddha and dropped the next bomb. 'I think Rusha did not commit suicide. I think she had been murdered.'

Trisha had gone to sleep a long time ago. She had her flight early the next morning. But Shraddha could not sleep. The conversion with Ray kept coming back to her. A stack of maroon leather bound executive diaries sat on her writing table. Ray's dead wife's diaries. She did not know what she felt about the task. But she could not say no to Ray when he asked her to read the diaries and update him about the content. The events related to the diaries evoked Shraddha's curiosity and made her agree to dive into them. Now, after bringing the diaries to her home, she became doubtful. Should she read them? Would she be able to stay neutral while reading about Ray's life with his late wife? With her index finger, she touched the diary which sat on the top of the pile. It was the last volume Rusha Ray had started before her death.

Even though it would not do her any good, she pulled the thick volume and opened a random page. The last three months were blank. Rusha died in September with the beginning of Autumn. Shraddha drew a long breath and began reading the entry made in March.

It has been a long day. I worked hard on my book. This one, I need to finish at any cost. Unfinished books are piling in my drive. Even though Rudra does not ask, I can see the question in his eyes. Why I make so much effort when I am unable to finish and publish anything. Probably that's the reason he is pulling away slowly. Or maybe, I am imagining things.

Shraddha moved her head from right to left a couple of times to release the tension from her neck. It had been a childhood problem. Each time she felt anxious, her neck began to throb. She turned a couple of more pages and went straight to the month of September. Rush died on 30th September 2007. So, she had the chance to journal throughout the month. It did not take a genius to know that she would write something about her discovery during those days. So, Shraddha began from 1st of September 2007.

I am astonished. How people could believe the impossible? Rudra's mother had killed herself. Or had she? Would a single mother kill herself? Ever? Taken that she had her father to take care of her child. But still, would she really kill herself? I doubted it before and now the more I dig into the matter, the more I am getting convinced that she could not have killed herself. She had been murdered. But I cannot prove that. Not right now. I cannot speak to Rudra about it either. First he is not speaking to me. Second he will not believe me. So, I will have to dig alone and find clues alone.

Shraddha started to flip through the pages to read more of her entries, but then her phone vibrated. A quick look at the wall clock showed that it was pushing 3 am. Shraddha reached for her phone, unlocked the screen, and started to scream.

Chapter - 26

With rising ray of the sun, he walked inside Delhi railway station to catch his train. It was better to catch a train after committing a crime. No one would recognize him. No one would remember. No one would have any records of him boarding the train. It was heaven. He chuckled to himself. Happy that everything turned out in his favor. A train smoothly pulled inside the station, and The Ripper got into it. He did not know where the train was going. He did not have to. All he needed was a little distance from Delhi and himself. He would wait three hours before getting down and catching a train to Lonavala.

The train was nearly empty. The Ripper took a seat by a window which overlooked the platform. He watched people ambling by in their own pace. No one had anything to worry about. No one even looked over their shoulders to see whether anyone followed them or not. A bad move, he thought with disapproval. They should watch their backs all the times. Then when people started to bore him, he looked down at his hands. This morning he had a very pleasant experience. A smile played on his face. He would live to relive the excitement he had while…

Did Shraddha get those pictures? Of course she had, he had waited till the massage app showed receipt notification. He leaned back and rested his head against the window. It immediately brought a rush of memories. All of a sudden he was a child again, travelling with his parents and grandfather. They were going to Banaras for some rituals. It was the only trip of his life which he remembered with a smile on his face. It was before his father lost his job and medical license for performing unlawful operation on patients. The domestic violence which kept him up most of the nights began after that and one night his mother died.

He let out a deep breath, probably, it would have been better had she not died the way she did. Probably, he would have turned into a better person had he had his mother by his side. Probably, he would have killed people less cruelly then. An elderly man took the empty seat beside him. He turned his head and look at the man for a fraction of second. Then he looked away. His eye lids began to turn heavy. A moment and sleep would sweep him off. But before he got the chance to drift into a state of peaceful slumber, his phone vibrated. With a startled gasp, he fished out the device and grimaced at the name flashing on the screen.

'Hello,' he said, eyeing the old man who had suddenly become very interested in the scenario outside the window.

'Where the fuck are you?' The question blasted in his ears. 'Do you have any idea what's going on here?'

The Ripper looked at his watch. He would have to bear this shit for a while now. With a long breath of resignation, he slumped against the seat, and said, 'I am travelling.'

'Really?' asked the caller. 'You are travelling. You fucker. Where are you travelling?'

That's none of your fucking business, he wanted to say. But he controlled his urge to blurt out the insult words. 'I am going to Mumbai.'

'You must come back to Kolkata right now,' barked the caller. 'Ashutosh went to Rudransh Ray.'

That got his attention. He sat straight, cursing. 'Ray,' he said the name with such hatred that he made his mouth nearly burn.

'Yeah, Ray and told everything about his dream.'

'Fuck,' said The Ripper. 'Has he given any name?'

'No, he cannot remember anything, you know that,' said the caller. 'But that does not mean, he will not remember. Now, that Ray knows about Ashutosh, it is only a matter of time, we all go down.'

The Ripper rolled his head right to left and then left to right. 'Fine, I am coming back.'

After the call got disconnected, he sat in silence for a long time. He needed to go to Lonavala. Ishant would be waiting for him. He looked down at the bag which he had placed on the floor, between his legs. If Ishant did not get the money, he would spill the bean to the cops. With a worried glance at his watch, he got up to his feet. Thoughts started to settle down. Slowly, he began to make plans.

Ishant looked at his watch. The meeting had been fixed at 11 pm. It was 10.50 pm now. Ten more minutes. He ordered another coffee. Since the morning he had failed to sit straight for even a minute. He let out a breath and took a long sip from the water bottle which the waiter had set on the table. Now, that he thought about it, the entire plan to extort money seemed a little too dangerous. He would just take whatever was being thrown at him and he would disappear forever.

At exactly 11 pm, a tall figure limped inside the small café. The man was wearing a black hoodie which concealed a major part of his upper face. The lower part of his face was hidden beneath a mass of heavy beard. Ishant's spine straightened at the sight of the dark hooded man. He had a backpack in his hand which looked to be heavy.

Without even glancing around, he came to occupy an empty chair opposite Ishant. Then he placed the backpack on the table, and sat back, waiting for Ishant to say something.

'Look,' said Ishant after clearing his voice twice. 'I hope you brought what I asked for.'

That earned a tiny nod of the hooded head. The waiter came with Ishant's order. He placed it threw a quick glance at the hooded face and then disappeared without a word. Ishant fidgeted on his seat. He had made a mistake in calling this upon him. He could feel the menacing stare of the man sitting across him.

'Look,' he said. 'I have a lot of evidence to get you all arrested. If anything happens to me, the package straight goes to Rudransh Ray.' His act of bravery slipped then. He noticed a slight tremor in his voice as he said the last two words. Ray would fry his ass if he come to know his whereabouts. But that would be better than being ripped apart.

Without a single word, the hoodie got up to this feet, took a moment to assess the café. Ishant knew that the guy was looking for CCTV cameras. When he was satisfied that none could have caught him properly, he walked out of the café. Ishant let out a breath of relief once the man disappeared. He finished his coffee, paid the bill, and walked out of the café to go back to his hiding place, oblivious of a tracking device stuck inside the backpack he carried with him.

It was after the clock struck 1 in the morning, Ishant heard a faint sound. In his sleep fogged mind, the intensity of the situation did not register. He pulled the blanket up to his neck and turned over to go back to sleep. Before sleep could claim him, he heard the sound again, stronger this time. Despite the cobweb of sleep clinging to his eyes, Ishant identified the sound. Footsteps. Someone was inside his cottage. Someone was…he sat up startled and saw the dark hooded man, standing at the door. In his right hand he clutched a cricket bat. In his left he held a knife, large enough to be called a dagger, sleek enough to pass for a small sword. Sharp steel gleamed even in the darkness.

Ishant did not know how did it feel like to look death in the eyes. He had never been the adventurous type. But tonight, looking at the shadow he felt his heart turning cold. A hot spasm snaked down his spine. It quickened his breath. Before he could speak or make a sound, the shadow charged forward. He raised the cricket bat and brought it down on Ishant's head. With a sharp crack his skull snapped into two.

The Ripper stood by the dead body with a satisfied grin on his face. Ishant had been a fucking liar. He had tried to bluff his way around, telling him about the evidence. But what Ishant did not know was, The Ripper had been raised to detect lies. He could understand when people tried to bluff their way out. For a moment, he stood still, savoring the moment, savoring his kill, and savoring the sense which told him that he was indeed the God. Once the feeling passed, he took his knife out from his backpack. It was time to polish his art and display it to the world.

Chapter - 27

Rudransh Ray rolled his head for the fourth time to make himself a little comfortable in the tiny steel chair. He sat facing Nishant who sat slumped in another steel chair and cracked his knuckles in every five seconds. Siddhanth stood leaning against the door frame. Akash chose to stay away from the drama. Ray's mind kept travelling back to the images The Ripper had sent Shraddha at exactly 3am that morning. If he had been as cold as he pretended to be, he would not have sat here thinking about the pregnant woman and her unborn child. To chase away the images, he rubbed his eyes.

A couple of minutes later, Chetan Bajaj joined them. The old man looked ancient to Ray, with unshaven face, and dark circles enveloping the eyes. 'We need to get this bastard,' said Chetan after taking his seat. 'He cannot go on killing people like this.'

Ray drew a deep breath as the HD images formed in his mind again. This time the killer had gone out of his way to take pictures of the dead woman from every single angle. Like Samir Shrivastav case, this time too, the dead body had gone through the killer's knife. The viciousness of the act clawed at Ray's heart. His hand itched to grab the neck of the asshole and snap it.

'This is Raghav Sinha's wife, right?' asked Nishant. He raised his eyes to gaze at Ray.

Ray nodded. 'Oliva Sinha.' He remembered Shraddha's face when she handed over the phone to him. She had kept blaming herself for the death of her best friend. Once again, everyone got down to the Rudransh Ray should have known game. Yes, he should have known that the killer would go after Samir's mother. He should have known that the man would travel to Delhi to kill Raghav Sinha's wife. He should have given up profiling killers and started psychic mind reading. A curse formed in his mind, then it vanished as he remembered Ashutosh.

'We must protect Ashutosh Khemka at any cost,' said Ray. Nishant and Chetan both looked at him questioningly. 'He came to me,' said Ray. 'He is having dreams in which he is seeing a man with a crutch getting killed with a cricket bat. The killer rips the dead body apart after the murder.'

Chetan stared at Ray for a whole one minute before asking. 'And when were you planning to tell us this?'

Ray took a deep breath and let it pass. He had assigned Nilesh and Chirag to track Ashutosh's whereabouts on the night of Samir Shrivastav's murder. But they had not presented any report yet. But Ray expected to get something as the day matured.

'We must keep an eye on Ashutosh,' said Nishant after a long moment of awkward silence. 'I think the unsub will go after Ashutosh now.'

Ray looked at his watch. It was 2 in the morning. His eyes burned from being awake two nights straight. The team which went to Delhi to assist Oliva Sinha's murder investigation had not come up with anything. Chetan had asked Ray to take Sid and Nishant and go to Delhi. But they all refused to go, saying that the killer would come back to Kolkata.

'If he does not go after Ishant Mullick first,' Siddhant said. He had been strangely quiet. The meeting with Natasha Mishra had shaken Sid like the way it had traumatized Ray.

'We cannot be responsible for Ishant Mullick,' protested Chetan. 'We have done our best to find him.'

Ray fidgeted in his chair, creating some irritating screeching sound. His back hurt from sitting on the same chair since early evening. His stomach growled, demanding food. 'No point in sitting here banging our heads,' Ray got up to his feet. 'I have handed over everything to you.' He looked at Nishant. 'You can speak to Ashutosh and his shrink.' Tired and desperate to go home, he thought of his quiet living room. Lack of sleep and rest had weakened him. To think straight he needed a couple of hours of sleep. 'I need to crash for a while.'

Chetan looked at Sid. 'What?'

Sid gave a nonchalant shrug. 'He needs to sleep.'

'Can't he speak English?' asked Chetan.

Again Sid gave a smooth shrug in reply. 'We will be available on phone. But officially you will be leading the case as per the instruction. So, we cannot be seen with you Nishant.'

Nishant's handsome face broke into a smile. 'Since when had that stopped you two from assisting anyone?' he asked. In the past, Nishant had been the ardent enemy Ray and Sid had in the department. Every case had been a struggle because Nishant made sure to create some obstacles. But now it seemed age and time had lulled the passion. The current Nishant had turned into a mellow shadow of his former self.

'True,' Ray agreed. 'It has never stopped us. But the current situation is sensitive. Death of a pregnant woman will hit everyone hard.' He paused, seeing Oliva's last photos in his mind. 'And the manner in which she had died…' He let the rest of the sentence hang in the air. 'I think you should speak to Ashutosh immediately.'

A commotion down the hall made them look at the door. Vivan rushed inside. His face looked white, and patchy. Fear and discomfort had masked his expression. He looked at Chetan, and then at Ray, and then said to Sid. 'He has released the photos on social media.'

Ray exhaled. He had been fearing this. 'Which platform?'

'All of them,' Vivan said. 'Under the name of The Ripper.'

'Fuck,' said Sid. He pulled his phone out of his pocket to check the latest damage.

Chatan dropped on an empty chair. His shoulders slumped as he buried his face into his hands. Nishant shifted his weight from one leg to another, not knowing what to do. Then said in a voice which sounded chocked. 'We must go and see Ashutosh the first thing in the morning.'

'Place a security guard at Ashutosh's door steps,' said Chetan. 'In plant clothe.'

After that they all moved together. No one knew where they should go to stop the mayhem which had suddenly taken them all by storm. Before Ray even reached his car, his phone vibrated. He cursed, anticipating some bad news. He halted in his track as he opened the message box. Ten images had appeared with a smiling emoji. Whoever had snapped those images had captured Ishant from every angle, dead, cold, and ripped apart.

It was half past 4 in the morning when Ray and Siddhant finally extracted themselves from the police station. Nishant stayed by to handle the media and the frenzy of people who had come to protest. Their collective voices echoed in the silence of night. Ray pushed his hands inside the pockets of his woolen hoodie. For the first time in five years, his hands had turned cold. Twice he flexed his fingers to savor the sense of being alive.

'You want to check on with Shraddha?' asked Siddhant.

Ray shook his head. 'There is nothing I can do for her,' he said. 'Oliva is dead. She had been killed in the most vicious manner. My agitated presence will not help her.' He paused to look at Sid through the rear view mirror. 'Besides, Trisha is there to console her.' Trisha had cancelled her flight and stayed with Shraddha. Not going meant not getting the dream job. Yet, Trisha appeared perfectly fine with the missed chance. She did not appear to be the least bit sad at not being able to go to Paris.

Siddhant said nothing to this. He looked out of the window at the deserted street of Kolkata. Usually, the city buzzed with life all the time. But the winter dawn had robbed Kolkata its usual zeal. Nothing stirred anywhere. They could not even detect a single stray dog while returning home.

'Drop me at my place,' said Siddhant. He looked shaken, pale, and ready to run away. Ray suspected that he matched Sid's appearance. Without speaking anything, he put the car on motion and headed for Netaji Nagar where Siddhant lived in a three bedroom apartment inside a housing society.

The dawning sky reflected the first tinge of the sun light when Ray dropped Sid at the entrance of his housing society. While driving home, he kept a watchful eye on the street but his mind whirled around calculating. The Ripper would be back to Kolkata looking for Ashutosh. If he caught a train, which was most likely, it would take him at least two days to reach Kolkata. If he came by the road, it would be longer than that. He needed to make a move and fast. The problem lied in the anonymity. Lack of motive could be dangerous. Here Ray failed to detect any motive to go on a killing spree like this. Why suddenly? What had triggered this frenzy?

He did not return home. In his state of mind, sleep was the last thing which would greet him back there. So, he continued to drive around the city, looking at the streets which he had grown to love. There was something about Kolkata, something in its soil, something in the air which kept him chained here. Even though he left after Rusha's death, he had to come back. When the sky cleared and the wind started to turn crispy, he pulled at the side of the road. In his trance, he had driven to Salt Lake Sector Three. A lone tea stall came to view. A dim light hung from the wooden roof of the stall. An old man was washing the utensils, getting ready for the day. Ray approached him with the hope of getting something to eat.

Scalding tea and egg toast were all he got in the wee hour. But it seemed like the tastiest food Ray had ever had. While he devoured his food, he made a call to Nilesh who was a self-proclaimed insomniac. He did not only stay up the night, he made sure to call everyone after midnight to prove that he was in fact an insomniac who failed to sleep. So, Ray never failed guilty calling Nilesh up at odd hours.

'Yes boss,' Nilesh's high energetic voice boomed. 'I cracked Ashutosh's phone location. It was switched on till 11pm on the night of Samir's murder. His was around New Alipore at 11pm. But after that there is no trace.'

Ray expected something like this. 'Anything else?'

'I ran a thorough check on Ashutosh,' said Nilesh. Ray heard the sound of papers being shuffled in the background. Nilesh was a by the book type of hacker. He made notes of everything he did. This habit worried Ray sometimes. 'He has three bank accounts, each one runs on a low balance. None is above 30 thousand which is pretty unusual given the fact that Ashutosh leads such a high lifestyle. He goes to Park Street to booze every day. He has membership of three posh clubs. He spends around 50 thousand every month for shopping.'

Ray took the information with his usual nonchalant manner. 'How does he pay his bills there?'

Nilesh chuckled at the question. 'He pays cash.'

'Thought so,' said Ray. 'Can you link Ashutosh to Samir or Raghav?'

'No,' said Nilesh. 'I ran all the sources. But technically these three have never met.'

'Who does he hang out with?' asked Ray.

'He usually hangs out with his childhood friend named Hemant Saxena,' said Nilesh. 'And there is another guy from his school Rahul Khatri. Ashutosh, Hemant, and Rahul are closest friends.'

'Ok,' Ray said, motioning the tea seller to prepare another round for him. 'What do you have on Hemant and Rahul?'

A series of shuffle of paper later, Nilesh spoke. 'Hemant runs a pottery store. He sells handmade potteries. Rahul is also a self-employed man. Works as tax consultant for small businesses.'

'Any girlfriend?' Ray pressed for more information.

'Ashutosh is in a on and off relationship with a girl called Poonam Doshi. Hemant is single. Rahul is on the verge of divorce. His wife Shalini Acharya suspects that Rahul is layering some property so she could not get her hands on them.'

A deep breath came out of Ray mouth. 'Ok, so what is she doing about it?' he asked.

Nilesh again chuckled. 'She has hired a PI to investigate him.'

'A PI?' asked Ray. For the first time since discovering Samir's torn apart body, Ray felt a little relieved. He sucked a much needed long breath and then said. 'Forward me the contact details of the PI.'

Chapter – 28

The call came when Ray was parking his car inside his residential building at Southern Avenue. It was Nishant who called to break the news that Ashutosh was missing since the last night. He walked out of his house and did not come back. Before Ray could get into his car, he got another call. The police officer who survived the hit and run accident, had finally succumbed to his injuries. A heartbroken Chirag lamented that now he would have to chase ambulance. Ray disconnected the call before Chirag could continue with his super irritating mourning.

He drove straight to the police station. Siddhant was already there, sitting with Nishant and sipping coffee. They looked at Ray with a bemused expression. 'How does The Ripper know that Ashutosh has contacted you?' Nishant asked.

Ray had the same question in his mind. 'I think Ashutosh himself has told him. We need to speak to his friends Hemant and Rahul.'

Sid let out a long breath before speaking. 'None is in the town right now,' he said. 'Rahul and Hemant both are in Mumbai for some professional work.'

Ray looked up at the ceiling. 'Let's speak to the great Arman Khemka then.'

Sid rolled his shoulders. 'Looking forward to it.' His sarcastic tone made the other two laugh despite the situation.

Outside Nishant's cabin, someone was watching a live news. A well groomed news anchor was screaming about injustice. Her heavily painted face looked like a mask. She spoke about human rights and it was getting violated by a man who was still uncaptured by the cops. She declared that Rudransh Ray who had been under treatment for chronic depression was the root cause of the entire problem. It was Rudransh Ray who had failed to find the killer and protect the victims.

Ray listened to the news while Vivan made a call to Arman Khemka to make an appointment. Every time something went wrong, people dragged his past out and made him look like a lunatic. It was time media and those who watched it changed their perception about mental health. Everyone who undergoes mental treatment is not crazy.

'Let's get going,' Nishant said after Vivan made the call to tell Arman Khemka that a team of law enforcement officers were going to meet him.

Ray shook his head. 'It is time we divide our force. You two go and meet Arman Khemka. I have someone else to pay a quick visit to.'

'Who?' asked Siddhant.

'A PI.'

Ekakshay Goswami operated from a two story building located near Kalikapore crossing. when Ray parked his car in front of the freshly painted house, it was 6.30 am in the morning. Akash was yawning like a man whose life depended on yawning.

'Will you stop that?' asked Ray.

'I can't,' said Akash.

Ray chuckled. 'It's cannot my friend. Cunt is a very bad word.'

Akash made a face at him. 'If you have not noticed, it is 6.30 am in the morning. Not office time.'

Ray looked around the empty street. 'He lives in the first floor.'

Akash looked up at the house. The owner had chosen to paint the exterior light yellow which looked both warm and pleasant. The sturdy two story house was at least one hundred years old. But due to proper maintenance it still looked dignified enough to be called beautiful. A long hanging balcony enveloped the front side of the upstairs unit. Just below the balcony was a small porch which led to the front door where lay sleeping a large street dog.

Ray walked up to the door ignoring the sleeping animal. He rang the doorbell and waited for someone to come and greet them. Five minutes later when no one answered, he rang the bell again. This time, they heard a faint sound of movement upstairs. Someone pushed a heavy furniture. Ray rang the bell before this someone went back to sleep.

'Who is it?' asked a clam male voice.

'Police,' Ray said even though that was the last thing he was. Sound of heavy footsteps resonated at the opposite side of the door. A moment later, the door cracked open and a tall, well-muscled young man appeared wearing only a thin cotton hoodie and a pair of black jeans. His alert eyes scanned Ray from top to bottom and then moved towards Akash.. After the once over Ekakshay Goswami relaxed. He pulled his hands which he kept buried inside the pocket of his jeans out.

'Rudransh Ray and Akash Bajaj,' he said with a flash of smile which showed a dimple on his left cheek. 'Please come in.'

Ray had been used to such greetings. It did not surprise him. They walked inside to find a modern setting. The interior of the house was also painted pale yellow. Lemon curtains hung from the windows. The fusion was so vibrating that it made Ray relax a little.

'Please have a seat,' said Ekakshay. 'I am getting coffee and cookies.'

'Please don't trouble yourself,' Ray said.

Ekakshay smiled, a lock of caramel brown curls fell on his fair forehead. It had an electrifying effect. 'I was about to make coffee for myself. If you refuse, I will not be able to have coffee today.'

'Really?' asked Ray. 'Why?'

'I don't drink coffee after 7 in the morning,' Ekakshay said.

'Why?' asked Akash. 'Coffee after 7 unleashes cruel monsters upon you or what?'

'It sabotages my metabolism.'

Before Akash could say anything else, Ray hurriedly said, 'Please bring the coffee.'

After settling with coffee, Ray said, 'We are here to talk about Rahul Khetri case.'

Ekakshay stiffened. 'What about Rahul Khetri?' he asked.

'To be precise, I am more interested in Ashutosh, Rahul's friend.'

Ekakshay's shoulders softened. 'Ashutosh is a spoilt brat. Lives to booze and take drugs.'

'Ok,' said Ray. 'Have you come across any link between Rahul and Samir Shrivastav?'

It made Ekakshay look at Ray sharply. 'Samir Shrivastav, the guy who got ripped apart?'

'The same,' said Ray.

'Not Rahul,' said Ekakshay. 'He does what he claims to do. The same goes for Hemant. He does run a pottery shop. You will find it at Gariahat more. Organic Pottery.'

'So, if not Rahul and Hemant, then can you link Ashutosh to Samir?'

Ekakshay let out a breath. He straightened his spine and then relaxed it again. After doing this twice, he finally decided to speak his mind. 'Well, the fact is,' he said. 'The rumor of the market is Samir Shrivastav used to run a porn business. One of Ashutosh's ex-girlfriends claimed to be drugged and raped in a Rajarhat apartment. She said that someone shot the entire event.'

Ray rolled his neck twice. 'This girl did not press any charges?'

'She threatened to press charge despite the availability of the video,' said Ekakshay. 'But then she disappeared.'

'How do you know all these?' Ray asked. Ekakshay shrugged. 'While investigating Rahul, I also did a quick checking on his friends. You never know who is hiding what asset.'

'True,' said Ray. 'So, when did this happen?'

'Last year,' said Ekakshay. 'The girl was an aspiring model.'

'Ashutosh is missing since last night,' Ray said finally.

Ekakshay shrugged. 'You might find him in a bar at Park Street if it is open. Otherwise, you may find him lying at the doorstep of the bar.'

'That bad?' Akash asked.

'Worse,' said Ekakshay. 'If Ashutosh is missing, you should speak to his friends. But none is in the town right now. I heard Rahul is coming back this evening. So, is Hemant.'

'And how you know this, may I ask?' asked Ray.

Ekakshay shrugged again. 'They both have called Arman Khemka to tell him that they are coming back to provide support.'

'Great,' Ray said. He placed his coffee mug on the table and got up to his feet. 'By any chance you have their train timing and seat numbers?' he asked.

Rahul was a huge man, getting heavier in the middle. He was also losing hair. But Hemant looked like he took care of himself. He was tightly built and had a slender body type which accentuated the fact that he was very tall. They both were surprised when Ray and his team greeted them at the Howrah station. After picking up the two friends in two police cars, Ray brought them to the station for questioning. They started with Hemant and left Rahul to sweat in a tinny chamber.

'Ashutosh is like a child,' Hemant said. 'He will never agree with you no matter what.'

'Do you know about the girl who accused Ashutosh of drugging her and shooting her porn videos?' asked Ray

Hemant was quiet. 'She,' he paused a moment. 'She wanted money from Ashutosh. Initially Ashu gave her the money she asked for. Then he refused to entertain her.'

'Okay,' Ray said. 'Then what happened?'

'She went to his home and accused him of drugging her and then taking her to an empty flat and then shooting her porn videos,' said Hemant. 'But that's not true. Ashu loved her. He wanted to have a future with her.'

Ray tilted his head. 'So, what Ashu did when she disappeared?'

'According to her mother, she ran off with a rich guy,' said Hemant. 'It shattered Ashu.'

Ray nodded. 'We tried to find this girl but found no trace of her,' Ray said.

Hemant shrugged. 'I hang out with Ashutosh and Rahul weekly at Park Street bars. But most of the times I remain busy with my shop and pottery manufacturing. I don't know much about Ashu's ex's personal life.'

'Do you know a guy named Samir Shrivastav?' Ray asked.

'I read about him in the newspaper,' Hemant said after a pause. 'Personally, no I don't know him.'

'What were you doing in Mumbai?' Siddhant asked.

'I went there on a business meeting,' said Hemant. 'One of my dealers live in Mumbai. I go there frequently.'

'Which dealer?' asked Siddhant.

'Pots & Glasses,' said Hemant. 'We are trying to manufacture some unique potteries.'

Sid pushed his notepad towards Hemant. 'Please write down the contact details of your dealer.'

Hemant jotted down the number quickly in neat handwriting. Once he was done, he handed the notepad over to Siddhant. 'Anything else?' he asked.

Sid looked at Ray who shook his head. Nishant got up to his feet. 'Please don't leave the town. You may have to visit us again.'

Hemant nodded good naturedly. 'I am glad to help you.' With that he left the crammed chamber which smelt of old paper and dust. Ray had spent countless hours in this chamber with Sid, trying to solve murders. But today the smell seemed a little too suffocating. Ray found it difficult to breath. Too much field work, he mused. A need to breath in outside air increased with time. But the ordeal was far from being over. A tired and angry looking Rahul walked in. He was on his phone and insisted on getting a lawyer before speaking to any of them.

Ray shrugged. 'Be lawyered up,' he told Rahul. 'Let his lawyer come down.' He looked at Sid who took the hint stood up. 'We will be outside. Give us a call.'

Outside the station, darkness had already thickened. But to Ray's relief the sky remained clean, stars shone like jewels, the wind smelt crisp. But there was no sign of rain clouds. 'What do you think?' asked Sid. 'It seems we are standing at the breaking point.'

Ray took a long drag from his cigarette. 'Yes. We are,' he said. 'Have you ever seen a hunter getting trapped in his own net?'

A smile played on Sid's face. 'Countless times.'

'The hunter will be hunted soon,' said Ray.

Rahul's lawyer appeared an hour later. Ray was sharing a meal box with Sid and Nishant, all being hungry. The lawyer slid out of a sleek black Audi, wearing a sleek black Armani suit. His violet silk tie looked to be brand new, just like his leather polished shoes. He looked around to seize the area in just one glance. Then his eyes came to rest on Ray. A smile played on the man's face.

'Rudransh Ray,' he said. 'Why I am not surprised?'

Ray shrugged, returning the smile. 'Probably because you already knew that you would find me here.'

Manav Trivedi, the most famous criminal lawyer of the nation, came towards Ray with extended hands. This was a man who believed in giving firm handshakes with both of his hands. Ray accepted the extended hands with a forced enthusiasm. He did not like criminal lawyers, he never did, and the feeling of distrust and dislike remained.

'So, what's new?' he asked Manav Trivedi.

'Rahul Khetri is my client,' he said. 'Who you have detained.'

Ray raised his brows in amusement. He threw a glance over his shoulder where Nishant and Siddhant stood smoking. They did not make any attempt to make pleasantries with the lawyer. 'We have not detained him exactly,' Ray said finally when the silence threatened to stretch for long. 'We have brought him here for questioning.'

Manav shook his head. 'That's not what Rahul says.'

To this Ray offered a silent shrug. He had no control over Rahul's opinion. 'We are looking for Ashutosh Khemka. I believe you know that he is missing.'

Manav nodded. 'I have represented him.'

Ray knew that Ashutosh's father Arman Khemka had hired Manav Trivedi to defend his son in the hit and run case. He decided to keep mum about the matter and resorted to give a small nod of his head to settle it. 'So, can we have a discussion with your client?' he asked.

Manav leaned forward and lowered his voice as if he was speaking to a close friend. 'Rahul is a little unsettled. He makes a fuss about everything.'

Again Ray decided to give a nod. He had no idea about Rahul and had no intention of poking deeper than it was required. His sole attention was fixed on The Ripper. The sooner they close the case, the better it was for everyone. Before they could proceed a flushed faced police officer in his late twenties came running. 'Ashutosh came home.' Ray straightened. From the corner of his eyes, he could see Sid and Nishant stiffening. Manav's face relaxed at the news. And they all crowded around the office. 'His father called to say that Ashutosh just walked back home.'

'Where was he?' asked Nishant.

The officer had no idea. He gave a swift shrug of his shoulders. 'The Chief asked me to give you the news.' He looked back at the police station. Then looked at Ray. 'He also asked you to let those two go.'

Ray looked at Manav with a sly grin. 'I am not holding them. They are free to go.'

Manav nodded, happily. 'Yeah, you were in a chatty mood.' He grinned back. 'I get it.'

'Cool,' said Ray. 'Now, we have to go and meet Ashutosh.'

Ashutosh had no idea where he had been. He looked at Ray with eyes which said he remembered nothing, not even his early morning visit to Ray's house. 'I don't know where I had been. I don't remember.' He appeared to be genuinely upset about the fact.

The meeting took place in Arman Khemka's massive living room. The walls of the room were painted milky white. A crystal chandelier hung low from the ceiling. Red velvety couch sets augmented the brightness of the room. The room could accommodate at least sixty people.

Arman Khemka, tall, a little bulky yet fit for his age, and stern looking, sat in a single couch watching over his son like a mother cat. His blank face revealed nothing. Ray did not find a tinge of guilt for forcing an innocent man to take the blame for his son's crime. Khemka kept looking at his watch as if Ray and his team were wasting his time. Probably they were, Ray decided and relished it.

'Do you remember going out?' asked Ray. 'Do you remember where you were going?'

Ashutosh looked down at his hand. He took a couple of deep breaths. Then he looked up and met Ray's eyes. 'No, I don't remember anything.' He shook his head, looking miserable.

Ray had a sudden suspicion. 'Do you remember anything Ashutosh? Your name? Your past life? Yesterday?'

Again the same lost expression appeared and this time Ashutosh's eyes watered. He lowered his head and gave a quick shake. No, he did not remember anything.

Ray understood they were wasting time here. Other matters need his attention. So, he straightened and got up to his feet. 'Thanks Ashutosh,' he said. 'We will be in touch.' Then he turned his gaze towards Arman. 'Mr. Khemka, I believe you understand that your son is a valuable asset in this case. So, please make sure that he remains home and does not leave unescorted.' Before Arman Khemka had a chance to say anything, he went on. 'I will have an officer guarding your house.' He paused, flashed a smile at Khemka and added. 'In plain cloth.'

Arman Khemka's jaw tightened then relaxed. He gave a short, forced nod and then disappeared from the room, leaving Ashutosh alone with them. 'Don't worry Ashutosh. We all are here to protect you,' Ray said, and drag you to prison if we can connect you to the murders, this he kept to himself.

They walked out in the street to be greeted by frosty air. Ray was getting used to the chills. He wished it lasted forever. But Kolkata did not like winter. Soon the city would sizzle, and people would sweat, and sodas would fly off the stores like hot cakes. Cakes did not fly off the store in Kolkata though, Ray corrected himself.

Nishant drove off to the station. Ray turned his car and headed towards Lake Gardens more. Sid leaned back in the seat and kept quiet. After a minute, he asked, 'May I know where we are going?'

'We are going to have mishti doi and baked rosogolla,' Ray said. 'I need some calories to build muscles.'

Sid let out a deep breath. 'Calories from mishti doi and baked rosogolla don't build muscles.'

'Says who?' Ray asked increasing speed.

Chapter - 29

A slender man in a black hoodie and a pair of black jeans sat crouched in the darkest corner of the spacious living room. His fingers were curled around a long blade which he carried everywhere. His pocket was heavy with a loaded pistol, secured with a silencer, ready to go at a moment's notice. Even though he had been advised to shoot and run, he preferred blades. It gave him immense pleasure to cut open a throat and then watch blood flow free. He warmed to the idea of slitting open the throat of The Ripper. He heaved a deep breath to allow his racing heart to calm down a little, then he moved his hips to get comfortable. The worst thing would be to get a cramp when his prey came within a stabbing distance. Silence echoed from outside. Not even a single car moved anywhere.

This part of the city was known for its deserted streets. In winter evenings, they turn doomlike. He preferred that. Any hired gun would prefer that. A slight movement outside made his sit straight. Blood rushed inside his head, making him both alert and itchy. A key slid into the keyhole and then he heart a click. It was time for the slaughter. The hunter was about to go down.

The Ripper walked inside his two story house. His head swamped with thoughts and ideas. He feared that the damn Ashutosh would spill the bin. But if he did, everyone would go down. A quick roll of his neck released the tension he had been holding. Then he closed the door behind him and instantly stopped. His living room had a different air. The vibe spoke of another presence. Someone was inside his home, he knew it like the way he knew that he breathed. Who could do it? He wondered. Who could send a hired gun after him? Who?

He lingered by the door, pretending to look for something important in his pocket. As long as he faced the living room, the intruder would not launch an attack. So, he had two options, one was to look for the intruder and kill the asshole. But it was his home, he could not just kill someone and then hide the body with ease. Even if he attempted to move the body, someone was bound to see him on the act. Therefore, he resorted to another option. He took a step back, unlocked his front door and slid out without taking his eyes off the living room. Better to run right now, than to call trouble upon himself and draw attention of the cops. He had been betrayed, he fumed at the thought of almost getting killed in his own house. In his rage, he pulled out his phone and dialed a number. After a couple of rings a voice answered.

'Your hired hand is still waiting for me inside my home?' said The Ripper without waiting for the person on the other side to answer.

'Don't be foolish.' Came the instant reply. 'Why should I send someone to kill you? Already a lot of damages have taken place. Why did you rip Samir apart? Why did you have to kill Ishant and those two old women and that pregnant woman?' The speaker paused. 'Do you even know what will happen now?' Spat the speaker.

The Ripper chuckled. 'So, you sent a hired gun to kill me,' he spat back. 'As for the murders, I don't give a fuck. People will know me. Everyone will know me.' He shouted. The empty street trembled as his voice rose. He looked at the sky and laughed at the emptiness. His home where he lived for the last ten years, now stood in utter darkness. He knew that he could not go back there. His own people had turned against him. They would kill him when they found him, he had no doubt about that. Then his mind stopped racing. Everyone was going to die someday. Everyone would cease to non-existence. Before he died, he would snatch what was his to claim.

Fame. He would make his name. He would leave his print in the history. Despite his trance, he noticed an yellow taxi. He hailed it and got inside, maneuvering his backpack behind him.

'Hazra Road,' he told the driver. 'Fast.' Just one more kill and then he would be gone forever, disappear like Jack The Ripper.

Chapter - 30

'You think Ashutosh has been drugged?' asked Sid.

Ray was driving in silence. 'I am sure he had been,' he said after a moment's consideration. 'His eyes spoke of being drugged. He does not know what he is saying or where he is.'

'Who do you think can do this?' asked Sid. 'It needs the expertise of a doctor to drug someone without killing them.'

Ray shrugged. He picked his phone and punched Akash's number. He briefed Akash while driving towards Shraddha's home. He needed to see her. Oliva's death must have hit her bad. He could not imagine what she had been through when she saw the images of Oliva's dead body. Even though he wanted to be there with her, his responsibility demanded him to be with his team. He did not even get a chance to call her once.

'Where should I drop you?' Ray asked.

Sid looked out the window and said nothing. He had not smoked a single cigarette in the last couple of hours. Ray smiled silently. Sid had always been a suffering soul, looking for a home stay. If Trisha could provide Sid the home he so longed for, no one would be happier than Ray.

Silently they drove. Kolkata smelt like it did in every winter, crisp, and burned. This smell dragged Ray back to his childhood days which he had spent in Rishop with his grandfather. His heart warmed as he thought of the old man, who had taught Ray to stand for the wronged one. He had not seen his grandfather for a long time. Probably the time had come for a quick visit after the pressing matter at hand finds its conclusion.

Shraddha was sitting in her living room couch wrapped in a thick blanket. Her head hung low over her chest. Thick mass of hair concealed her face. So, Ray could not guess her current mental state. Trisha sat in a single couch, also wrapped in a thick blanket. In her hand she held a thick paperback. A ceramic mug sat in front of her, condensing the air. She looked up when Ray walked in with Sid.

'I should change the lock,' she said jokingly when she saw the two friends.

Shraddha raised her head and looked at Ray. A hot mist of rage rose in Ray's heart at the sight of her face. It had paled completely. Her eyes had sunken in these few hours. She looked tired and fragile. Relief flooded over her face as she saw Ray. He smiled at her, assuring that everything would be fine soon, though he knew that nothing would be like before. She had already seen the darkness, and experienced its power. Now, nothing can be the same again. She had seen too much, experienced too much. He let out a deep breath. The murder of Lisa Brown had only scratched the surface. The Ripper had not only ripped his victims apart. He had done a lot more damage than that.

'How are you doing?' Ray asked. From the corner of his eyes he saw Trisha getting up from the couch and moving out of the room with Sid behind her. Immediately after that he heard utensils being moved in the kitchen.

'I don't know,' she said with a sad expression. 'I told Oliva over and over again to go to her parents' place.' She looked down. 'Why did he do it? Why did he kill Oliva?' A sob escaped and she heaved the words out. 'She did not know anything.'

Ray stood rooted to the ground. He had no answer to this question. Fame, the bastard was chasing fame. He wanted to be famous and for that he could do anything. But it was not the right time to talk about this. So, he went over to where she sat and dropped beside her. Gently he took her hand in his and squeezed.

'I am sorry,' he said, not knowing why he was saying sorry to her, not knowing how that would alter the situation. He only knew that he would have to say something to ease her pain. Something which will work as a balm to the wounds which had her captivated. Shraddha's shoulders shook a little. A lone drop of tear slid out of her right eye. Ray wiped it with his thumb. He squeezed her hand again, cursing himself for giving her the photos of Samir's dead body. He should not have done it, he know that now. If he could go back, he would alter that moment. But it had been done. He could do nothing to change it. He could only work hard to catch the killer and put an end to the whole thing.

His phone vibrated. With a sigh and a silent curse, he fished out the device. It was Ekakshay. Ray had an instant liking for the young PI. The young man seemed to be on a mission. A mission to save the world, Ray smiled a sad silent smile. Soon Ekakshay would discover that things were not as rosy as it seemed from outside and frequently people destroyed themselves trying to save the world.

'Ekakshay,' greeted Ray.

'Please, call me Eka,' came the polite request.

'Eka?' asked Ray.

'Yes, Eka,' said Ekakshay.

'Eka as in Lord Shiva?'

Ekakshay chuckled. 'The one and only,' he said. 'Glad to know that you know.'

Ray was pulled back in time just that moment. A sweet face formed in his mind. The face smiled at him causing him to draw a deep breath to keep control of his emotion. 'My late wife was a Shiva devotee.'

'Oh,' said Ekakshay. 'Rusha?' he asked.

'You know?' Ray asked, surprised that Ekakshay knew so much about his life.

'Yes, I do,' said Ekakshay. 'I read your book and then read about you on Internet.'

'My book,' Ray said. He reached out to touch Shraddha's nose with his fingertips. It had turned cold and red. 'I wrote it a long time ago.'

Ekakshay chuckled again. 'But the one you wrote is a masterpiece,' he said. 'Mr. Ray, I called to tell you something.' He paused. 'Might not be important. But I think you should know about it.'

'Nothing is unimportant in a murder case,' said Ray. 'So, tell me.'

Ekakshay paused for moment then spoke. 'The Ripper, the one who has killed Samir knows about human anatomy, right?'

Ray pushed himself up on his feet, feeling adrenaline rushing in his guts. 'Yes.'

'So, it can be someone who has seen or got trained under a professional physician, right?'

'Right,' Ray said.

'Hemant's father, grandfather, and great grandfather were all medical practitioners,' said Ekakshay. 'Surgeon. Hemant's father had been dismissed from his duty because he used to perform surgeries without any valid reason.'

Ray closed his eyes and summoned Hemant's face in his mind. The young man had vulture's eyes. He could kill people. He could rip them apart, after that. Ray exhaled. 'Go on,' he said.

'A close source, a nurse said that Heman's father Dr. Jatin Saxena was passionate about operating people. It was as if he loved to cut people open.' Ekakshay stopped for a breath after this.

Ray rolled his head. 'What made you look for this information?' he asked finally.

'Rahul's wife suspects that Hemant is hiding Rahul's assets. She has asked me to look Hemant up,' said Ekakshay.

'What can you find out about Hemant's mother?' asked Ray.

'She died of some unknown disease,' came the reply. 'Not much is known about her.'

Ray let out a breath. 'Great,' he said. 'Thanks for the tip. I will get back as soon as I verify the information. Good job.' He added after a beat.

'Pleased to be helpful,' said Ekakshay.

Ray met Shraddha's questioning eyes. But he did not have time to answer her questions. He turned and rushed towards the kitchen. He could hear Sid speaking to Trisha in a low voice.

'Sid, we gotta get going,' he said coming to stand at the threshold of the kitchen where he had kissed Shraddha not so long ago. The memory bloomed in his mind like an explosive and made him heave a deep breath. With force, he pushed it away. Not now, he cursed himself.

Sid sat on the kitchen marble kitchen top, looking calm and at peace. Trisha had a bowl in her hand, in which she mixed something using a stainless steel spoon.

They both looked at Ray as he spoke. Sid got off the tabletop with a frown. 'Anything wrong?' he asked.

Ray nodded, 'Ekakshay called. He says Hemant's father and grandfather were surgeons.'

Sid raised his brows. 'So?'

Ray made a face. 'So, nothing we gotta go now.' He turned and started to walk towards the front door when Shraddha held his hand.

'Be careful out there,' she said. 'This man is not in his right mind.'

Ray shook his head. 'Wrong this man is too much in his right mind.' He let out a deep breath. 'That's why he is dangerous.'

Ray zoomed past a blinking yellow light narrowly missing a speeding auto. In his rear view mirror, he saw the traffic police to jot down his car number. Ray detested rash driving. But unfortunately he always ended up driving his car like he flew it.

'So, his father and grandfather both were surgeon,' said Sid for the tenth times. 'That does not make Hemant a serial killer, does it?'

'No,' said Ray. 'Fiona is looking into his files. She will come up with something, I am sure.'

'So, why are we going to his place?' asked Siddhant. 'What makes you think he has killed all these people?'

Ray calculated his words then thought fuck with it. 'This guy has a strange attitude. I expected him to freak out like Rahul when we picked him up from the railway station. But he did not even flinch. This shows that either he is too composed or his brain does not work like the normal human beings. Usually psychopaths are composed and you know that.' Ray stopped to take a sharp left turn to enter a narrow lane. 'But I did not react based on that because being composed does not turn anyone into a criminal. But when Ekakshay told me about his family, I thought it will be worth taking a look at.'

Fiona called just before they reached Hemant's Baruipur house. He lived in a two story stand alone. It had a touch of melancholy which made it discomforting to look at. It stood dark and lonely among a row of houses equally dark and lonely. The area was deserted with mostly empty houses and streets.

'So, what did you find?' asked Ray.

'Jatin Saxena was a famous surgeon, just like his father Mahesh Saxena,' she said. 'But they both had a shady past. Mahesh had been accused of operating and deliberately killing people several times. Jatin also had a similar reputation.' Fiona's voice trailed in the end. She cleared her throat and began speaking again. 'Jatin had a promising career but he had been fired from his job when he operated a patient who did not need operation. The patient died. His family threatened to press charge. But the hospital authority suppressed the matter by compensating them heavily. After that they fired Jatin and there ended his medical career.'

'Does he live?' asked Ray.

'Yes, according to a digital news channel, Jatin lives in a private mental hospital at Hazra Road,' said Fiona. 'Apparently, he has been living there for quite some time.'

Ray listened to the story while walking around Hemant's neighborhood. It was a quiet locality which reflected middle class life style. Houses even though well maintained had a withered look. Hemant's house was similar to the other houses. But it had a polished look which the other lacked.

'What do you know about Hemant's mother?' asked Ray.

'Nothing much,' said Fiona. 'She died of some unknown cause after Jatin got fired.' Fiona paused to consult some notes. 'People close to her claimed that she had been murdered but no one could prove anything.'

'Is there is distant relative?' asked Ray.

'An aunt lives in Bardhwan,' said Fiona. 'If you want I can try to speak to her.'

'Fix an appointment, I want to speak to her,' said Ray. 'Also, tell her to be careful. Hemant, if he is the one, might be out of his sanity line right now.' He thought for a moment then added. 'Call Nishant and tell him to send someone to check on Hemant's father.'

'On to it boss,' said Fiona before disconnecting the call.

'Can we get inside?' asked Ray.

Sid had been hovering by the front door which was tightly locked. He tested the door twice. 'We can always get inside, you know that.'

Ray gave a smooth shrug. 'Then what are we waiting for?'

It took them less than two minutes to get inside. No one even noticed two able bodied male entering the house. They padded their way through a wide living room, furnished by wooden chairs, a wide dining table, and a cream colored couch set. Ray stopped short as his eyes fell on a wall. It was adorned with knives and daggers of different shapes and sizes.

'I think he manufactures all these,' said Ray, eyeing the sharpness of the stainless steel blades. Dark red stains glared from one of them, recently used. 'We should send this to the lab for blood analysis.'

'We are not authorized to search this house,' Sid said. 'I believe you know that.'

Ray grinned at his best friend. 'I sure do.' He pulled out a handkerchief from his pocket and using it plucked the knife with red stains. 'I am sending it to my special lab.'

'Knowing would not help us put him behind the bars,' Sid said.

Ray looked at his friend, astonished. 'You think he will go behind the bars?'

Sid shook his head, exhaling. 'Nah, I don't think so.' He paused to look at his best friend. 'I believe he will get a bullet between his eyes.'

Ray shrugged without looking even tiniest bit guilty about the whole scenario. He noticed a staircase leading down. 'Oh a basement,' he said. 'My favorite place to hunt for evidence.'

Chapter - 31

Hemant sneaked past a half asleep security guard at the front gate of a bruised building. From experience, he knew that no one took patrolling this mental hospital seriously. All the patients who lived there had long ago lost their minds and were too fucking old to make any serious harm. So, the hospital authority had placed an old asshole at the front gate to guard the dismal looking three story house. If anyone caught Hemant sneaking around, he would tell them how he had been missing his father. It would make a teary story, sad and attractive. He chuckled as he climbed a long winding staircase, made from wood.

The stairs creaked under his weight, making him wince. He wanted to make it fast and get it done with. This man had contributed without restrain in making him what he was today, he stalled on the stair for a moment, memories began to flood in his mind, making him a little dizzy. He clutched the iron railing to steady himself. Then he started to climb again. Jatin's large frame formed in Hemant's mind. He remembered the pride he felt each time his father walked home from work. He remembered the lessons his father had given him. He remembered the first time he had been taught to take a life.

The staircase led to a wide passage. Rows of rooms stood silently at one side. A long evolving balcony embraced the passage from the opposite. The building overlooked a narrow lane, lit by yellow street lamps which elevated its gloomy status. Hemant looked at the lane just once then he walked through the passage. His father lived at the furthest end in a wide room. He had not seen it eight years ago when he dragged his derailed father here for the first time. He could not bear the thought of his hero being constrained in a mental hospital. But Jatin needed treatment and Hemant had to bring his father despite his unwillingness to part with the old man.

Jatin Saxena was sitting by the only window of the room, staring outside. The old man's eyes had a lost and distant look which Hemant had seen many times before. He stood by the threshold of the room and watched his father. The memory he held of his father shattered in that moment. In place of the large robust man, sat a shrunken old one, with bent back, and defeated shoulders.

Hemant drew a deep breath, suddenly unsure of what to do. The blade he carried inside his sweatshirt seemed to be getting heavier with time. Because he could not get to his collection of knives because of the man hiding in his house, he had to buy a knife from a store which he disliked as he preferred to use his artwork when making his art.

Hemant closed his eyes and allowed a piece of memory to emerge from the depth his soul. It was the singular event which evoked something within him, something sinister enough to scare people away. He leaned his back against the shabby wall of the hospital room and went back to the day when he was only eight year old and worshipped his father like the way a fan worshipped their superhero.

It was a gloomy Sunday morning which promised a downpour as the day matured. Hemant's grandfather was busy in the basement making a dagger which he boasted about for months. Hemant's mother Abriti Saxena was in bed, recovering from a beating and a harsh all night expedition which kept her screaming till the dawn broke free.

Hemant had been out in the front yard of his home, playing with a cricket ball when his father called him inside.

'Hey boy,' Jatin called him. 'Come inside.' Jatin never addressed Hemant by his name. It was always *hey boy* when he was a child and the gradually that changed into *you sneaky ripper* as he grew up.

Hemant, eager to please his father, ran inside with his ball. 'Yes daddy,' he said.

'Let's go check what grandpa is doing,' his father said.

Hemant followed Jatin, excited at the notion of being able to see the interior of the basement where he was not allowed to enter. His grandfather, an enormous man in his sixties, was standing by a long wooden table with a dagger in his hand. The white light of the basement room fell on the edge of the blade, making it look both shiny and unnerving.

'Hey kiddo,' said the old man as Hemant entered. 'Come inside and see what I have made.' Pride and something else sparkled in the eyes of his grandfather. Hemant shuddered as he started into the pair of shiny gray eyes. 'What do you think of this?'

Before Hemant could answer, a painful moan made his look under the table. He saw a boy of his age or may a little younger tied to one of the wooden legs. The boy had a drowsy expression on his face. He tried to raise his head, but could not. Hemant remembered this boy. The child came asking for food the previous night. When he looked back at his grandfather, he saw the old man smiling at him.

'Today, you are going to get your first surgery tutorial,' said Jatin.

Surgery tutorial, exhaled Hemant. He closed his eyes, letting his head lean back against the wall, reliving the moment, savoring the smell of blood, experiencing – once again, the exhilaration of sliding a sharp blade through human flesh. Air turned heavy all of a sudden, and Hemant felt the need to smell blood. His dagger, the blades he had sharpened with care every night after coming home, were at his home. But he had a knife. He would have to satiate its thirst. His father dozed, leaning forward. The old man's head almost touched the iron railing of the window. At that moment, Jatin looked like the man who had taken Hemant down the basement that day. The same man who told Hemat with the indifference of a pallbearer, that his mother had died of heart attack. Hemant knew the truth though. He had heard his father beating his mother the previous night. He had remained awake in his bed and listened to the screams the poor woman made. Slowly as night matured, her voice lost its strength, and her screams turned into desperate moans. Then everything stopped, and a doom like silence echoed in the emptiness of his room. Hemant knew instantly that his mother had died and felt no remorse for the woman who had allowed herself to get tortured for so long. If anything, she had invited the treatment which his father had lavished upon her by staying back. Every night when her wails of misery kept him awake, he wished for her to run away, to disappear, to die – if nothing else worked.

'Dad,' Hemant called in a low voice. He rushed here in desperation to speak to his father. But now that they were in the same room, he had no idea what to tell him. Hemant, driven and misguided though he was, had no misconception about Rudransh Ray and the treatment the criminologist would shower upon him lest he got arrested. Ray had a reputation to be ruthless. When he was in the CID, he used to punch first ask question later. So, Hemant had just this moment. He needed to speak to his father, plead for understanding, fish for compliment, he had no idea what to say. 'Dad, I kept my knife sharp and my hands bloody, as you always told me to do.'

When the old man did not reply, neither did he turn or acknowledge Hemant's presence, he plodded inside the room, careful not to make even the slightest noise. 'I thought you would want to know that I have carried forward our family legacy and never wasted any opportunity to showcase your and grandpa's teaching.'

Wail of siren rose in the distance. Hemant straightened his spine and tilted his head. Those fucking cops, he thought with disdain. They were coming for him, he had no doubt about it. They knew his identity. Rudransh Ray had discovered him. Now, he had nowhere to run. He would not run, Hemant decided. He would die fighting. But before going, he would give his dagger what it demanded. Blood. Strong, passionate blood. Blood which boiled with fury and flowed with rage.

'Dad, take care of yourself,' said Hemant, before creeping out of the room, unseen, ever the shadow, ever the paleness who had never been noticed, not by his grandfather, not by his father, and never by the woman he had loved with all his heart.

Hemant climbed down the stairs, three at a time. A commotion had already started to take place downstairs. He could hear hurrying footsteps. Did Ray think he would kill his own father, he wondered stepping into a heavily shadowed corner to allow an elderly woman to pass. A blast of cold air hit his face, almost burning his naked flesh the moment he stepped outside. Hemant inhaled the frosty air. He always hated winter. From its smell to its air, winter bugged him since the very days of his childhood.

A white Scorpio materialized in the fog. Had it not been for the headlights, Hemant would not have seen the vehicle coming. As it moved forward towards him, Hemant dived sideway and slipped through a narrow passage between two old and silent houses. The Scorpio sped past the lane and vanished in the fog. Hemant remained in the darkness for five minutes, waiting for other vehicles to pass through. When none came, he pulled the hood of his woolen jacket over his head, hunched his back forward, and began to walk. Anyone who saw him from behind would take him for an asthma patient, trying get some air.

Temperature started to drop again, making the already cold wind turn frosty. Hemant cursed as he made his way towards the main road. To be safe, he remained close to the corner of the street. His dark woolen jacket and black jeans merged with the shadows and concealed his existence. Another pair of headlight came to view. Hemant stopped at the sight, and moved deeper into the darkness. A few moment later a cherry red Honda City sped past him. It headed towards the building where his father lived. Rudransh Ray, he thought with disdain. This man had done nothing to deserve the fame which he enjoyed. A fortunate man which a favorable family, and high education, bitter taste formed in Hemant's mouth. Without waiting for the thought to find its conclusion, Hemant spat at the wall against which he stood hunched. The weight of the blade he carried felt heavy against his ribs. Again he heard the demand of his knife. His grandfather used to say that every object spoke in silence. It was up to them to hear the muted words. He heard his knife's call. He would act upon it soon enough.

Chapter - 32

An acidic odor sneaked past Ray's nose as he entered the sorry looking building. Whoever had built it tried to bestow an appearance of enormity upon it. But instead of looking formidable and regal, the building looked unplanned and disorganized for some reason. A group of elderly men and women greeted him as he entered with Siddhant at his toe. Nishant had to go to Delhi to supervise Oliva's murder investigation. He looked glad to be away from the pressure of bringing The Ripper down.

'Why are we here?' asked Sid in a guarded voice.

'Because we have nothing else to do,' replied Ray in equally guarded voice. They had placed a plain clothed police near Hemant's home, though Ray had strong doubt that Hemant would return home ever again. 'Because, this is the point from where we start fighting for our lives. Because, all hell will break lose after this.'

Sid threw Ray a disgusted look. 'If you have not noticed my friend, all hell has broken lose already.'

Ray did not acknowledge the jab as he walked up the stairs. Dull lights from yellow bulbs sketched a sleepy stairway. It reminded Ray of settings straight from old Bengali movies which he dreaded to sit through as a child. With each flight he climbed, smell of unwashed clothes, and human waste grew strong. Once he had smell sensitivity, Ray recalled. As a child he would refuse to eat anything which had strong smell. He refused to enter puja alters lest he smelt strong incense fragrance.

Fate, Ray reflected, had a weird sense of humor. His line of work in CID frequently made him stand by dead bodies which smelt rotten enough to twist his stomach and make him want to vomit. He still remembered the first time he inhaled the smell of decaying flesh. It sent him out of the building, shuddering. Since, that day, a lifetime had passed, reflected Ray. His head felt heavy due to the sharpening smell. But he had to go up and meet Hemant's father. He needed to look the man who had created such a monster in the eyes.

Jatin had been sitting by the only window of the room, looking at something outside, when Ray walked in. The sound of so many footsteps did not rouse the old man from his reverie. He remained seated, without moving, bent and broken. Ray could not summon any sympathy for the old man despite the dismal scene.

'Dr...Mr. Saxena,' Ray called. But he received no response from the old man. 'This is Rudransh Ray. I am helping the police catch a killer. This guy rips his victims apart after murdering them.' The last information did something as the old man stirred from his motionlessness. Jatin tore his gaze away from the yellow streetlight and fixed his unfocused eyes on Ray. 'We believe it's your son, Hemant.' Ray gave away the information without stopping for a reaction. 'He has not returned home,' said Ray. 'Can you tell us where he can go?'

Jatin's eyes narrowed as he stared at Ray. The old man's head tilted. 'You?' he asked after a couple of heart beats.

'Rudransh Ray,' said Ray. 'I want to speak to you about your son Hemant.'

A moment passed, then another, the old man's face changed then and a cruel smile formed on his face. 'I trained Hemant. He is good with knife.'

Ray greeted his teeth at that. 'Really?' he asked. 'How good?'

'He can slice people,' said Jatin.

'He does slice people,' Ray said. 'He is good, really good.'

'Yeah better than you Doc,' Sid said. 'His cutting is better than yours.'

The old man's face fell. He looked down at his feet. 'Can't be. I am the best one here.'

Ray took a step towards the old man. 'If you allow him to continue to cut people, he will get better than you someday,'

'Stop him.' The order came fast and sharp.

'Where can we find him?' Ray asked the question without letting a moment pass.

The old man went quiet and remained silent for a long time. Then he parted his lips and said, 'We have a farmhouse at Joka.'

Ray looked at Sid who had already started to move towards the door. But a call from the old man stopped them both. 'He cannot be better than me,' said the old man.

Ray was about to drive off the narrow lane, when his phone rang. Shraddha's name flashed on the screen. Ray put the phone on speaker and answered. 'Yes, tell me.' He raised his voice despite the silence inside the car.

'I just received a package,' Shraddha said. Her voice barely above whisper. 'It is from Raghav.'

Ray turned the car and pulled at the side of the road. 'Ok, what's inside?' He heard the sound of paper being handled on the other side of the phone.

'Photographs,' Shraddha said after a while. 'A pen drive, a notebook, and a file.'

'Anything else?' asked Ray. He knew that she would go through the items one by one, even though it was police evidence now.

Shraddha hesitated for a second, then she said, 'The notebook is 500 pages thick,' she said. 'Looks like Raghav had kept daily accounts of his work with Samir.'

'Okay, has he mentioned Hemant?' asked Ray.

'Yes, Hemant, Ashutosh, and Arman Khemka,' said Shraddha. 'According to the images and the videos of pen drive, Arman Khemka is the leader of the porn racket. It's all in there,' she said without enthusiasm. 'There are videos of Arman Khemka with young girls.' Her voice dropped and Ray heard her drawing a deep breath. He was sorry that she had to see this. But with her line of work, there was nothing he could do to protect her. 'He has been engaged in the act of...' She allowed her words to hang in the air.

'Got it,' said Ray. He looked at Sid, who nodded. 'Call a cab and come down to Elgin Road right now.'

'Kevin is here,' said Shraddha. 'We will have him drive us there.'

'Tell him to bring his full team along. Send me clips of the images and some of the diary pages,' Ray said before disconnecting the call. 'We have a live coverage to take care of.'

'I don't get it,' said Sid. 'Hemant works for Arman. He kills to secure Arman's business.' Ray remained quiet, allowing Sid to speak. Sometimes it helped to listen to others rather than thinking continuously. 'Yet, he rips people apart and draws attention to his boss's business.'

Ray drove out in the main road without speaking for a long time. 'Hemant is an attention seeker,' he said. 'If my guess is not wrong, he has been deprived of attention as a child. His father and grandfather had been dominating men and Hemant must have felt rejected and unworthy. His suppressed rage had him act in this manner. I am sure he has killed many other to satiate his rage. But Samir's death had changed everything for him. Once he killed Samir and got the media attention, his lifelong desire to be noticed came to life.' Ray paused. 'I am sure once he gets caught he will speak to anyone and everyone. Arman Khemka should have seen the danger of hiring someone who is emotionally fragile. People like Hemant live for limelight. They do anything to get people's attention.'

Sid drew a deep breath. 'Price of fame,' he mumbled.

'Price of fame,' Ray said. He turned his car and drove towards Jadavpur Police Station. 'I need to speak to Chetan. We must act fast and pick Arman Khemka before the man flees.'

Sid looked at his watch. It was nearing 10.30pm. 'Where do you think Hemant may go?'

'Anywhere but his farmhouse,' said Ray. 'We will worry about Hemant after putting Arman and his son in the prison.'

Chetan readily agreed to issue a warrant which a judge signed despite the late hour. They raced towards Elgin road in silence. Four police cars zoomed through the darkness of the night. When they reached Elgin road crossing they met a full team of Kolkata Breaking's reporters. Shraddha got out of the car as she saw Ray's cherry red Honda City approaching. She had been wrapped in a black woolen coat and dark blue jeans. Trish slid out of the car and followed Shraddha. Trisha wore a thick sweatshirt and a pair of faded blue jeans. Her face looked impassive, expressionless. Ray had expected her to be excited with the development. But she did not seem to have grasped the intensity of the situation.

'I will wait here,' said Trisha. 'I don't think I should be a part of a criminal investigation.' Trisha's voice sounded bored. 'Shraddha dragged me here, so I came.'

Ray chuckled. 'Get in. Within a few hours the entire nation will witness this manhunt.' That made Trish look at Shraddha, who nodded his approval.

'Okay,' Trisha said.

Once the girls got into the car, Ray entered the lane where Arman Khemka's house sat with pride. As they neared the front gate, it opened without warning and a black Scorpio zoomed out like a hungry monster. Ray turned the wheel of his car expecting a sudden collision but the Scorpio took the opposite side of the lane and plunged into darkness.

Ray overcame the sudden jolt in a fraction of seconds. He turned the wheel and went after the Scorpio. Behind him shrill sound of siren began to ring. Empty road allowed the Scorpio the luxury to speed up. Two minutes in the race, Ray turned his steering wheel again, making a sharp U-Turn.

Sid fished out his phone and made a call to the drive of one the cars. 'You guys continue the chase. We will join you soon.' With that he disconnected the call.

Then he called Chetan. 'We are going back to Arman's house. Join us there.'

Arman was stashing Ashutosh in a navy blue Breeza when Ray's car pulled at the front gate, blocking the way. Arman pulled out his gun at the sight of Ray's car. But then he saw the helplessness of the situation when Chetan's white Hyundai i20 joined the show. Half a second later another unmarked car slid to stand by the other two cars.

'Mr. Khemka,' Ray said. 'We have a full force which will be difficult to shoot with one gun. It is better you give yourself up.'

Arman Khemka grinned at Ray's challenge. 'You think you can keep me in prison.'

Ray got out of the car after throwing a warning look at the two girls and gesturing them to stay inside. 'No, I am not a fool Mr. Khemka. I know I cannot keep you there in the prison.' He took a step towards the front gate. Arman raised his gun as a warning but Ray did not pay any attention to the weapon, he continued walking. 'I will just damage your reputation.' He smiled at Arman Khemka's expression. Color drained from the man's face. 'I will make so much noise that the next time people hear of you or your son, they will cringe. You may walk free, but you will walk free a guilty man.'

That hit the mark. Arman Khemka's back hunched and the proud man melted on the ground. Ashutosh came out to stand by his father. His face looked pale and expressionless as he looked at his father and then at Ray, not knowing what to do or say.

Ray pushed the front gate open. 'Who took your Scorpio?' he asked. 'You always find people to take your fall, don't you?'

Arman looked up at Ray's face. Sid and Chetan entered the front yard after Ray. Usually when Ray dealt with criminals, no one interrupted or intervened. They stayed put and allowed Ray his space to work.

'I did not kill Samir, Raghav, or Ishant,' said Arman.

'Probably,' said Ray. 'Probably, you have not ordered Hemant to kill them either. But that does not make you any less guilty. You have been engaged in porn. You have raped innocent girls and took video shots of them. You sold their videos, blackmailed them.' Ray felt a stab of disgust at the man and for a fraction of second considered pulling his gun and pouring bullets in the head of Arman Khemka. But he controlled himself before his hand reached for his gun. 'Raghav has documented everything. He has left a series of photos and video clips of you and your band of criminals on act.' Ray stopped speaking, allowing his words to sink in. 'A true crime fighter continues to fight even after their death. The game is over for you Arman Khemka.'

Before anyone could move, Arman Khemka straightened, he looked around with wild eyes, then seeing no escape route, he put the muzzle of the gun against his temple and pulled the trigger with his thumb. The sound of the blast pierced the silence and made Ashutosh cry out loud. He jumped shrieking like a child. Two police men went ahead to restrain him, but he continued to thrash and scream. People swamped out of the house at the sound. A woman in her late fifties, possibly Arma Khemka's wife wailed at the sight of Arman lying on the ground, his skull shattered and his blood everywhere. She started to run towards the dead body when her eyes fell on the windshield of the Breeza. It was sprayed with blood and brain particles. A large chunk of Arman's brain had splashed in the middle of the windscreen. The sight of the raw meat stopped the woman on her track. She swallowed hard, then she covered her face with her hand and ran inside.

Chapter – 33

It was past 4.30 am in the morning, when Ray finally made his way back home. The sun had not emerged out yet. It would take time for the sunlight to break free. Ray smelt the copper odor of blood as he got out of his car. The gate keeper of his building slept peacefully on a metal chair. The middle aged man was wrapped in a thick coat and woolen cap. Ray stopped to admire the gatekeeper's ability to sleep so deep on such an uncomfortable chair for a moment. Then fatigue, day old fatigue and anxiety took over. He walked towards the elevator. The case had reached its climax. They had sent a team of investigators to Jatin's Joka farmhouse. As expected the farmhouse sat empty and dark.

Hemant could be anywhere right now, Ray thought with discomfort. The guy could be doing anything. He had weighed the decision of dropping Shraddha and Trisha at their house. Hemant would go for a last kill which would earn him a last bout of fame. Ray knew that Hemant had the intelligence to understand that the game was over him. Either he went for a big one now, or he went undercover for a long time. A serial killer with Hemant's merit would not go for the former one. It worried Ray. Who would a killer like Hemant attack now? The question lingered in his mind as he unlocked his apartment door at 11th floor.

Hemant sat on the plush three seater couch with his leg up on the coffee table in front of him. His stomach twisted with anticipation and excitement. When surrounded a warrior went after whoever they find. Snakes delivered a last strike before dying. He would too.

For this kill, he had chosen his a long knife. It looked like a gift from his grandfather. The old man had used that blade to slit up at least twenty people. Before he died, he handed the knife over to Hemant, saying, 'Carry forward the legacy boy. Make me proud.' And Hemant did, in his own way, he did make his grandfather proud of him. He still remembered his first murder, like the way he remembered his first kiss. The muffled cry of the small scrawny boy as his throat was being cut open still echoed in Hemant's mind. For a whole week, he could not sleep at night after the murder. But then something in him started to demand for more.

Hemant drew a deep breath as he allowed his head to fall back on the headrest. His back screamed for a little break. But Hemant resisted the urge to relax. If he lay down, he would fall asleep, if he fell asleep…the train of his thought broke at a sound. The front door stirred as someone unlocked it with a click. Within a moment Hemant sprang out of the couch and dived towards the nearest door which led to the kitchen. He placed himself behind the kitchen door. From here he could get the full view of the hall. He was accustomed to attacking his victims from behind. The element of surprise had always worked. Raghav did not see the cricket bat coming. Samir did not see the deadly blow either. Those two old ladies were fruitcakes, his easiest till date. Ishant was asleep when he got attacked. He lamented not being able to carry a cricket bat or a stick. A blunt weapon made the job easier. This time, he would have to rely on the blade to do his job.

Rudransh Ray, hopefully would be too tired to restrain him or launch a counter attack, he thought. This would be his last work of art, the best work, the one which would place him in the history. The door opened moment moments later and Rudransh Ray stepped in. Hemant remained crouched and watched Ray closing the door shut. He waited for the criminologist to remove his jacket, and shoes. Ray dropped on the couch, pulled out his phone, and texted someone. He remained seated for a few minutes then go up to his feet. With discomfort, Hemant saw that Ray had not removed his gun from his waistband even though he had taken off his wristwatch. Did the man sleep with his gun around his waist, thought Hemant.

Finally, Ray unclasped the waistband and removed it from his body. He picked his gun and caressed it with his long fingers for a few minutes. Then he went to his bedroom carrying it. Hemant had combed the entire house to satiate his curiosity. He wanted to know a little about Ray. But other than books and work related notes, he found nothing to know the man a little better.

Not that it mattered. They both would die within half an hour.

Ray emerged from his bedroom ten minutes later, dressed in a pair of black track pants and a full sleeve gray sweatshirt. He carried a thick book and a blanket to the couch. Hemant watched Ray getting comfortable with the blanket and his book. He lay down on the couch and started to read. Getting impatient could ruin everything, Hemant knew that. Rudransh Ray was not like his previous victims. This man had been trained to fight and kill. Sneaking past a sleeping old gatekeeper was one thing, and sneaking upon Rudransh Ray was another. So, he would have to wait till Ray fell asleep. Fifteen minutes passed then finally Ray put his book down on the floor and reached for the switch on the coffee table. Within a moment a sleepy gloom fell around the hall. Hemant waited ten more minutes, holding his breath and bracing for phone calls or text messages. None came. Sound of Ray's heavy breathing began to stir the air. Peaceful, he reflected with approval, a great time to rip Ray apart.

Hemant held his knife tight in his grip and padded out of the kitchen. His sneakered feet made no sound at all. Yet, he did not take any chance. It was an Ex CID he was dealing with and he did not underestimate Rudransh Ray a bit. He had planned each of his moves while waiting for Ray to fall asleep. Because he did not have a blunt object to cause restrain, he would go for the throat first. It would be exhilarating to cut it open and watch Ray chock in his own blood while he ripped the body open. The vision brought a smile on his face. It made him happy to be able to go like this.

After approaching Ray's sleeping form, he stood for a moment, savoring the glory and then he leaned forward to take away the blanket, stab Ray on the throat and then pull the knife down all the way to his stomach. But before he could reach down, something hit directly on the face, breaking two front teeth and sending an excruciating pain up his skull. It took him a moment to realize that he had been hit by Ray's tight fist. Before the pain subsided, something slammed against his lowered abdomen, probably Ray's feet. Hemant collapsed on his knees at the blow. He started to gasp for breath, seeing colors in front of his eyes. Lights flashed and Hemant saw Rudransh Ray stood towering over his crouched form. In his hand, Ray held his gun.

'Next time you go to kill someone,' Ray said. 'Don't sit on their couch. Warm cushion in the winter time seems a little strange, you know that?'

'Killing comes naturally to me,' said Hemant. The conversation took place in the police station. Hemant's hands were cuffed. Ray sat facing him, Sid stood by the metal door of the cramped cabin. 'Since the childhood, I have been killing.'

'Killing humans?' asked Ray.

'Humans, animals,' Hemant said with a shrugged.

'Whatever was available.'

'Where did you get your victims?' Sid asked.

Hemant pressed his lips together for a moment, reliving the murders. A strange expression settled on his face, as he leaned his head back and thought about his past life. 'Usually, grandfather brought street children, promising food and work.'

'Your grandfather was a doctor, I believe,' said Ray.

'Yeah, one of the best,' Hemant said. 'But he had this passion for killing. It made him feel god like. Same goes for my father. He was a great surgeon. But he could not control his urge to kill.'

Ray sat back and watched Hemant, speaking as if he was discussing the weather. Relaxed, and at ease, Hemant did not display even the slightest tinge of tension or fear. Ray noted with discomfort that the killer had nothing close to guilt or remorse in his manner. This was the aspect of human behavior which disturbed Ray. He had seen this body language in every organized offender. They did not care.

'I am just like them in many ways,' Hemant said with pride. 'I cannot control my urge to kill or to rip people apart after killing them. It's god like, being able to take life.'

'Why did you kill Samir Shrivastav?' asked Ray, jotting Hemant's statement and circling the godlike part.

'Samir thought he was the leader. He directed all our movements even though he reported to Arman Khemka,' said Hemant. 'But Samir was stealing money from Arman. He was cheating everyone. He needed to die. Arman Khemka himself had ordered me to take care of Samir.'

'But you did not stop at that,' Ray said. 'You had to rip Samir apart and gain attention.'

Hemant shook his head. 'I was not chasing fame when I killed Samir. I would have hidden the body had it not been for Ashutosh. He suddenly ticked at the bloodshed and ran from the scene, making enough noise to unnerve…' He stopped suddenly.

'Unnerve?' asked Ray. 'Unnerve who? Dr. Natasha Mishra?' Ray smiled at Hemant's reaction. 'Her father worked in the same hospital with your father, didn't he?'

Hemant sat back, looking down at the metal table. All of a sudden, he paled and color drained from his face. With a swift movement of his head he looked away before anyone could see his eyes.

Ray smiled at his behavior. Love, he sighed, could make people act irrationally. 'I have checked her background and bank account details. She is one of the regular customers of your shop. You two go to trips together.' Ray pulled his phone and pretended to check messages. Then after a moment when he felt Hemant mellowing down, he looked up. 'On the night of Samir's murder she had been near the murder location. We have checked her phone network.'

'That will not convict her,' Hemant snapped.

'No, of course not,' Ray said. 'But possessing porn movies could implicate her and ruin her career.' He chuckled when Hemant shuddered. 'Right now, a team of investigators is combing her house and clinic for evidence. Raghav had mentioned her in his diary, do you know that?'

Hemant's jaw tightened at the mention of Raghav's name. 'Raghav,' he chewed the word out.

'Yeah, Raghav,' Ray said. 'How did you discover his true intension?'

'Raghav came through Ashutosh,' Hemant said. 'He convinced that fool that he could bring fresh girls for our movie business. I had my doubt from the beginning. But Ashutosh was the boss' son. So, we had to keep quiet.' Ray could feel Hemant's anger like hot air blowing inside the tiny cabin. But then I got a little suspicious when Raghav failed to bring a single girl. I questioned him several times. But Ashutosh came to Raghav's aid whenever I confronted him. Raghav had been supplying drugs to Ashutosh and the idiot did everything to get a little more of that thing. Finally, I discovered his identity.'

'How?' asked Ray. He held a ball point pen in his hand and tapped its nib on the table, leaving blue dots all over the surface. He was unmindful of what Hemant said. His whole focus lay on Hemant's body language. A perpetrator said a lot about themselves from the way they spoke, they sat, or the way they held themselves. Not only perpetrators, every human being revealed themselves continuously as they communicated with others.

'I went to his hostel,' said Hemant. 'He was not there. So, I took the liberty of looking around a bit. He had files on all of us. We had to do something. Arman signed his death warrant without a single question. We did a little research and discovered everything about Raghav.'

Ray placed the pen on the table before him. Then he leaned forward a little. 'Where is he now?'

'Raghav?' asked Hemant. 'We buried him behind an abandoned construction site on National Highway 31.'

Ray pulled out a writing pad from his pocket. He pushed it towards Hemant. 'Give me the nearest landmark of the construction site.'

Hemant jotted down the name and direction. 'Can I talk to Shraddha Basu?' asked Hemant as Ray started to pull himself up from the chair.

Ray stopped mid-air at the request. His eyes narrowed as he looked at Hemant. 'Shraddha?'

'Yes,' Hemant said. 'I want her to write my story.'

Ray considered the request for a moment, then he said. 'I need to speak to the authority. If they permit, you can talk to her.'

'You are welcome to sit while we talk Mr. Ray,' said Hemant. 'I will be a pleasure to let you hear my story. I wanted to talk to her after ripping you apart but somehow you got away.'

Ray gave him a half smile before walking out of the cabin. His head felt light as he walked down a narrow passage towards the front door of the police station. The horror was over, he thought with relief. A killer was behind the bars and would stay there for a long time.

'How did you know Hemant was there inside your house?' asked Sid once they came out in the sunlight and stopped to inhale fresh air.

'Behavior,' said Ray. 'I knew he would go for a last kill before going down. The kill should be a big one to earn him his quick fame.' Ray fished out the packet of cigarette which he had been denying for a long time now. 'I considered his options. He could have gone after Shraddha. But then again, if something happened to her, who would write his story? So, that left me. I knew he would come after me. But I did not anticipate that I would find him waiting for me inside my home.' Ray took a big drag of his cigarette. 'I am going to change to traditional latches today. So much for modern security.' He shook his head in disgust.

About the Author

Anasua Ghosh

Anasua Ghosh is a professional writer based in Kolkata. She has written and published two books already. Her first book Miles Apart is a rom-com that follows the theme of twin flame reunion. Her second book Kingdom Of Clay Book 1, published by Ukiyoto is the first installment of a high fantasy trilogy. The Ripper is a dark modern-day psychopath thriller, set in a winter-frozen Kolkata. The Ripper follows the story of criminal profiler Rudransh Ray hunting down an organized offender who not only kills his victims but also rips them apart.

The Ripper is the first book of Rudransh Ray series. The next one is going to be a classic whodunit murder story set in the picturesque backdrop of a hill town.

www.ingramcontent.com/pod-product-compliance
Lightning Source LLC
LaVergne TN
LVHW091701070526
838199LV00050B/2239